Breathless for Him

Breathless for Him

SOFIA TATE

New York   Boston

Copyright © 2014 Ulyana Dejneka
Excerpt from *Devoted to Him* copyright © 2014 by Ulyana Dejneka
Cover design by Elizabeth Turner
Cover copyright © 2014 by Hachette Book Group, Inc.

Forever Yours
Hachette Book Group
237 Park Avenue
New York, NY 10017
hachettebookgroup.com
twitter.com/foreverromance

First published as an ebook and as a print on demand: July 2014

Forever Yours is an imprint of Grand Central Publishing.
The Forever Yours name and logo are trademarks of Hachette Book Group, Inc.

The publisher is not responsible for websites (or their content) that are not owned by the publisher.

The Hachette Speakers Bureau provides a wide range of authors for speaking events. To find out more, go to www.hachettespeakersbureau.com or call (866) 376-6591.

ISBN: 978-1-4555-5736-3 (ebook edition)
ISBN: 978-1-4555-5741-7 (print on demand edition)

For my mother
My opera 411 & 911
I love you, Mama

"Non, je ne regrette rien."
—Edith Piaf

Acknowledgments

As a writer (and now published author!), I have had one of my greatest dreams come true—an acknowledgments page of my very own. The person I must thank first and foremost for making that a reality is my rock-star editor extraordinaire, Megha Parekh. Your e-mail to me from that life-changing day in September is still up on my bedroom wall, where it will remain for a very long time. You take such good care of Davison and Allegra, for which I am so grateful to you! They are in the best hands with you. I'm so excited to continue Davison and Allegra's journey with you!

A huge thank-you also to the entire team at Forever Romance / Grand Central Publishing! I am in awe of everything you do for your authors, and I am so lucky and proud to be a part of the family!

Linda Judge, my BFF from Buckinghamshire: we've been through it all, and I wouldn't change a thing. You are my rock! Love you!

Aliza Mann, my critique partner: thank you for always knowing exactly what to do when I don't. Love you! And special thanks to our mutual friend, Richard Sorensen, for introducing us! *Merci mille fois!*

Victoria McKillip, my kick-ass beta reader: You just get it. You always do. For that and so much more—thank you! Mushes! Xoxoxo.

Holly Wright: you provide the sustenance for my soul. No words are ever necessary. Love you, sweetie!

My support system, near and far: Maria Royce, Melissa Siket-Ouari, Soraya Shalforoosh, Amy Almond, Orna Silverstein, Rebecca Post, Lisanne Kyle, Lora Mehrer, Cindy Chang, and Kathy Robinson. I may not see you on a daily basis, but knowing you have my back means the world to me. Love you all!

Victoria Routledge: thank you for your friendship, support, advice, and encouragement over the years. You're a star! Xoxo.

Kennedy Ryan, my Forever Romance pub buddy: what can I say? Because of one tweet from you, I have someone in my life who can make me laugh until it hurts. No smoke. No BS. Love you!

To my RWA/NYC fellow chapter members: thank you so much for your friendship and support! Special thanks to Lise Horton, Kwana Jackson, and Jeanine McAdam for your advice and letting me vent and making me laugh when I need it most, and for introducing me to *Strike Back* (Jeanine) and *Scandal* (Kwana)! Extra-special thanks to Katana Collins for my amazing author photos!

Logan Belle: I'll always be grateful for business cards with book covers on them! Meeting you that Saturday last May was an unexpected surprise and a beautiful gift in my life. Thank you for our leisurely lunches and always being there for me! Xoxo.

Paola Savoia: thank you so much for your invaluable help! Any errors are entirely my own. *Grazie mille! Baci e abbracci!*

My MFA family: I miss seeing your lovely faces and laughing with you in the MFA lounge every week. You are such treasures in my life!

My Twitter and Facebook families: you know who you are. You mean the world to me. (((HUGSTIGHT)))

My wonderful family: thank you for the nonstop laughter and hugs! To my grandmother, Nancy Bushnell—I can't imagine what my life would've been like if you hadn't become a member of our family thanks to Grandpa—what a wise man! I'm so proud to be your grandchild number one (in age only, not importance). Thank you for everything you do for our family! I love you so much! Thank you also to my aunts, Natasha Suter and Jeannie Salfen, for their love, support, and encouragement.

Dad, Wendy, Tor, and Daa-Daa: I wish you weren't so far away. I'm always thinking of you, sending you much love.

My sister, Taissa, and my brother, David: I know I can always count on you. I love you very much. And to my niece, Kvitka—are you sure you're only five? You are the coolest person I know. You're going places, kid. Your aunt/godmother loves you so much!

My husband, Victor: thank you for your love, patience, and understanding during this entire process. Love you!

And to my mother, Kvitoslava: I dedicated this book to you

not just to thank you for your superior knowledge of opera, but also for everything you have done and sacrificed for Taissa, David, and me. Your courage and strength humble me, always inspiring me to do better because nothing is impossible. I love you so much, Mama!

Breathless for Him

Chapter One

hank you. Enjoy the rest of your evening."

I watch as the last of the patrons don their camel-hair coats and calf-length sable furs. Before they leave, the owner makes sure to shake each of their hands. As they exit, the black velvet curtain that covers the front door swishes like a whisper against the marble floor, shielding the interior of the restaurant from the chilly November air. They shuffle their way out to begin the search for their town cars, a fleet of which stand outside on Broadway, engines idling, waiting to be claimed.

I'm standing inside my work space, which happens to be the coat-check room of Le Bistro, a restaurant that is an institution on the Upper West Side of Manhattan. Like Sardi's in the Theater District, Le Bistro is its equivalent, except it serves the opera buffs, cineastes, and ballet lovers of Lincoln Center. Its owner is Elias Crawford, one of New York City's most well-known restaurateurs, known for his charm, sophistication, and meticulous attention to detail.

Dressed in my standard uniform of a white long-sleeved blouse with French cuffs, black trousers, and black ballet flats, my dark brown hair done up in its usual chignon, I turn and take in my surroundings. Technically, my work space is a closet, lined with clothing rods for coats and jackets and shelves for handbags and briefcases. Since I began working there, I have checked an eclectic collection of items, from a famous rock star's red leather jacket pockmarked with cigarette burns to a vintage Louis Vuitton trunk that took up most of the traffic pattern.

Lola, the statuesque hostess, pokes her head in the door. "We're done, Allegra. You can start closing up."

I nod. I begin to wrap the plastic check numbers in an elastic band, stowing them into the shoe box that I use as a Lost and Found. I count my tips and tuck them into my purse.

As I take one last survey of the room, I spot two objects on the floor. One is a black-and-white silk scarf, the name "Hermès" imprinted in the lower right-hand corner.

The other is a man's driving glove, brown lambskin, cashmere-lined, with initials stitched on the inseam—DCB.

I stow both items in my Lost and Found shoe box. Perhaps the owners will collect them in the next few days.

* * *

"Did you hear about Davison's latest venture? He's flying to China to check out some new company that's doing amazing stuff with voice technology."

"Ha! 'Voice technology,' my ass! The only voice he's concerned about getting away from belongs to that shrew girlfriend of his, Ashton. She's got a hot body, but she's a total bitch—at least that's what I've heard."

That's what gossip is to me. Hearsay. It's common for someone to approach me while I'm working, offering me monetary compensation for any kernel of gossip that involves a celebrity. Because of its trendy status and location, Le Bistro attracts everyone from politicians to film stars to opera divas, basically anyone who's ever appeared in *Vanity Fair*. I knew since I began working here six months ago that if someone really wanted the truth about a scandal, the people to eavesdrop on were the doctors and lawyers who came into the restaurant. But I treat my place of work as a confessional; whatever I overhear will never be passed on to a third party.

The two men retrieving their coats are discussing the couple whose names and faces were featured almost every day on Page Six—Davison Cabot Berkeley, the Manhattan billionaire and heir to the Berkeley Holdings fortune, and Ashton Lane Canterbury, the heiress of the Canterbury family. Since they're the "it couple" of Manhattan, their histories are well known thanks to the tabloids and business pages. They're childhood friends. He has the proper pedigree: age thirty-one, prepped at Exeter, undergrad and MBA from Harvard, while she went to Miss Porter's and Wellesley.

A match made in WASP heaven.

It's funny, though, because every time I see their photo in the paper, she always looks much happier than he does, as if he would rather be anyplace else than with her. My life is far removed from the circles they travel in, but seeing such a handsome man so miserable with the woman he supposedly loves, I wonder if he is truly in love with her. I'm twenty-four, a butcher's daughter, but I don't envy their social or financial status in society.

I'm putting away the men's tips in my purse when a sharp knock on the flat ledge of the coat-check room's half door brings me back to the present moment.

"Excuse me? Are you working or not?"

At the door stands a tall woman with platinum-blonde hair that cascades down the back of her fur coat, a black crocodile Birkin hanging in the crook of her elbow.

"I said, did you happen to find a black-and-white Hermès scarf two nights ago?" her voice shrills above the cacophony of the restaurant. Her thin, oval-shaped face holds an exasperated look, while her blue eyes burn my face like a set of lasers.

"I did. Just a moment, I'll retrieve it for you."

As I pull out the Lost and Found box, I hear the woman speaking to her female entourage. "Oh my God, Davis is the biggest nerd. He never wants to go out. All he wants to do is stay home and read books or watch movies. He's *so* boring." She sighs. "But at least we're going away for the holidays to his family's chalet in Gstaad. I can't wait to see his new jet. We have invitations to *so* many parties when we're there."

Suddenly, I know whose scarf I'm holding. It belongs to the shrew herself, Ashton Canterbury.

Ashton's friends giggle in enchantment over the gilded life she is supposedly leading.

I walk back to Ashton with scarf in hand. I observe her, concluding that the tabloid photos actually make her look better than she does in person.

"Took you long enough," she huffs. "I hope nothing's happened to it."

"It's in pristine condition, madam. I kept it safe," I reassure her.

"Yes, well, it looks fine. Let's go, girls."

The lack of a gratuity from her does not come as a surprise to me.

* * *

"O mio babbino caro?"

Two days later during the lunch service, I'm bent over picking some dust off the floor humming the aria to myself when a deep male voice interrupts me.

I'm still distracted when I reply to the man. "Yes, how did you know?"

"My family has a private box at the Met."

When I stand up and turn to the door, I see in front of me what no photo could ever do any justice, now that Davison Cabot Berkeley is standing in front of me. He has to be over six feet tall, with dark brown wavy hair that borders on black. His eyes are deep green with flecks of amber in them. On any other man, his lips would look odd because of their lush shape, but on his chiseled face, they are perfectly suited.

He's dressed in a navy-blue wool coat, open to reveal underneath it a dark gray pin-striped suit and tie, accentuated by a button-down shirt in a lighter palette. A cashmere scarf the same shade as his coat is tied around his neck.

His eyes meet my dark brown ones, and in a flash, my throat goes dry. Shivers run up and down my arms. My pulse increases because of the way he stares at me. His head rears back slightly, and he takes in a deep breath through his aquiline nose. But it's the intensity of his eyes that paralyzes me. They sear me, as if they have the ability to read my inner thoughts without having to speak a word.

After a few seconds that seemed more like a full minute, I clear my throat. "You're very fortunate. May I be of service, sir?"

A small grin appears on his face. "Yes. I seem to have misplaced a glove. By any chance, would you happen to have found it?"

"I believe so. Could you describe it?"

"Brown driving glove, cashmere lined. My initials are on it. DCB. Davison Cabot Berkeley."

The sound of his voice warms my body, as if it were a cashmere blanket that tightly wraps around me. When he speaks, he speaks deeply, but it's more like a rumble, as if something is inside him on the verge of erupting. Even though he's only spoken a few words to me, I have a vision of him commanding others with that voice, and how intimidated I would feel, which is actually beginning to happen to me at that precise moment.

All I can do is nod my head. "Yes. I have it. I'll be right back."

As I turn to retrieve the Lost and Found shoe box, he says, "You have a lovely voice."

Thankfully, I'm looking away from him when he says that because as soon as he does, my face turns hot. "Thank you, but I was just humming, sir."

"I can still tell, though. Are you a singer?"

My face now cooling down, I finally turn around. "Yes, I am

actually. I'm a graduate student of voice at the Gotham Conservatory."

"Opera?"

"Yes."

"So I suppose the fact that you work across from one of the most famous opera houses in the world is not a coincidence?" His lips lift in a sly grin.

I laugh slightly from my nerves. "No, it is not."

He smiles at me. "Umm, may I…" he asks, gesturing to the glove in my hand.

I shake my head in embarrassment. "Oh, I'm sorry. Of course."

He takes the glove from me, running his fingers over the stitched initials. "Hmm. I wonder…"

"About what, sir?"

"I wonder when my parents named me if their goal was to see how many surnames they could slap on their newborn child."

I smile, laughing slightly. "I can imagine."

His head tilts at me curiously as he leans in closer to me. "What's your name?"

I swallow in my throat as his warm breath caresses my face. "Allegra."

"Allegra what?"

"Allegra Orsini."

He pauses for a moment. "That's a lovely name. Italian?"

"Yes, sir."

I look into his eyes, which are still boring into mine. I can't move. Something is…there. Something…powerful. It takes my breath away. We both seem to be stunned into silence.

He pushes back the tail of his coat to retrieve something from his pocket. He pulls out his wallet and shuffles through the bills.

A fifty-dollar bill appears on the flat ledge of the door.

I push the money back to him. "No, that's not necessary."

"Please take it. It's not just for the glove. It's been a long time since...I just want you to have it."

"Truly, I can't accept it. For the same reason."

He nods in understanding. He puts his hand over mine, the hand that's trying to return the money to him. He doesn't move, and neither do I.

Without warning, he begins rubbing his thumb over my hand, slowly. So slowly. My breaths begin to increase. His emerald eyes turn darker, hooded with a look that both scares me and arouses me. The warmth from his touch permeates my skin, setting the rest of me aflame. I can feel myself turning wet at the apex of my thighs. I press my lips together, determined not to break this moment. He is powerful and commanding. I can't look away. And I don't want to.

Then he moves in closer to me. His lush mouth opens to say something, his thumb still moving again and again over my hand.

"Do you think I could make you come just by doing this?"

"What?" I manage barely above a whisper.

"Answer the question," he commands huskily.

Before I can answer him, a cell phone begins to ring inside his coat, which effectively breaks the moment. I step back as he shuts his eyes, emitting a low growl, then pulls out the phone, grimacing when he checks the caller ID. He lets it continue to ring as he shoves it back into his coat.

He pauses a moment, then takes the fifty and returns it to his wallet. Like a magician, he then reveals the glove's mate from his coat, and I watch him put on both of them.

His hands now fully gloved, he looks at me again, both of his green eyes fixed onto my own. They seem darker, ominous almost.

I swallow. "Have a good evening, sir."

He leans into my space, mere inches from me. His scent, something laundered with a hint of spice permeates my nose, his hot breath caressing my face once more. "Good night, Allegra."

Once Davison Cabot Berkeley leaves, shaking Mr. Crawford's hand on the way out, I step into a corner of the coat-check room, leaning against it in the darkness. I press my head against the wall as I try to catch my breath.

No man has ever affected me like that before, mostly because I would never allow it. I know it was just a moment. That's what I tell myself. We will never see each other again. And it's just as well, because I never let in a man far enough to know my deepest secrets.

Chapter Two

When my mother was alive, I loved waking up in the morning to the smells that came from our kitchen. She was an early riser, so she would start cooking and baking just after dawn. On any given day, I detected anything from the thick cheese and robust sauce of pizza margherita to the sweet cream and sugar of cannoli.

"Mia Allegra, taste this."

My long brown braids bouncing on either side of my head, dressed in my freshly pressed first-grade Catholic school uniform, I came running up to my mother in the kitchen as she held out a mixing spoon of fresh cream.

"What do you think? Too sweet?"

"It's yummy, Mamma. What are you making?"

"Just a surprise for your father. He's been working so hard, and I just wanted to bake him a special treat."

"I hope one day I can be a good cook like you."

She touched my cheek. "You will be, cara. *Someday you will meet the one man who you will want to cook for and he will love you for it."*

After she died when I was five, my grandparents on my mother's side came over from Italy to help my father take care of me. They also liked to get up early, but all I ever smelled in the morning was the strong aroma of espresso. My father spent as much time as he could with me while he ran his butcher shop downstairs. Once I reached my teenage years, my grandparents returned to Naples, and then it was just Papa and me.

The kitchen in our fourth-floor walk-up has never been the same since.

The morning after my encounter with Davison Berkeley, I'm sitting at the breakfast table eating my usual—a hard-boiled egg, whole wheat toast, and a cappuccino. My father sits next to me, sipping his espresso.

"How is school going, *cara*?"

"Fine," I mumble.

"And how was work last night?"

Work…last night.

Do you think I could make you come just by doing this?

I shiver.

Answer the question.

"Allegra, are you listening to me?"

I shake my head to snap myself out of the memory.

"*Scusa mi*, Papa. I was distracted."

"Is something troubling you?"

I pat his hand reassuredly. "No, everything is fine. I just have a lot on my mind."

"Maybe we could do something this weekend. I don't see you enough."

My heart starts to break, hearing that from my father. "I would like that very much. We can see if there's something Italian playing at Film Forum. I can check the listings."

"That would be very nice." He smiles at me.

I glance up at the clock on the wall. "Oh God, I have to run!" I push back from the table, grabbing a banana from the fruit bowl. "I can't be late for class."

"Will you be home for dinner?" he asks.

"*Sì*. I'm not working until tomorrow night."

"*Bene. Ti amo, cara.*"

"I love you too," I tell him, leaning down to kiss him on the cheek before I dash out of the kitchen.

* * *

The following night, I'm back at work inside the coat-check room at Le Bistro. It's a Friday night, so the restaurant is more crowded and hectic. But everything is running smoothly. I'm arranging the tote bags and briefcases on the flat metal shelf that lines the top of the coat racks when I hear a loud voice, akin to scraping one's nails on a chalkboard, declare:

"You know, you really should have a small bell on the counter here so you can actually know when someone is waiting for you to assist them."

I grind my teeth together and take a deep breath before I turn around because I know who is at the door.

It's Ashton Canterbury. With Davison Berkeley standing right next to her.

Shit.

Her eyes are narrowed at me in anger, while he has a look of complete shame on his face, his head shaking in embarrassment.

They're with another couple; the man is checking his phone, while the woman is smirking at Ashton's comment to me.

Professional. Be professional.

"Of course, ma'am. That's a very good idea. May I check your coats?"

"Well, that would be nice, seeing as that is your job," she tells me, her voice dripping with pure, unequivocal disdain. She looks back at her friend, exchanging a shared look of triumph.

"Ashton…" Davison admonishes her.

"Am I wrong, Davis?" she asks him, almost as if she's horrified that he would disagree with her.

"Just give her your fucking coat already!"

Along with Ashton's and the other couple's, my eyes widen at his outburst, but I'm the only one whose mouth hasn't dropped. His face is red, which I'm guessing is from both impatience and anger. But why would he be angry?

"Fine," she huffs as she takes off her floor-length sable fur. "Don't do anything to it," she warns me as she hands it over to me.

"Enough, Ashton!" Davison admonishes her again.

He lets the other couple check their coats before him, while he hangs back.

"Go on. I'll be right with you," he tells the three of them.

We both watch as Ashton and their friends walk away, leaving me behind with Davison.

He turns back to me, stepping in close enough to the counter that I can feel his warm breath on my face, sending chills up and down my arms, my pulse racing.

"I'm so sorry for Ashton's behavior. I'm completely mortified."

"It's okay, sir. You really don't need to apologize. I'm fine. No harm done. Truly," I reassure him as best I can.

"Don't do that, Allegra," his voice growls in warning.

"What?" My voice lowers slightly at the sound of my name from his mouth, and I'm stunned that he remembered it.

"Pretend that it didn't hurt."

My hands grip the edge of the counter, trying my best to keep calm as a million thoughts rush through my head, number one being why it matters so much to him in the first place. But I can't help but be touched by the fact that he cares that what Ashton said affected me, despite what I tell him. I need to put a stop to this, whatever it is.

"May I take your coat? I don't want to keep you from your party."

His eyes blaze at me as he exhales deeply through his nose. He removes his navy-blue wool coat, giving it to me. I try to keep cool when what he's wearing underneath is revealed—a charcoal-gray pin-striped suit, a white shirt, and a red tie. He looks so damn good.

Our hands brush briefly, but enough for me to feel his thumb brush against the top of my hand, igniting a thrum of pure electricity throughout the entirety of my body. Goose bumps pop up on my skin as I hand him his coat-check number, sliding it to him along the wood of the counter so he can't touch my hand again.

"Thank you, Allegra. I'll see you later," he tells me with a sly smile before he picks up the small piece of plastic and walks away.

* * *

The end of my workday nears, and luckily there are only a few customers left. My chest tightens as I watch four of those customers approach me to collect their coats.

Even though I don't need their numbers, I wait patiently as they come closer, with Ashton engaged in a high-volume conversation with her friend, while Davison looks straight at me as the man is talking to him, oblivious to the fact that Davison is ignoring him.

"Ashton, give me your number," Davison tells her.

She continues chattering away.

"Ashton, do you mind? Your number," he repeats, more short with her this time.

"Davis, drop the attitude, will you?" she tells him, finally reaching into her clutch and handing it over.

The other man gives Davison his numbers as well. I quickly take them from his hand to prevent any lingering rubs from his thumb. I return with all four coats, watching as Davison helps Ashton into her fur. For a moment, a flutter of jealousy waves through my stomach, which I swiftly sweep away, mentally reprimanding myself.

I watch as the party of four moves toward the entrance. I turn my back on the open door, taking a step farther inside, shutting my eyes and biting on my lower lip to keep myself from getting upset that Davison didn't say good-bye or leave me a tip. It doesn't matter.

"Allegra?"

I inhale deeply before I turn back around to see Davison standing at the door.

"I'm sorry. I totally forgot. This is for all of us," he murmurs, sliding a twenty-dollar bill underneath my hand on the counter.

"Oh yes, thank you, sir," I stammer like a complete idiot.

Professional. I am a professional.

"Don't you think it's about time you called me by my name?"

"Why would I?"

"Because I would like to hear my name cross your lips."

My heart starts pounding inside my chest. Suddenly, I don't feel my legs holding me up as he leans in closer to me and his thumb starts to stroke my hand again like it did two nights ago.

I swallow in my throat before I answer with a smile plastered on my face. "Have a pleasant evening, Mr. Berkeley."

"There, now," he whispers, his warm breath caressing my face, "was that so hard? I'll see you again soon because I'm still waiting for something from you."

"What's that?"

"An answer to my question."

A shock wave hits my lower body, sending fiery pulses of blazing heat to my nerve endings from the top of my head to the pads on my toes. His eyes turn hungrier, more dangerous as he waits for me to say something, his thumb still sliding back and forth across my hand.

"What question?" I ask innocently, my voice cracking slightly.

"Really, Allegra, acting coy doesn't become you at all," he teases me. "But I'm not worried. I'll have my answer soon enough, because I always get what I want."

He sweeps his eyes over me with a hooded look one last time before he turns and heads for the front door.

I finally start breathing normally again, shutting my eyes as my heartbeat regulates. I push away from the counter, but then I feel the money Davison left me under my hand. I open the twenty and, tucked inside it, a fifty is staring back at me—the fifty I didn't accept from him the night he claimed his driving glove from me.

I fist my hands, crushing the money inside my right palm.

Damn him.

Chapter Three

The Gotham Conservatory is located in a former grand hotel from the 1920s near Gramercy Park. It doesn't have the cachet of Juilliard or Manhattan School of Music, but it's the only graduate school that accepted me and offered me a partial scholarship.

"Hey, Alli!"

I turn to see my best friend, Luciana Gibbons, dressed in a tight white sweater and boot-cut jeans, perfect for her shapely and voluptuous figure. We always joke that thanks to our physical shapes, I'd be perfect as the ill-fated Mimi who dies from tuberculosis in *La Bohème*, with my long dark hair and wide-set brown eyes, while her dream casting, with her honey-blonde hair and blue eyes, would be as the strong, fierce warrior maiden Brünnhilde in *Die Walküre*. I'd practice my coughing while she'd learn how to handle a shield of armor.

She looks me over closely. "Did you study much for the exam? I pulled an all-nighter."

"It's Puccini, Lucy. I practically started listening to him in utero thanks to my parents. I could pass it in my sleep."

"Ugh, I hate you," she jokes, bumping her shoulder with mine.

Luciana and I met on the first day of classes in our first year at the conservatory. We decided then that we would give each other nicknames because our first names are so formal. We are the only ones who call each other by those names.

We take our seats in the classroom, where our professor, Signora Pavoni, is already waiting. Once the entire class is present, she clears her throat to get us to settle down. The exam is passed out, and we begin.

When the last person turns in the test, Signora Pavoni stands in front of the class.

"Ladies and gentlemen, I have some very exciting news to share with you. I wanted to wait until after you completed the exam because I feared you wouldn't be able to focus after I'd told you."

I see everyone's eyes are focused on our professor, just as eager as I am to know what had happened.

"I received word from our dean this morning that an anonymous donor has arranged for all of us to take a private backstage tour of the Met."

A smattering of "No way!" and gasps of awe can be heard throughout the room.

"I don't know yet when the tour will take place, but I think it might even be as early as two weeks from now. I will keep you posted when I receive further details. You are dismissed."

Lucy and I can't contain ourselves as we join our classmates in the whoops and hollers of our shared excitement as we leave the room.

* * *

A week later, my classmates and I, along with Signora Pavoni, exit through the front doors of the Metropolitan Opera House. We can't stop reveling over what we had seen. Some costumes and scenery were even brought out from the archives for us, which was unexpected and very exciting. Lucy and I are excitedly showing each other the pictures we'd taken on our phones, pointing out the details in the background scenery from Verdi's *Aïda* and in the water nymph costume for the lead role in Dvořák's *Rusalka*.

Signora Pavoni allows us to go home after the tour. As we begin walking across the plaza, Lucy clamps her hand over my arm. "Oh my God. Look at him."

"Who?" I ask indifferently, my eyes scanning the open space.

"That hot guy leaning against that car right in front of us."

I look to where Lucy's eyes are fixed, and I freeze on the spot.

It's Davison Berkeley. Standing next to a sleek black Maybach, he is staring right at me. Dressed in his long navy-blue wool coat and matching cashmere scarf, his green eyes are fixed on mine.

"Davison…" I murmur.

"What did you say? Don't tell me you know him."

"Umm, kind of. He came into the restaurant a few weeks ago to pick up a glove he'd lost."

"You talked to him?"

"I am the coat-check girl, you know."

"Who is he?" she asks excitedly.

"Davison Berkeley."

Lucy's grip on my arm tightens. "Wait, you mean the guy who's like a gazillionaire and is dating that blonde chick?"

I wrestle my arm out of her grasp. "Ow! I don't know how much money he has, and frankly, I don't care."

"But why can't he stop staring at you?"

"How the hell should I know?"

"Let's go find out."

I shiver in fear, my heart threatening to explode from my chest. Lucy begins to pull me by the arm toward him, but I stay firmly in place. However, the more I resist, the more she pulls. I realize I'm just putting off the inevitable, so I give in.

As we get closer to him, I notice the glare in his eyes begins to soften, as a sly grin takes over his face. I start to feel like a mongoose about to be snatched up into the cobra's mouth.

His voice still possesses that hypnotic rumble. "Hello again, Allegra."

Lucy looks at me curiously as my throat suddenly goes dry. I barely manage to get a word out. "Good morning, Mr. Berkeley."

"Did you enjoy the tour?"

"We did…Wait…how did you know? Did you arrange that?"

He nods. "I thought your class would appreciate it."

In a flash, Lucy thrusts her hand out to him. "Hi, I'm Luciana Gibbons. It's so nice to meet you. Thank you so much for the tour."

He returns her handshake. "You have an interesting name. Did your parents name you after Luciano Pavarotti?"

Lucy giggles as I roll my eyes in exasperation. "I know, right? I have zero Italian blood in my family, but my mom is a total opera buff."

"That's charming."

I can't tell if he's being sincere or patronizing her. But it's his voice that hypnotizes me with its low rumble, the words oozing out of his mouth like melted caramel. But before I can come to a conclusion, he speaks again. "May I give you a ride home, Miss Orsini? And you as well, Miss Gibbons."

That is the last thing I want. "No, thank you. I'll just take the subway."

"It wouldn't be any trouble at all," he counters.

"Thank you, Mr. Berkeley," Luciana says, "but I'm meeting my mom for lunch at Boulud Sud."

I catch her gaze, narrowing my eyes at her with a knowing glare.

Liar.

"Really, I'll be just fine," I protest. "Anyway, it's too far."

In a not-so-subtle manner, Lucy coughs, clearly signaling that I should take him up on his offer.

"I insist," he says, practically commanding me to get into the car.

He stares at me long and hard. The voice in my head is screaming to walk away, to stay detached as I have been up to this point, to keep my secrets safe. But something in me makes me answer, "Okay."

As he turns to open the door for me, Lucy gives me a quick *Call me* gesture with her hand. "It was nice to meet you, Mr. Berkeley."

He nods in her direction. "A pleasure, Miss Gibbons."

Davison stands behind the open door, waiting for me to get into the car. As he presses his lips together, his jaw locks, as if he's anxious for me to get into the car without any further delay.

I sink into the cream leather seat, my head lolling back into its caress. The other passenger door opens, and he slides in, confident and self-assured. He crosses his long legs and turns to me.

"Where am I taking you?"

My folded hands start fidgeting as my feet start to tap the floor of the car. I can't say it. I'm too embarrassed. He's one of the most popular bachelors in Manhattan and I'm a butcher's daughter from Little Italy.

But that's why it doesn't matter, since you'll never see him again after this.

"Allegra, I can't drive you home if you don't give me your address."

Finally, I whisper the words, "Little Italy. Mulberry Street between Kenmare and Broome."

He shouts to the open partition, "Did you get that, Charles?"

An older man with white hair dressed in a dark suit sitting in the driver's seat turns his head back toward us. "Yes, sir."

The car pulls away from the curb and begins its long journey downtown.

* * *

Through the tinted windows of the Maybach, I watch the West Side neighborhoods of Manhattan rush by me as the car heads south on Ninth Avenue. I can feel his eyes on me, but we don't say a word to each other until we hit Hell's Kitchen in the West Forties.

"It's lovely to see you again, Allegra."

I nod my head in silent reply.

"Did you enjoy the tour?"

"Yes, thank you," I tell him, hopefully sounding gracious.

"Is something wrong?"

"No," I reply, praying that sounds convincing enough for him to stop questioning me.

Wrong.

"Have I offended you in some way?"

I finally turn back to face him. Even though I don't want to be with him, he doesn't deserve me being rude to him.

"No, Mr. Berkeley. Not at all. It's just that now I feel like I owe you something in return, and I don't want to be in that position."

"Allegra," he sighs. "I paid for the tour because I wanted to do something nice for you."

I become more confused. "Why? You don't even know me."

"But I want to know you. You didn't take that fifty from me—"

Before he can say something, I pull my wallet from my purse, removing the fifty-dollar bill, holding it out to him.

"Which reminds me. I can't keep it," I tell him determinedly.

"For crying out loud, Allegra, are we going to keep going over this? I want you to have it."

"But I don't want it. I already feel like I owe you for the tour."

"You don't owe me anything. I just wanted…"

"What?" I ask, eyebrows furrowed.

"To do something nice for you," he repeats.

"Why?" I need to know, even more confused now.

"Because of how Ashton treated you last week. Because you don't fawn over me, even though you probably knew who I was from the moment you saw me."

I let a small smile escape my lips.

His eyes brighten. "You wouldn't believe how many times a day people ask me for something just because I am who I am. I get so fucking sick of it. And you...you don't want a damn thing from me, and not only is that something new for me, but it's also sexy as hell."

My mouth drops at his last admission.

"You are, Allegra. And you know what else?" He smiles mischievously.

I shake my head, unable to form a coherent word.

He leans in closer to me, his breath warm on my face. "The fact that you were carrying around that fifty means you were hoping to see me again."

"But I could've seen you at the restaurant when I was working," I counter, hoping to dispel what he was thinking.

He takes my hand, the one holding the money, and begins that thing with his thumb, the thing that makes my pussy moist and my insides constrict in arousal. His thumb begins to stroke the top of my hand, slowly, so fucking slowly.

"Spin it any way you want, Allegra. You just wanted to see me, time and place be damned."

He's right. He's fucking right.

But I wasn't going to tell him that.

"Those same outlets that report on you where I read about you also never neglect to mention that you're with Ashton Canterbury, Mr. Berkeley. So carrying around that money doesn't mean a thing since you're dating her."

"I'm not."

I tilt my head at him, completely stunned, trying to comprehend what he just told me. "What? Since when?"

"The night I gave you the fifty."

"But why?"

He smiles widely, extending his right hand to stroke my cheek. "Why do you think?"

Oh God. No. No. No. This is moving way too fast.

I need to end this before it starts, whatever this is between us. It's for the best. I can't be with him, knowing I'll be thrust back into the spotlight the second we're seen together in public.

Neither of us speaks for the rest of the trip.

A short time later, the car comes to a halt.

"Which building, ma'am?"

At the sound of the chauffeur's voice, we both turn our heads to the front of the car. I glance out the window. "On the right. Sergio's Meat Market."

"Very good, ma'am."

I look back at the man sitting next to me. He has a curious look on his face. "Your father's a butcher?"

I take a deep breath. "Yes. Sergio is the man he bought the shop from."

I expect a sarcastic comment or condescending remark, but nothing comes out of his mouth. Only a small smile crosses his face, as if he were genuinely pleased about something.

As I grab my bag from the floor and reach for the door handle, his voice rumbles, "Wait." He checks the traffic outside, and then opens his door, rushing over to my side of the car.

He extends his hand to me to help me out. I carefully alight from the car, with him leading me to the sidewalk, holding on to my hand the entire time.

Now standing on the pavement, I sling my purse over my shoulder, turning back to him.

"Thank you for the ride and the tour. It was very kind of you."

With one hand on my left elbow, he leans in and brushes his lips against my cheek. His scent of laundered fabric and spice assaults me, making me woozy.

He whispers in my ear, "Good-bye, Allegra."

He pulls back slightly from my face, waiting for me.

I hold out the fifty to him in my hand, praying he'll just take it from me. And, with a grimace, he does. But he doesn't let go; he just keeps looking down and staring at my hand as if it were something precious.

I need to tell him something because I know this will be the last time we ever speak to each other.

"You know the question you asked me that first night we met?"

He begins to caress my hand again with his thumb and nods, silently replying to my question.

Before I say it, I take a deep breath. It comes out in a murmur.

"My answer would've been yes, Davison."

His head snaps up, his beautiful emerald eyes shining, his mouth gaping at me.

I walk to my door and don't look back.

Chapter Four

Wʜo was that man, *cara?*"

I look up at my father from my half-eaten turkey sandwich. Giacomo Orsini's light blue eyes hold a playful, curious look, his lips forming a knowing smile.

"What man?" I ask him, glancing down at my sandwich, which now has suddenly become more interesting.

"You know who I'm talking about."

"He was nobody, Papa. Shouldn't you be in the shop already to give Luigi a break?"

My father's voice grows louder in frustration, and I hear a sigh of exasperation. "Allegra, don't change the subject. I don't think he was a 'nobody' driving in that fancy car dropping off my only child. I just want to know you're safe."

I give in and turn to face him. "You know I'm always careful.

And I never cross Bowery to go to the Lower East Side. It's too painful. Too many memories."

He nods as I continue, "He's a customer from the restaurant. I found something of his at work, so he repaid me by giving me a lift home. But don't worry. I won't be seeing him again."

"What's his name?"

"Davison Berkeley."

"He should've come into the shop and introduced himself."

I get up from the table, putting the plate in the sink and my sandwich in foil to take with me. "Didn't you know? Chivalry is dead."

He sighs. *"Sì. Morto."*

I lean down and kiss my father's ivory-white hair. "I'm off to work. See you tonight. Love you."

"Ti amo anch'io, cara."

* * *

I know something is wrong the minute I step into the restaurant. The noise inside is close to ear-shattering. The waitstaff is working at a faster pace than usual to set up for the dinner rush. The hostess on duty is shouting "No comment!" into the phone with all of the lines lit up. She holds her hand over the receiver when she sees me. "Allegra. Thank God you're here."

"What happened?"

"Elias had a heart attack."

"Oh my God!" I clamp my hand over my mouth in shock.

"Someone walked into Elias's office and found him on the floor and we called 911."

I gasp. "Is he okay?"

"We don't know yet. He's in critical condition at St. Luke's. Of course the press found out, and the phone lines are lighting up like a damn Christmas tree."

"Is there anything I can do?"

"Actually, go see William in the office. He wants to talk to everyone before the dinner rush starts."

I don't even bother taking off my coat. I head straight to the back of the room and take a left into a small corridor where the restrooms are located. I knock on the door marked PRIVATE. I hear my manager, William Fitzgerald, telling me to come in.

When I open the door, I find William sitting behind Mr. Crawford's desk. He is not the only person in the room.

Davison Berkeley is standing to William's right.

* * *

What the hell is he doing here?

My body begins to go through the same motions every time I'm near him—heart palpitations, sweaty palms, dry throat.

William motions me in. "Close the door."

With the door shut, I take two steps forward. I know Davison is staring at me, but I refuse to return the look. I don't want to appear unprofessional.

William clears his throat. "Allegra, I'm sure you know Mr. Berkeley."

I nod, still ignoring Davison's eyes on me. "Yes, we've met."

"Mr. Berkeley is the other owner of Le Bistro."

I tilt my head, my eyes widening. "What? I thought Mr. Crawford was the owner."

Davison comes around the desk, stopping within a few feet of me. "I'm a silent partner. When I was little, my parents liked to bring me here every Sunday for brunch. The place grew on me, so when I heard Mr. Crawford was looking for investors, I was more than happy to oblige. This place is a part of me."

I can't help but smile at that admission. "I see."

"But after tonight, it won't be a secret anymore."

"What does that mean?"

William leans forward in the desk chair, placing his hands down flat in front of him. "Because of what happened today, Mr. Berkeley is fully agreeable to losing his anonymity about his ownership. That brings me to what I needed to tell you. With you working in the coat-check room, I know many people will be hounding you tonight asking you about Mr. Crawford. Just be the way you usually are—discreet, offering a sympathetic comment, hoping that he'll be back soon. But if anyone hassles you, I want you to tell me or Mr. Berkeley."

I hope my mouth didn't drop as low as I think it did. "Mr. Berkeley?"

"Yes, I'll be here managing things until Elias returns."

I look back at Davison. His black suit is slightly rumpled and his tie is missing. His white button-down shirt is open one button, revealing his bare skin. Scruff is starting to appear on his strong, chiseled jaw. And his hair is messy, as if he's been running his hands through it in worry. I've only ever seen him with every hair and thread in place. Never like this.

Like a total fucking sex god.

The grin on his face melts my insides the more he stares at me. His stare doesn't waver, only becoming darker and hungrier with each second, arousing me until my nipples grow hard against my bra. I can feel myself blushing from the look in his eyes, as if he were looking into my soul, nurturing it with the care and attention that he's given me not just now, but ever since I met him.

The sound of a chair scraping against the floor echoes throughout the room as William pushes back from the desk, successfully ending the moment between Davison and me. "I'd better go out front and see how things are going. Just remember, Allegra, if anyone gives you trouble, let us know."

"Certainly, sir. I'll come with you. I need to start setting up."

Davison takes another step closer to me. "If you wouldn't mind giving me another minute, Miss Orsini, I need to ask you something. Is that all right with you, William?"

"Of course. Take all the time you need."

I shut my eyes in frustration. With William gone and the door closed, Davison walks right up to me, taking my hands into his. "Are you all right?"

The familiar rumble makes me shiver. "I'm okay. I just feel badly for Mr. Crawford. Do you know how he's doing?"

Davison shakes his head. "Nothing yet. They're running tests. That's all I know."

I nod. "Look, Mr. Berkeley—"

"Davison."

"I can't call you that. You're going to be here every day."

"I know."

I scoff at the glint in his eye, pulling my hands from his. "We can't do this. You're my boss now. We have to be professional. I don't want to lose my job."

"That will *never* happen," he growls. "I won't let it."

I believe him when he says that. Completely. The heat from him overwhelms me, and more than anything, I want that heat to consume me.

"But this won't lead anywhere," I whisper. "We're from two different worlds."

He takes hold of my hands again. "I don't care who your parents are, where you live, or how much money you have."

Oh God. This can't happen. Every fiber of my being wants this…wants him…but I can't let it.

He smiles slyly. "And since I finally have the answer to my question, we'll have to test that theory out, won't we?"

He leans in and softly brushes his lips over mine. The taste of them sends my mind reeling, my heart threatening to explode out of my chest. No man has ever made me feel like this before—safe, cared for, and most of all, desirable.

I didn't go out at all in high school, and when I was in college, I dated one man on and off for four years. I can count the number of men I've slept with on one hand. It doesn't matter because when I actually tried to be in a relationship, it never worked because I closed myself off if the guy wanted more from me, and then I'd eventually stop seeing him.

But none of them compare to Davison. He's the most incredible man I've ever met. So self-assured, so confident, and I want that in my life. I need it. I need *him*. I've kept to myself for so long, and now I want to try with him. He makes me want to actually step outside the box that is my life.

His lush lips are so soft on mine, the tip of his tongue just escaping his mouth almost as if he's testing to see how I would react.

I take his lower lip into my mouth, sucking on it just barely to let him know I am letting him in. And from the soft moan he lets out, he knows he has my total permission.

He pulls back, smiling at me so widely. "You'd better go."

I take a deep breath and nod. "I'll see you later."

Standing at my spot in the coat-check room, I watch Davison walk around the restaurant, making sure everything is in place before the first dinner patrons arrived. His black suit is now smoothed out, with a purple tie tightly knotted around his neck. His hair is combed and in place. He oozes self-confidence with every step. He's probably never done anything like this before, but he takes up his new role with such ease that he seems like a natural.

Until Mr. Crawford comes back, for the unforeseen future, work is going to be complete torture.

Chapter Five

Opera is my passion. I love everything about it, from the costumes to the lyrics to the music. Learning how to sing it is a challenge that I welcome. I try to put as much of myself as I can into each line that I sing. Being able to read a music score brings me joy. The feeling of reaching the high notes is indescribable.

However, there is one component of opera that presents great difficulty for me—diction.

I grew up in a bilingual home. I consider both English and Italian to be my first languages. French is a Romance language, and it rolls off my tongue. *Pas de problème.*

German is an entirely different matter. Between the umlauts, diphthongs, and the guttural word endings, it poses a huge problem for me, as does singing it. I don't picture myself playing the lead in any Wagner operas, which isn't a disappointment for me.

There are people more talented than me who can sing Wagner beautifully, like Luciana. I'm more of a Puccini girl anyway.

But I have to pass my diction class, which is the reason for my presence in the conservatory's language lab a few days later. I'm using a computer app that lets users tape themselves, then the program corrects their pronunciation.

"*Mein Gott!* You suck, Alli."

I jump in my seat at the sound of Luciana's voice. "'Oh My God' yourself! You scared me. What are you doing here?"

"I took a wild guess. You know I can tutor you."

I sigh, watching as she plops down into the chair next to me. For some unknown reason, German pronunciation comes naturally to Lucy. "I might have to, judging by the zero progress I'm making with this thing."

"Okay, time to spill."

"About what?"

"Don't play coy with me. Money Boy. What's the latest with him?"

I shut off the computer and take off my headset. "He's going to be at the restaurant until Elias recovers."

"Has he made a move yet?"

"Nothing major. Just a peck on the cheek."

Lucy's face drops. "That's it?"

I stand up and start shoving my notebook into my tote bag. "It doesn't matter. Nothing is going to happen between us."

She grips my arm. "Hey, stop it. Sit down, okay? Why do you say that? Tell me."

"Because I'm being realistic, Luciana." I sigh, back in my chair. "I have to keep my distance."

"Because…" She looks at me knowingly.

"Yes, *that* 'because,'" I confirm for her.

"Jesus, Alli, do you really think he'll care about all that?"

"He might not, but his family will. As will the tabloids. So this is a preemptive strike against shit hitting the fan."

"That's all well and good, but what's it been like seeing him every night?"

I shake my head. "How do you think? Like nothing I've ever felt before. Pure joy seeing him within a few feet of me, and utter hell knowing I can't be with him, even though he said he broke up with Ashton because of me."

She frowns at my admission. "Wow. Does he talk to you? How does he act around you?"

"Like the gentleman he is," I tell her helplessly. "He pops by to make sure everything is running okay, and then I'll see him across the room and he's staring at me with this look that just kills me and makes me regret my decision."

Luciana pauses. "God, I can't imagine…"

"Yeah, it sucks," I say resignedly.

"And you're sure…"

I give her a firm look with my eyes. "Completely."

She rises to give me a hug. "You know I'm here for you, sweetie."

"Thanks. So if I need to call you at midnight after my shift is over to vent my frustration over my sound decision…"

"I'll have my phone on twenty-four/seven."

* * *

I don't see Davison when I walk into Le Bistro. I say hi to everyone and head for the coat-check room. After hanging up my coat and bag, I take the Lost and Found box down from the shelf to remove the coat-check numbers.

A gorgeous single red rose is lying on top of the tickets, a BlackBerry, and a lone pearl earring.

I gently put the box down and take the rose out. I lift it to my nose, inhaling its intoxicating scent. I study its rich red color, touching the petals with my fingertips so as not to jostle one loose.

"Like it?" a voice asks deeply and huskily.

My heartbeat turns rapid as I lose my capability to breathe. Once I take in a lungful of oxygen, I pivot to the open door, where he is standing, his eyes fixed on me. Dressed in a navy-blue suit, white shirt, and yellow tie accentuated by a platinum Rolex on his left wrist, Davison is the epitome of a man who exudes power wherever he goes.

The energy between us is a live spark that makes my blood rush, heightening all of my senses. He makes me lose all rational thought when I'm around him. I want to know what his tongue feels like in my mouth, what his cock feels like when he's thrusting into my pussy again and again and I'm begging him not to stop.

But I made my decision.

"I love it," I tell him sincerely. "Thank you."

"I did some research." He smirks. "Roses are one of the most popular flowers in Italy, and it's associated with the Roman goddess of love, beauty, and sex."

"Venus."

"A gold star for you." He smirks again.

"I am Italian, after all," I reply pointedly.

He smiles and shakes his head, laughing slightly.

"Well, thank you," I murmur. "Again."

"My pleasure. Ready for tonight?"

"Yes."

He nods. "Good. I'll talk to you later."

Davison leaves just as quickly as he appeared. I shut the lower half of the door, taking the rose in my hand and putting it in my bag.

I close my eyes, mentally telling myself, *Don't encourage him. You made your decision. Now you have to live with it.*

* * *

Just after midnight, I finish my shift, heading for the downtown 1 subway across the street. The temperature has dropped several degrees during the course of the night, and I burrow my chin into the warmth of my black wool peacoat, raising its collar around my face.

I place one foot on the top step of the station entrance when I hear a voice call me.

"Miss Orsini?"

I turn to see an older man with white hair dressed in a dark suit, a chauffeur's cap on his head.

"Yes?"

"Mr. Berkeley would like to give you a lift home."

I glance over and see the familiar Maybach logo on the back of the car parked at the curb. I didn't see it at first with my attention focused on reaching the warmth of the subway station.

"You're Charles?" I ask him. "The same driver who took me home to Little Italy with Mr. Berkeley?"

"Yes, ma'am," he smiles warmly, saluting me with a light tap to his hat with his index finger.

"Is Mr. Berkeley inside?"

Another voice pierces the air, sounding like it's coming from inside a closed space. "For God's sake, Allegra, will you please get in the car before you freeze to death?"

My question asked and answered.

I pause for a second, then step over to the car as Charles opens the door for me. I slide inside and sink into the heated leather seat. My head falls back as my body returns to a normal temperature.

"Took you long enough."

I smirk and glance over at Davison. He looks annoyed.

"I'm here, aren't I?"

"Once you finished interrogating Charles."

"Well, you know, there are so many Maybachs in Manhattan, I just wanted to be sure it was the right one. Can't be too safe these days," I tease him. "Wouldn't you agree?"

He finally smiles at me, shaking his head again.

"Sorry, I didn't mean to be punchy. It's been a long night."

"Please. Don't apologize for that. I wish you would tease me some more."

His comment stuns me. I have no idea how to take it, so I sit forward in my seat, stretching my legs. "Owww."

"What's wrong?"

"Nothing. It was just a long night. My feet are killing me."

"Come here."

I look over. "What?"

He flips up the seat console between us and leans down, pulling my left leg toward him. My body shifts as he brings up the right one as well. I'm now fully lying across the seat horizontally, my head propped up by the armrest. My body is tingling with anticipation.

"What are you doing?"

Davison takes off my winter boots one by one and drops them onto the floor.

"What does it look like I'm doing?"

Before I know what's happening, he begins to rub my feet, starting with my toes all the way down to the heels. I can't help but smile as he continues with an intense look on his face, as if he's making sure that every nerve is relaxed. I'm sure Harvard doesn't offer a course in reflexology, but wherever he learned to do this and on whomever he chose to practice, I honestly don't care at this point. Everything he is doing at this moment is pure nirvana.

The warmth of the seat eases me into a lambent state. All of my muscles are slowly becoming looser; my body is turning into liquid jelly.

With each stroke, I become more aroused. My thighs soften with each rub from his hands, my panties soaking with desire. I bite down on my bottom lip to keep me from making any provocative noises that would arouse him. I'm just grateful that I'm not wearing a skirt. The temptation of taking his hand and placing it on the apex of my thighs for him to explore there would have been too great.

I stare at him, his jaw clenched in concentration on what he's doing.

I know I told myself that I would stay away from him, but I find it incredibly futile. When he told me about liking me for not wanting anything from him, it moved me. He arouses me, and the fact that I can do the same to him gives me such self-confidence, something that I only find when I'm singing. The more I get to know him, the more I think he just wants someone to like him for him, and not how much money he has or who his family is. Maybe the feeling I had when I saw him with Ashton in those pictures in the tabloids wasn't off base at all. Maybe he really was miserable with her. But are those reasons good enough to make me want to be with him, knowing I'll be thrust back into the public eye?

I don't even hear him until he repeats the question.

"How did you become interested in opera?"

"When I was growing up, my parents listened to the Met opera broadcasts on the radio. It became part of our weekend routine. Saturdays at home listening to the opera, Sunday at church." I smile, recalling my mother joyfully singing along with the radio and with the church choir. "Opera is the other religion in my house."

"How long has your father been a butcher?"

"Since before I was born. When he immigrated from Milan in the sixties, he settled in Little Italy and became an apprentice to the original owner. When the owner died, he took it over, and the rest is history. Then he met my mother and they married. She was from Naples."

"Was?"

Shit.

"Yes," I whisper, turning my head so he can't see my eyes.

"How old were you when she died?" he asks quietly.

"I was five."

"How did—"

"Davison, I don't talk about it," I tell him firmly, still looking away.

He pauses, looking down at me. He stops massaging me for a second and takes my left hand, gripping it tightly. "Okay. I'm sorry. I didn't mean to push."

"It's all right." I nod and shut my eyes.

As the car speeds down West Street, I feel every bump and pothole hit the chassis of the car under my back. Davison resumes massaging my feet. The more he does, the more he and I become relaxed. Very relaxed, to the point where his hands begin to travel from my feet to my calves. His hands never stop. Back and forth, back and forth.

Without warning, the car comes to a halt. I would've fallen to the floor had Davison not grabbed for my right side.

I sit up. "I guess we're here," I announce in a slightly disappointed tone.

As I reach for my boots, I notice Davison adjust himself. I look down at the floor so he can't see my eyes and mouth open wide at the sight of seeing the huge bulge in his pants. Then I smile at the thought of him wanting me as much as I want him.

Thank God it's not just me.

Like he had the previous time, he gets out, goes to my side of the car, and opens the door for me, putting out his hand to help me out. We stare at each other not saying a word. We don't need to speak.

Davison lifts his hands to caress my face with his fingertips. I shut my eyes, softening from his touch. He then wraps his hands around the nape of my neck.

"Allegra," he whispers, his breath circling my ear.

Suddenly, with a low growl, his mouth is clamped over my lips, his tongue seeking mine. I gasp before I open my mouth, greedily accepting what he is offering me. He pulls me back into the wall of my building as our tongues tangle, his hot breath exhaling from his nose onto my face. We moan in tandem, finally releasing the desire we have both felt for so long. My hands run through his soft, silky hair, until I reach around for the back of his neck, pulling him into me as close as I can.

I want him. God help me, I want him so damn much.

A passing car honks as someone yells out from it with a cackle, "Get a room!"

The moment effectively broken, we start laughing helplessly. We pull away from each other, but still inches from each other's faces, holding on to each other and panting for fresh oxygen.

"Do you have any idea how long I've wanted to do that?" he asks, my face between his hands, a huge smile on his face.

"As long as I have," I confess, smiling right back at him. "It's late. I think I'd better go in."

He nods. "Yes, I guess you should, as much as I don't want you to."

He pulls me in and softly kisses me on the lips. "Good night, Venus. My goddess of love, sex, and beauty. See you tomorrow."

"Yes. Tomorrow." I sigh contentedly.

I step into the lobby of my apartment building, shutting the door behind me, leaning against it.

I shut my eyes in frustration, angry at myself. "Fuck."

Why did I let that happen?

Because I wanted it. I wanted him. So badly.

But I can't let it happen again, no matter what I feel for him.

* * *

"Davison, are you crazy?"

"We know who she is. Wanna guess?"

"Not the best choice, dude. I'd think again if I were you."

"She's got a past, man. Walk away now."

Flashbulbs of blinding light attack my eyes, my hand tightly gripping his. A huge pack of paparazzi are shouting vile things at us as we're walking down Fifth Avenue.

Suddenly, my hand is empty, a strong breeze blows across my palm where Davison's hand once held mine.

I yell out, "Davison? Davison, where are you?"

The paps are descending on me like hungry vultures. I drop to the ground, curling my body into itself. I'm crying so hard, my body shaking from the wracking sobs.

"Don't leave me! Davison, come back!"

* * *

I wake with a start, shooting up from where I was lying in my bed. My heart won't slow down. I put my hand over my chest, as if that will do anything to slow down my heartbeat.

I start breathing deeply, mentally willing myself to calm down. I grab the ends of my sheet, twisting them in my hands to give myself support.

It feels like it's been eons when my heartbeat finally regulates. I reach for my water bottle and take a few long gulps for my parched throat.

I lie back down, my eyes wide open.

I'm playing with fire and I know it. But damn it, I want to allow myself this. Being with him. Just to finally know what it feels like to be with someone who makes me forget my past, who actually wants to be with me, and who doesn't care if I'm a butcher's daughter.

Deep down, I know the obvious truth. It's still playing with fire.

Chapter Six

From that night on, Davison and I follow the same routine when I'm working at the restaurant. After my shift, I walk across Broadway to where the Maybach is parked at the curb near Lincoln Center. Charles waits by the car to open the door for me, with Davison already in his seat. I slide in, take off my coat and shoes, and lie down across the backseat, the console already in its nook, nothing to separate me from him.

It's true that we live in opposing worlds—moneyed versus working-class, Upper East Side versus Little Italy. But as intimidating and dominant as he is, he brings me comfort. I enjoy being with him. I find his honesty refreshing and touching, imagining how difficult it must be for someone like him to not feel like he's being constantly being taken advantage of.

During the drive to my house, we usually talk about our day, the people we encountered in the restaurant that night. He asks about my classes. But I still haven't asked him about his own life for two reasons. The press covers his life on a regular basis, so there's really not much to know in general. But the more important reason is I don't want to know. I know whatever this thing we have is, it's fleeting, and I just want to enjoy it for what it is. I don't want to get invested in him, to protect both myself and him from being exposed to my darkest secrets.

However, there is one question I'm dying to ask him, and a week before Thanksgiving, I finally find the nerve to do it.

We're just starting the drive down Ninth Avenue, my feet in Davison's hands.

I take a deep breath. "Okay, Harvard, give it up."

"And what is it that you'd like me to give up?"

"How you learned to give such amazing, toe-curling foot massages."

He grins slyly as he shakes his head. "Sorry. That's classified information."

"Ugh. You're infuriating." I roll my eyes at him and sigh in frustration.

He lets out a deep laugh as he keeps massaging my heels. I close my eyes. When I open them again a few minutes later, he has a serious look on his face.

"What's wrong?"

He puts my feet down in his lap, staring at them, caressing them.

"I'm leaving for Shanghai tomorrow. On business."

The high I'm on from the massage plummets.

So that wasn't hearsay. Those two men who were talking about him when I returned their coats at the restaurant weren't wrong.

"How long will you be gone?"

"A few days. I want to be back before Thanksgiving."

"I see."

"But Charles will still take you home after work."

"He doesn't have to."

"Yes, he does," his voice rumbles. He pauses. "Will you miss me?"

I answer as passively as I can. "No."

"You need to work on your poker face, baby. I don't believe you."

"Well, it's true," I insist.

"The hell it is."

Without warning, Davison yanks me up across the seat, positioning me on his lap, my knees straddling him. His eyes are fixed on mine, ablaze with fury. His hands roughly grip my hips, pulling me as closely to him as he can.

I glance back behind me.

"Don't worry. That partition is always closed now."

Stretched across his muscular thighs, I brace my hands on his own, breathing faster, nervous to see what he does next. I can feel the bulge of his hard cock hidden under his suit, rubbing against my pants. I can't look away from his eyes, mesmerized by the severity in them.

"Ever since I heard you humming that aria, and then when you finally turned around...I can't explain the effect you have on me. I see you. I hear you. I feel you. I dream you."

My heart begins to beat harder, pounding against my chest. Whatever I expected him to say, that's not even close to the reality.

"Davison..."

With a growl, he pulls my face to his, crushing his lips over mine, his tongue pushing into my mouth, desperate for entry. I accept him hungrily, dying to taste him, to feel his guttural moans vibrating against my chest when he is savoring my tongue in his mouth. With his left arm diagonally pressing across my back and his hand on my shoulder blade, he pins me tight into his chest, hard and solid against my curves.

We begin to devour each other. I want him so fucking much. My hands coil around his neck, one fisted in his hair, the other around his shirt collar. The taste of him is pure ecstasy for my mouth. I can't stop, and neither can he.

Once we come up for air, he stares at me in wonder. He begins to softly stroke my face with his hands as I lean with my head into his touch. His hands travel down, caressing the sides of my throat, along my shoulders. Reaching the front of my shirt, he rubs my breasts, rolling his hands repeatedly over the cotton fabric. When my nipples pop up, sharp and pointed, his eyes widen, and he takes a deep breath.

"I have another question for you," he asks me, gravelly and rough.

"Yes," I reply without hesitation.

"'Yes,' what, Venus?"

"Yes, you could make me come just from doing that."

"Let's test that theory, shall we?"

Davison starts to unbutton my shirt. He pushes it back from my shoulders as I shimmy it down my arms to let it fall to the floor, never removing my eyes from his burning gaze.

He sees my white cotton bra, inhaling deeply at the sight of my nipples pushing out prominently against the bra's cups.

"Off," he commands, pulling at the bra's straps.

I unhook the back of my bra. His eyes roam over my breasts, hooded with desire, a low growl emanating from his throat. Like a panther about to devour his prey.

He licks his lush lips. "So beautiful."

With his arms holding my lower back, he dips his head down and clamps his mouth over my left breast. He suckles until my nipple is fully extended, then bites down hard on it.

"More," I moan, and he obeys, moving to my other breast to give it equal attention. He suckles it while massaging the other one.

If he doesn't do something more soon, I'm going to explode. My pussy is soaked and I'm on the verge of coming unraveled.

We aren't acting like horny teenagers. We are primal creatures in heat.

Suddenly, Davison picks his head up from my breast. I whimper from the loss, begging for more. He leans to his left, pressing a button on the wall and speaking into an intercom. "Charles, take the scenic route."

That piques my curiosity. "Scenic route?"

"Stoplights."

Oh God, yes.

"I need time for something I've wanted to do for weeks."

"What?"

"Making you come."

His answer sends me into a frenzy. I want him more than anything at this moment. I want to know how it feels when he makes me come with him inside me. His finger, his cock, I don't care how. I need him now. Right fucking now.

I push off from him, my hands fumbling as I reach for my belt buckle, then my zipper. He's panting as loudly as I am, the sounds echoing in my ears, his urgency making me even hotter. At the sight of my white thong, he grunts, "Fuck yes," as he rips the thin fabric from around my hips.

Now entirely naked, I settle back onto his lap, my hands bracing his shoulders.

"Touch me, Davison. I need you," I beg him.

I have never desired a man as much as I do at this precise moment. No man has ever made me so aroused, so brazen, making me want things I never have before.

He massages the opening to my slit, finally plunging one finger inside. My back arches from the first contact. "Oh God... more..." I plead.

He thrusts another finger into me and begins pistoning me with them. With my head thrown back and my eyes shut, my entire body bucks as I clamp onto his fingers, sheathing them with my cleft, wishing that it was his penis inside me instead. I grip his shoulders harder, digging my fingernails into his jacket. I hold nothing back. "Yes! Yes! Don't stop!"

Then when he places the heel of his hand at the exact angle on my pussy to rub my clit, I lose all sense of self. I almost don't hear him when he rasps, "Look at me, Allegra."

I open my eyes and lock my gaze on him, the amber flecks in his eyes alight in lust. "Come for me. Now."

My orgasm comes over me as I ride its glorious wave. "Ahh-hhh!" My entire body collapses. I can't tell which heartbeat is mine. Our bodies match—panting breaths, shaking limbs.

Through heavy-lidded eyes, I watch as Davison tucks a hand

under me, coming back up with his fingertips covered in my warm cream. He sucks on each one, long and deep, his eyes never leaving mine. "Mmmm. Delicious," he declares. I mewl, smiling like a contented feline.

His arms encircle my naked back, pulling me into his body. With no stitch of clothing on, my breasts pressed against the rough fabric of his shirt and his hard chest, I become aroused again. It's the most erotic sensation I've ever experienced. I feel alive, sexy, every nerve ending pulsing with electricity. Even though I'm naked, I feel safe with him, as if he would do anything to protect me.

I lay my face against his chest. I close my eyes, taking in the scents permeating the car—my come, his cologne, fresh male sweat. I know we're driving over bumps and potholes, but I feel nothing, as if I'm gliding. Davison tilts his head slightly to whisper into my ear. "You undo me, Venus."

Completely sated, I drift off blissfully for what seems like an eternity. A pair of hands tucks my hair back. "Allegra, wake up. We're here."

I open my eyes and see my neighborhood through the tinted windows. I reluctantly pull myself out of Davison's arms. He envelops my face in his hands.

"Are you all right?"

I nod. "How long was I asleep?"

"Ten minutes. You looked so peaceful. I wish I didn't have to wake you up."

I touch his face. "Kiss me good-bye here so we don't give my neighbors something to talk about."

He smiles, pulling my lips to his. We kiss more softly this time, our lips swollen from our previous exchange. But the emotion between us is just as electric as before.

I look down at my naked state. "I'd better get dressed."

"Good idea."

I slide off him, reaching for my clothes. With my pants on, I reach for my bra, but before I can get ahold of it, Davison grabs it, holding it behind his head.

"Give it to me!"

"Not until you kiss me again."

I frown for a second, then lean in and peck him on the lips.

"You're joking, right?"

I roll my eyes and kiss him a bit harder, licking his lips with my tongue.

He smiles. "Better."

As I'm trying to hook my bra behind me, Davison starts stroking my breasts, flicking my nipples. I look up, and he's smirking like he's doing something naughty, and having too much fun doing it.

"You don't play fair." I sigh.

"Never said I did," he says, still playing with my breasts.

Finally, my bra is in place, and I lean down to the floor for my shirt. I shove my arms into the sleeves, but Davison stops me from buttoning it.

"Allow me," he murmurs.

He does one button, then kisses me. Button, kiss. Button, kiss. When he reaches the last button, he grabs my head and slams his lips over mine, kissing me longer this time, his tongue tangling with mine.

When he pulls away, he smiles. "There. Now I know you'll miss me while I'm gone."

I shake my head at his bluntness, laughing at his bravado. But he's right, arrogant as it may have sounded. His self-confidence arouses me, making me braver and wanting to be with him even more, despite what I vowed to myself about staying away from him.

As is now standard practice with us, Davison steps out of the car and comes around to my door to open it for me. I grab my torn thong from the floor and shove it into my bag.

The cold air hits my face. I take in a deep breath, feeling more alive than I have in a very long time.

We smile at each other. I don't want him to go, but it's freezing outside.

I smile at him. "Have a good trip. Call me...Oh, wait. You don't—"

He holds out his hand expectantly. I know what he wants without him having to say it. I rummage around in my purse until I feel the hard metal rectangle in my hand. I give him my phone and watch as he punches in a few numbers. Then he presses a few more until I hear the thin ring of a cell phone coming from his coat.

"There. Now I have yours, and we can reach each other anytime." He touches my face one last time. "You'd better get inside."

I nod. "I'll see you soon."

He embraces me with a final kiss on my lips.

Once inside my building, my phone vibrates in my purse. A text is waiting from him already.

Remember, Charles is taking you home after work while I'm gone. We'll pick up where we left off tonight. I'm counting the hours already, Venus.

I wait until I'm in my bedroom to reply.

God, you're a pain in the ass. Fine. Tell him I'm off tomorrow night so he doesn't have to wait for me—forgot to mention that before. And I am counting them too. Sweet dreams, Harvard. xoxo

Another text comes in just then, but it's from Luciana.

Hey, Alli! My mom can't use her La Traviata *tickets tomorrow night. Wanna go?*

I quickly write her back.

Hell yes! I'll meet you inside at seven. Thanks so much! Can't wait!

* * *

Dressed in my standard operagoing outfit of my favorite black knit dress, black stockings, and black patent leather kitten heels, I wait for Luciana the next night inside the lobby at the Met.

I open my clutch to check the time on my phone. I always bring two small pieces of my mother with me whenever I come to the Met—her black satin clutch with a gold rose clasp that she bought before I was born, and on my left shoulder, I wear her diamond rose brooch that my father gave to her as an anniversary gift. She would have both with her whenever she and my father went out for dinner or dancing when I was little. I remember her leaning over me, wishing me good night, and kissing me on the cheek as I inhaled her favorite perfume.

Luciana comes rushing through the door, her coat buttoned up to her chin. "Damn, it's freezing out there!" she exclaims as she hugs me.

We have about thirty minutes until curtain time. "Got the tickets?"

She opens her purse to search for them. "Yeah, yeah. They're in here somewhere." Finally, she pulls out a white envelope. "Got them!"

This is my favorite part of going to the Met—taking the walk up the red carpeted stairs to our level. I love ascending the stairs with the others, seeing what everyone is wearing, feeling the hum of anticipation in the air.

Lucy's mother's seats are on the third level, known as the Grand Tier, on the front-row side aisle.

"I'm going to the bathroom," she says, dumping her coat on her chair. "I'll be right back."

"No problem." I cover the back of my seat with my coat, looking out at the familiar scene. I take out my opera glasses from their tiny case and hold them up to my eyes, eager to check out the house.

As I turn from left to right, someone catches my eye diagonally across from me on the second level, specifically in the second box from the left. My glasses fix on a woman flipping her platinum hair back over her shoulder after she removes her fur coat. Once I focus the lenses, I can see a man embrace her shoulders as he leans in to place a kiss on each of her cheeks. An older couple is sitting behind her. After she sits down in her chair, the man remains standing within full view of me.

I gasp.

Motherfucker.

It's Davison. I know even without seeing her face that the blonde is Ashton, his supposed ex-girlfriend.

I begin to shake, my breath caught in my throat. I'm paralyzed, unable to look away. My entire body is so focused on the sight ahead of me that I don't even feel Lucy's hand on my arm until she squeezes it harder.

"Jesus, Alli, what's wrong?"

I hand over the glasses to her. "The second box from the left on the Parterre level, the one with the blonde."

She shifts her body to the correct angle and freezes. "Oh my God. Is that who I think it is?"

"Yes," I sputter.

Lucy puts down the glasses and sees my face. "Okay, what's going on with you two? Because it's obviously become more serious since I last saw you if you're reacting like this."

I lean over and whisper into her ear what happened the night before in the Maybach.

A variety of exclamations come out of Lucy's mouth as I recall the events, ranging from "Oh my God!" to "Holy shit!" I end with him telling me about his "trip" to China.

"So that's what he told you?"

"Yes," I barely manage, choking back my tears and my anger. "But he's not in Shanghai. He's here. At the Met. With Ashton."

I begin to pull on my coat. Lucy clasps her hand over mine. "Whoa! Where are you going?"

"Home. I can't be here."

But it's too late. The decorative house lights that hang above the orchestra seats, the ones that look like glistening snowflakes falling from the ceiling, are being pulled up, indicating the start of the overture.

Lucy knows what that means as well as I do. She reaches around my shoulders with her left arm. "We'll leave at intermission," she whispers. "If we go now, they might see us."

As much as I'm dying to get out of there, I know she's right. I nod in agreement.

"The second the lights come up," I confirm.

"We'll be outta here."

The audience applauds the arrival of the conductor. The overture ends and the lights go down.

I can't help myself. I reach for my glasses and look across the house again to the second-level boxes. Davison is sitting to Ashton's right. Because his box is close to the stage, its lights provide me an ample vantage point from my seat to see their box clearly. Ashton is constantly leaning into his side, placing her hand on his shoulder, whispering into his ear as he nods in reply to whatever she is saying. I can even see him smiling at times in reaction to her comments.

When I see her right arm lift and move to her right, and then Davison's left arm move slightly and shift to the left, I know exactly what's happened. Her hand is now on his left thigh, and his left hand is on top of hers, holding it in place.

I shut my eyes and bite down on my lower lip. Taking a deep breath, I start mentally admonishing myself.

I should've known better. I ignored the voice in my head, and look where it got me. Used and thrown away like I was a fucking distraction.

I thought he was different, but he isn't. He's a player. He gets off on it.

Well, we're done. At least I know now before I got completely invested in whatever it was we had. And more important, I'm still safe. Safe from the press and the public eye.

I sense the weight of Lucy's eyes on me. She takes the glasses from my hands, first placing them on her lap, and then my hand in hers.

I adore Verdi's operas. I can recite the lyrics along with the singers. But I'm not enjoying anything—not the staging, the costumes, the music. None of it. All I can do is close my eyes and pray for the first act to end quickly. As the last lines are sung, I pull on my coat, ready to make a quick escape. Lucy follows my lead and does the same. The curtain comes down, and we scurry out even as the lights are still coming on.

I quickly walk down the stairs, pushing my way out the lobby doors. Lucy is right behind me, guiding me to the fountain that sits in the center of the plaza, sitting me down on the black marble.

"It'll be okay. Just let it out, sweetie," she coos, rubbing my back.

I turn to her, surprised. "I'm not going to cry over him. Did you think I would?"

Her eyebrows furrow in confusion. "Yeah, kind of."

"Well, I'm not," I reassure her. "He's a player, Lucy. I should've fucking known better. He made me feel things I never have before, and then he goes to the opera with someone who he told me was his ex. I'm done being taken for a fool. And frankly, I'm glad it's over because I don't have to worry about anyone finding out about me. I can go back to my life as it was, no one the wiser."

"That's bullshit, Alli, especially after what you told me happened last night between you two. You can't just end it without talking to him first."

"Of course I can," I tell her determinedly.

"No, you can't. You need to talk to him. Get the truth from him. Then decide what you want to do."

I stand up. "All I want to do now is go home."

She gives in with a sigh. "Okay." Now on her feet, she pulls me toward the front of the plaza that faces Columbus Avenue, but then a thought strikes me. "Wait, we need to take the side stairs. Charles will be waiting out front for Davison."

"Who's Charles?"

"Davison's driver. He'll see me and tell him."

She nods. "Good idea. Come on, let's go."

Arms linked, we hurry for the stairs that open onto West Sixty-Fifth Street. Lucy raises her hand in the air for a taxi.

I grab her arm. "What are you doing? Are you crazy? I can't afford a cab all the way back to Little Italy!"

She waves me off. "It's on me. No way are you taking the subway home after tonight. And Tribeca's not that far away from you. I can practically walk home if I wanted to."

I smile at her as a cab pulls over to the curb.

We don't say a word to each other as the taxi takes the same route that Charles has taken with Davison and me these past weeks—except for last night, that is, with all of the stoplights.

Before I get out of the cab, I give Lucy a hug. "Thank you."

"Call me if you need me. And remember, talk to him before you do anything."

At that moment, the thought of talking to him unnerves me, as resolute as I am in my decision. I can only nod. "Night, Lucy."

"Night. Try to get some rest."

Thankfully, my father is asleep when I walk in. Once I'm in my room, I strip off my clothes and leave them on the floor. I dive under the covers and attempt to go to sleep, but it's useless. I stick in my earbuds and turn on my iPod, choosing Chopin's "Raindrop Prelude" to calm my restless, anxious mood.

* * *

I'm grateful that Davison doesn't show up at Le Bistro the following day. Not that I expected him to, since he told everyone he was going to be in China. He obviously had to keep that as a cover. I do my best to keep up an upbeat demeanor at work, but physically, the lack of sleep from the previous night has taken a toll on me.

When my shift ends, instead of crossing Broadway, I walk around the corner and head one block east for Central Park West. I don't want to risk the chance of Charles seeing me or even Davison surprising me. He'd probably assume I would be so excited to see him and fall all over him—*Oh my God, Davison, what are you doing back so early? I can't believe you're here! I'm so happy to see you!*

But I know better than that now.

I head down Central Park West to Columbus Circle to catch the subway there. After the past weeks of enjoying the luxury of being driven home, I do miss it for a second, but then I remember *La Traviata*, and I know I made the right choice.

When I get to my street, I start to search for my keys. Then I hear a car door slam. I don't look up until I hear his voice roar at me.

"Where the hell were you?"

Davison is leaning with his arms crossed against the Maybach parked in front of my building. I refuse to look at him and walk right up to my door.

He pulls me back roughly by my arm, turning my body to his so he can look into my eyes.

"Don't ignore me, Allegra. I was waiting for you. Aren't you even pleased to see me?"

Fuck, he looks so good. He has that messy look after a long day at work—hair askew, his suit all wrinkled, but still sexy as hell.

Get a fucking grip.

I reply coolly, "No, I'm not."

He shakes me by the shoulders. "Hey! Talk to me! What the hell is going on with you?"

I decide to play this out and ask him point-blank. "Where were you last night, Davison?"

He pauses for a second and stares at me confusedly. "Why?"

"Just tell me."

"At the Met. With my parents."

"Anyone else?"

Say it.

"Ashton." He sighs. "Let me explain—"

"Don't bother," I tell him pointedly, still rummaging for my keys. "I was there too. I saw you."

He pulls on my shoulder so I would look at him. "Fuck! Will you just listen for a goddamn minute?"

"Fine. One minute. Go," I tell him impatiently.

His jaw clenches in frustration. "The trip was canceled at the last minute. I was going to call you, and then my mother called and asked me to go to the opera. I didn't know Ashton was going to be there. My parents asked her to come. It wasn't my idea."

"Then explain to me why your hand was on her thigh," I demand from him.

"Because she put her hand on my leg, and I was placing it back on hers so she would get the point that I wasn't interested. Anything else?" he asks exasperatedly.

I hate myself for believing him, but something still bothers me.

"You could've called or texted me. You have my number. You put it in my phone yourself, remember?"

He reaches for my hand. "I fucked up. I'm so sorry. I—"

I shake him off me.

"Please, Venus…"

Hearing his nickname for me now twists my insides, my blood boiling. "Do not call me that ever again!"

"Allegra, si sente bene? Ti sta dando fastidio?"

I turn around and see my neighbor Pietro walking his bulldog.

"No, Pietro, he's not bothering me."

He looks over at Davison, then the car, then back at me. He nods, satisfied I'm not in trouble. *"Bene. Ciao, cara."*

"Buona notte, Pietro."

We watch him stroll across the street into the building directly across from mine.

"What was that about?" Davison asks curiously.

"My neighbors. They're very protective of me."

"Why do they need to be?"

Shit.

"I meant we're very protective of each other. People who care about others tend to be like that."

"Meaning I'm not."

"I never said that." I've never felt so deflated. "Look, Davison, this is getting way too complicated for me. The two of us together doesn't make sense. We're from two different worlds."

"That's bullshit and you know it, Allegra!" he roars.

How can he not see it like I do?

"It's late." I sigh. "I'm tired and I want to go to sleep."

"Fine. I'll let you go. For tonight," he warns me, his eyes heated, the emerald tint of his eyes even darker now, as if he's about to erupt.

I don't want to argue with him anymore. Honestly, I don't know what I want.

Actually, I do know. I want to forget I ever met him. "Bye."

Before I can stop him, he takes a step closer to me to tuck a strand of my hair behind my left ear. I quiver at his touch. "Good night," his voice rumbles.

His hand drops, letting me pass. I put my key in the lock and walk into my building. I refuse to look back to check if he is still there.

For the second night in a row, I strip off my clothes and go straight to bed. This time, I have no trouble falling asleep.

* * *

"Mamma!"

"Run, Mia, run!"

"No! Stop hurting Mamma!"

"Go, Mia! Hide! GO!"

Someone is shaking me. I'm still screaming when I open my eyes and see my father hovering over me.

"*Cara*, stop! Wake up! It's just a dream. I'm here."

I'm hyperventilating. My father reaches for an empty plastic bag on the floor next to my bed. He holds the edges close together so I can breathe into it. My sobs diminish as my heart rate begins to normalize. I drop the bag from my hands.

My father grabs a bottle of water that's sitting on my nightstand. He unscrews the cap and gives it to me. I take slow sips as he runs his hand across my upper back to calm me down.

"What happened? You haven't had a nightmare in such a long time."

"It was a bad night. I don't want to talk about it."

I know why I had the nightmare. It was Davison. I closed myself off for so long from possessing any true emotions, and then he woke me up. He allowed me to feel, to care, to hope. And now that we're finished, I'll have to go back into my hiding place, pretend that he never affected me, and seal myself off for good.

Damn him.

"Maybe you should go back to see Dr. Turner."

"After one nightmare? No, Papa."

He sighs. "Fine. But if it happens again—"

"It won't."

"All right. I'll let you get back to sleep. *Ti amo*, Allegra."

"I love you too."

He kisses me on the head and walks out of my room.

Once he's gone, I take a small prescription bottle from my nightstand drawer. I stare at the label and the pills inside through the tinted plastic. I have fought the demons before. I can't go back. This time, I will fight off the beasts with my own whip and chair, everything I have, whatever it takes.

I put the pills away and try as hard as I can to fall back asleep, praying for one night of peace before they return.

Chapter Seven

For the next ten days, I live my life as if I'm in a daze. Nothing holds my interest. My professors reprimand me for not focusing in class. I am numb. I feel nothing.

I can't say the same is true for Davison.

He won't leave me alone.

Being at work is complete torture. He's at the restaurant every day. I do everything I can to avoid glancing over at him. But it's futile. Seeing him in his custom-made suits that accentuate every muscle of his body, with his dark hair and commanding presence, I can't help being aware of wherever he is. He is just *there*. We catch ourselves now and then when we sneak looks at each other, but they only last for a second so it won't be obvious.

He leaves me two flowers in my Lost and Found box every time I'm at work. One blue rose and one yellow rose. The first night they appeared, I looked up the colors on my phone. Each had several meanings, but I took the ones that applied to me—yellow was for an apology, the blue for love at first sight.

Then there are what I call the "drop-bys." He thinks of any ridiculous excuse to stop by my post at the coat check. He'll ask the most inane questions that he knows I won't have the answers to, ranging from "Do you know where the sommelier went?" to "Was the bread delivered?" I mean, really? Doesn't he have better things to do with his time—like run a financial empire—than ask me such ridiculous questions?

And then there are the drop-bys when he thinks he has something in his eye or asks me to fix his tie. It's like having a root canal without any novocaine; that's how painful it feels. I manage to evade those requests nine times out of ten, but then when he's persistent, I can't help myself. I lean in to check his eye for some imaginary speck of dust, and then his hot breath caresses my cheeks, I inhale his scent that's all Davison, he touches my arm lightly with his fingers, and I lose all rational sense. Then when I finish helping him, he smiles like a contented fox that just consumed its prey. And I'm left trembling and aroused, my pussy soaked with desire.

Why can't he see that we're not right for each other? He needs someone who's part of his world, who doesn't mind the spotlight. He just doesn't get it. And I need to keep my life as uncomplicated as I can.

The worst part comes at the end of my shift. The first night I came back after our argument, I took my alternate route down Central Park West to get the subway at Columbus Circle. But somehow, he found out about it. A few nights later, there it is on

CPW: the black Maybach with Charles waiting to open the door for me. I don't need to ask if Davison is inside.

I would ignore him, but Charles doesn't deserve that.

"Hello, Charles."

"Good evening, Miss Orsini. Mr. Berkeley would like to give you a ride home."

"That won't be necessary. I'm going to take the subway."

"But Mr. Berkeley—"

"I don't need Mr. Berkeley anymore. For anything," I tell him firmly.

Charles swallows. "I'll be sure to pass that along to him."

I step closer to the tinted passenger window and stare right into it. "Oh, I don't think you'll need to do that. I'm sure he heard me," I say to the closed window, trying my best to sound passive and detached.

I turn back to Charles and give him a kind smile. "It was lovely seeing you again, Charles. Have a good night."

It doesn't come as a surprise to me when I see the Maybach trailing me as I walk south to Columbus Circle. Just to piss him off, I duck into the Time Warner Center and wait a few minutes, then walk back out to use a different subway entrance. But, damn him, he is still waiting for me on my street when I finally get home. The one blessing is that he doesn't get out of the car. He knows better than that. If he had, though, I don't know if I would've been able to resist him.

On the eleventh day after our fight, he texts me, which immediately puts me on alert.

I find sometimes the best things in life happen when you least expect them. Don't you?

Now I'm scared. Not of him, but of what he does to me.

I have no idea what he means by that text. I try to forget it, but it's always in the back of my mind. With Davison's money and connections, anything is possible.

* * *

"Number thirteen! Who has number thirteen? *Tredici?*"

It's a typical Saturday morning downstairs in Sergio's Meat Market. All of our friends and neighbors are gathered in our tiny shop, not just to buy meat, but also to exchange local gossip. With Luigi, Papa's employee, out sick, I volunteer to help out. I don't mind since I don't have to be at work until later and I know how Papa likes to run things. I handle the orders, while he rings up the sales and chats with the customers. When I was little, I used to sit in the corner behind the counter on top of wooden crates, drawing in my coloring books, watching my mother help my father.

"*Sono tredici*, Allegra."

I look up and see Mrs. Gregorio holding up a torn piece of paper from the shop's counter machine with "13" written in bold black numbers.

"*Buongiorno, Signora Gregorio.* What can I get you?"

"A pound of prosciutto and two pepperoni sticks."

"Coming right up."

I carefully slice up the ham nice and thin just like Mrs. Gregorio likes it, wrap it up in parchment paper, weigh it on the scale, and mark the price on the outside with my father's ever-present black grease pencil.

Once I wrap up the pepperoni, I hand the order to my father. "Mrs. Gregorio."

"Okay, *cara*." He puts the meat on the counter and begins to punch the numbers on the antiquated cash register he still insists on using. "And how are you, Mrs. Gregorio?"

I yell out to the customers, "Next, please! Fourteen! *Quattordici!*"

Our next-door neighbor Mr. Torino waves his number at me as high as his hand will let him.

He always wants the same thing. "Sweet sausage, *Signor*?" I ask.

"*Sì*. And…"

"I know. Cut it up so you don't have to."

The old man nods at me. "*Grazie*."

Mr. Torino suffers from arthritis, so it's difficult for him to cut anything with a knife. I pull the foot-long sausage from behind the glass and am about to reach the counter when something stops me. The two words seem to boom over the cacophony of voices that bounces off the walls in the small space.

"Hello, Allegra."

I freeze in place. The hush that falls over my father's customers is something I've never encountered before on a Saturday morning. Everyone turns to stare at Davison. He looks completely out of place in my father's butcher shop—smooth, perfect. Too perfect for me, a butcher's daughter from Little Italy…with a past that still haunts her.

I bite the inside of my lower lip to keep myself calm as I start taking deep breaths. My eyes roam over him. His cocoa-brown suede boots contrast against the bleached white of the shop's tiled floor. In a similarly colored suede jacket over a cream crewneck sweater, pressed blue jeans, topped by a cashmere scarf wrapped around his neck, he is too beautiful for words.

However, the image he is seeing when he looks at me does not project the same sophistication.

With a white paper hat pinned to my head, my clothes hidden under a white apron stained with meat juice, and holding a lengthy sausage in my hands, I can't imagine a greater way of mortifying myself in front of this man.

His last text about the best things happening when you least expect them now makes sense to me.

Calm. Remain calm.

I can feel everyone's eyes on me, most of all Davison's. I take a deep breath and exhale.

I stare right back at him. "I can't talk now. I'm busy."

"Then I'll wait."

"Suit yourself."

He doesn't move. He keeps staring at me. His attention doesn't waver once.

Feeling the weight of the sausage in my hands, I realize I'm holding up Mr. Torino. I turn back to reach for the cutting knife, but seeing the other equipment at my disposal, I grab the meat cleaver instead.

With my left hand holding the sausage on the cutting board and the cleaver in my right, I look up at Davison. "Well, go ahead."

He clears his throat. "Fine. Look, Allegra—"

THWACK!

I bring the cleaver down hard onto the sausage. When my eyes shift back to Davison, he is cringing, his eyes narrowed in imagined pain, his eyebrows furrowed.

It has the effect I hoped for.

"This has gone on long enough, and—"

THWACK!

"Jesus, will you stop for a minute?"

"I'm sorry, Mr. Berkeley, but this is how Mr. Torino likes his sausage. He can't cut it himself because he has arthritis. Right, Mr. Torino?"

The old man nods at Davison, smiling. Davison grimaces as he acknowledges Mr. Torino.

"Please, I just want you to talk to me."

THWACK! THWACK! THWACK!

"If you're trying to make me leave, it won't work," he declares.

I roll my eyes as I wrap up the sausage pieces, weigh them, and watch as my father takes them from me. But he doesn't let go of my hands.

"*Cara*, is this the man who drove you home?"

"Yes, Papa."

Davison steps up to the counter and stretches out his right hand to my father. "Forgive me, Mr. Orsini. I'm Davison Berkeley."

"You're the one with the fancy car."

Davison nods. "Yes, sir."

My father puts down Mr. Torino's order next to the cash register. He gives Davison a once-over, then extends his own hand to him. "Giacomo Orsini. Nice to meet you."

"I was hoping I could get Allegra to have some coffee with me."

"It's up to her, Mr. Berkeley. She has a mind of her own."

Davison smiles. "Yes, she certainly does."

I stand in place with my hands on my hips, eyes rolling. "I'm standing right here! And the answer is 'no.'"

Pietro, our neighbor who was walking his dog the night of our argument, comes forward. "He's obviously sorry, *cara*. Give him another chance."

Mrs. Gregorio pipes in, "He's very handsome. *Ma che bell'uomo!*"

Suddenly, the whole shop erupts in English and Italian versions of "Go!" and "Such a gentleman," and "If you don't want him, I'll take him."

I watch all this in shock. "I thought you were my friends!" But I know they aren't going to stop until I put an end to it.

I glance back at Davison, who's brushing away some stray hair that has fallen into his face. He keeps looking down at the floor. I've never seen him look so unsure before. So nervous.

I sigh as I pull the pins out of my hair that are holding my hat in place. I untie the apron behind me and hang it on a hook behind me. "Okay, I'll go as long as you take it easy on my father, since he'll be working the counter all by himself," I announce to our customers.

Out of the corner of my eye, Pietro comes around the counter and takes the apron down, tying it around his body. "Don't worry. I'll be here." He pats me reassuringly on the shoulder.

When I look back at Davison, he is smiling at me. He takes in a deep breath and exhales in relief. I hope it's because I have just given him what he so desperately wants—another chance.

* * *

Davison follows me out of the shop onto the street, where I find Charles standing in his usual spot next to the Maybach.

"Hello, Charles."

He greets me with a slight bow of his head. "Always a pleasure, Miss Orsini."

Standing behind me, Davison's breath warms my neck. I take one step and turn to him with a straight face. "I'm going to change clothes. I'll be right back."

"I'm not going anywhere."

Deciding not to dress up for him since technically we aren't seeing each other anymore and I have no need to impress him, I wear my old yoga pants and a ratty Gotham Conservatory sweatshirt over a T-shirt under my winter coat. Back downstairs, Davison is still waiting outside, as are countless pairs of eyes staring out from my father's shop window.

"We can go to the café around the corner. It'll be quiet there."

Davison smiles slightly. "Wherever you want is fine with me."

I lead the way. Davison never reaches for my hand as we walk, but I know he is there. At times, I feel his left hand on my lower back, but he quickly removes it, probably to prevent a reaction from me.

When we walk into the café, some of the tables are already occupied, but I lead us to one in a far corner. A petite blonde waitress with a pixie haircut comes over to take our orders.

Once she walks away, I take a deep breath and look across at Davison. Now that I see him close-up, I can see his face is a bit sunken. The usual spark in his eyes is missing, and I begin to feel guilty for my part in its absence.

We just stare at each other until our coffees arrive—espresso for him, cappuccino for me. Once we take our first sips, we place our cups down on the table simultaneously.

His first words come out in a rasp. "You have no idea how much I've missed you."

I stay silent as he continues.

"I totally fucked up that day. I should've called you and told you my trip was canceled. And you were right. It would've taken me less than a minute to text you. I thought I'd have time, but then my mother called about the opera, and I was in a rush to get to the Met. And then when I saw Ashton waiting in the box, I was totally surprised, and I got agitated and just wanted to get the hell out of there."

I sigh. "Those are just excuses. Knowing that you couldn't take a minute of your time to call me really hurt me. It still does, especially since I can't help but wonder what would've happened if I hadn't gone to the opera that night."

He stays quiet, seeing I have more to say when I hold up my hands, silently asking for him to wait.

"But honestly, I think I am glad I saw you that night because it just proved to me that I shouldn't be with you. You're always in the public eye, and I don't want to complicate my life that way."

"Okay, *that* I don't understand," his voice rising in frustration.

"Please, you just have to trust me on this. We can't be together," I plead to him.

"And you have to trust me, Allegra. I don't know what's going on with you, but I don't care. I've wanted to be with you since the first second I saw you. I never stop thinking about you. You shut me out because I broke your trust in me. I want to start over. I want you to give me another chance. I want you to see what kind of man I can be with you, the kind you deserve."

"What about Ashton?"

"We're done. Our families are old friends. I think our parents always assumed we'd end up together, but that's not what I want. I want to be with someone who's warm and kind, someone who likes to argue with me and challenge me, someone with a big heart. And that's you."

He slides his hands across the table over mine. They're strong and warm, solid and unyielding.

I look down at my cappuccino as tears begin to form in the corners of my eyes.

His eyes soften when I raise my head up again. He sees the tears streaking down my face and grips my hands tighter.

I choke slightly when I open my mouth. "I missed you too. And I want to try again because not being with you all this time was unbearable."

"Oh, baby…" His voice breaks.

Before I can stop him from making a spectacle of himself, he leans in and pulls my hands to his mouth, kissing the knuckles on both of them. I let go and cup his face as he places his hands over mine again, stroking them back and forth.

"Thank you, baby. Thank you."

"I missed you so much, Davison."

He licks his lips as he starts to stroke my hand with his thumb, the same motion he made that first night we met when he asked me that question. My torso starts to flutter, sending goose bumps up and down my body. I can feel my cleft clench with heated desire.

"If we weren't in public right now..." he murmurs.

Any other time, I'd be pissed off at his rude connotation, but at the moment, I don't mind at all because I feel exactly the same.

"Get the check, Harvard. Now."

He replies with a wicked smile and doesn't even bother asking for the bill. He pulls out his wallet, throwing a twenty on the table. Yanking me by the hand, we fly out of the café. His grip on my hand threatens its circulation, but the pain only increases the heat that is close to erupting inside me. Our attached hands are a live current, the energy pulsating between us, just proving to me how much we had truly missed each other.

We're almost running, not saying a word to each other. We need to be somewhere private. It hits me that it's Saturday, the busiest morning for my father at work, and I just left him in the shop.

"Follow me," I command him.

We finally get back to my building, and thankfully I don't see anyone familiar outside. I don't want anyone reporting back to Papa that I'm taking Davison inside our home without him there. Even though I'm a grown woman, I still live under my father's roof. My traditional, old-school father's roof.

By the time we reach my apartment on the fourth floor, we're both panting from exhaustion. I grab the key Papa and I keep hidden on top of the door frame and let us in.

Within seconds, Davison takes my hand and slams me against the door, shutting it with a thud. We devour each other, just like we did the first time in his Maybach. The taste of his hot tongue twisting with mine is the food I have been craving all this time.

We moan and whimper as we kiss, our grips on each other's bodies becoming corporeal vises.

"Allegra," he rasps between kisses.

I need more. I tug him to the living room, pulling him down with me onto the couch. His long, solid body stretches over mine, his hard cock straining against his zipper. He shoves his hands under my sweatshirt, then groans in complaint when he feels my T-shirt underneath.

I hear Davison mutter, "Fuck. You're killing me, baby," as I laugh to myself.

He pushes both up with his hands, feeling for my breasts. With a growl, he clamps his lush lips over one nipple as I throw my head back in ecstasy, kneading the other breast with his left hand.

"Yes, Davison…" I moan.

The sensation of his warm tongue on my body, sucking, nipping, biting, pushes me to the brink. I need him to make me come, to feel him inside me.

As if he'd read my mind, his right hand travels down under the waistband of my yoga pants, blindly searching for my cleft. Once he finds my pussy, he shoves two fingers inside me, massaging it, sighing in the feel of my wetness that is for him, that was caused by him.

"Oh, baby, you're soaked already. You want me, don't you?" he rasps into my ear.

I whimper in reply to him, not at all able to form a coherent word.

With the heel of his hand, he presses down on my cleft at the precise angle over my clit, and I bite down on my lower lip to keep me from screaming aloud, knowing how thin the walls are in my building, but the rest of my body shudders from the release of my orgasm.

Davison sits up, yanking me with him. I cover myself up as he pulls me into his arms. We kiss each other gently, our lips swollen. Wholly spent, I rest my head on Davison's shoulder.

"Baby?" he pants.

"Yeah?"

"How do you say 'crazy' in Italian?"

"*Pazza.*' Why?"

"Because you are fucking *pazza* to bring us back here for a heavy make-out session when your father is working downstairs."

"Hey, we needed someplace private to do what we just did. You're not complaining, are you?"

"Are you kidding? That was…"

I look up at him when he pauses, and he's staring at me, his eyes soft, his lips smiling fully across his face.

"I'm just really happy right now," he says, stroking my face with his thumb.

"You can be such a sap, Mr. Berkeley, but I promise I won't tell."

He laughs. "It would ruin my reputation."

He continues staring at me, his eyebrows narrowing.

"I'm almost afraid to ask," I say to him.

"Dinner. My place," he announces.

"When?"

"Your next night off."

I smile. "It's a date, Harvard."

"But one thing won't be on the menu."

"What?" My curiosity piques.

"Sausage," he says.

I glance down at the enormous bulge in his pants.

"The Italian kind," he corrects himself, his face cringing at the thought of what I was doing in the shop not even two hours ago.

We both laugh, and it's a laugh of catharsis. What happened between us is now over. We are together.

God help me.

Chapter Eight

After that Saturday, which I still love to replay in my head, things between Davison and me are still fragile, but we know we want to be together. There is no disputing it—there is something between us and I'm done fighting it, mostly because of two things that remind me why I should.

I find a flower from Davison in my Lost and Found box every day I come to work. One day it's a pink tulip, another day it's a cornflower. He's definitely keeping some lucky florist in business. The other is the ride he gives me after work. It's not a question anymore of whether he'll take me home—it's a given.

Right now, we're doing what we usually do at work: exchange heated stares since we can't touch each other. Davison is wearing a midnight-blue suit with a matching vest and tie over a crisp white shirt. Every stitch fits him perfectly, as his suits always do.

He is standing behind the bar talking to the bartender. As if he senses my eyes on him, he looks over at me. A sly grin takes over his entire face, as it does on mine. He winks at me, then walks to the front of the restaurant to talk to William, the manager.

The holiday season is now in full swing. Business is always busier at this time, which means more tips for me, but also customers who like to celebrate the spirit of the season in excess, especially on the weekends. This Saturday night is no exception.

As closing time approaches, my feet are truly killing me. I'm thinking about Davison's foot massages when a man in a wrinkled brown suit steps up to the coat-check door. He grips the door to steady himself.

"I need…my coat," he spits out at me.

The overpowering stench of alcohol punches me in the face.

I take a deep breath and steel myself. Even though I've already grown used to dealing with inebriated customers, it's never pleasant.

"Do you have your claim number, sir?"

He starts searching through his pockets for the ticket. He almost falls backward, but steadies himself at the last minute and leans into the open door. "I can't find it…c'mon…you remember me," he slurs.

I take a step back. "Sir, I've had a lot of customers today."

"I'll bet you have," he mutters.

I lean in closer to call out to get William to help him when the guy suddenly grabs the collar of my shirt with both of his hands. I try to pry his hands off me, but they won't budge. He tries to kiss me as I fight him off, screaming, "Let go of me, you pig!"

In a flash, an arm dressed in midnight blue is pinned around the guy's neck. "Get the fuck off her!" Davison growls under his breath, his face bloodred, his eyes narrowed and menacing. He locks him in a choke hold. The guy's hands let me go in a second as William and another waiter come over to throw him out.

I'm frozen, trying to catch my breath, when Davison reaches over and unlocks the door to let himself in. Before I can stop him, I'm in his arms.

"Are you okay, baby?" he asks worriedly. "You're shaking."

"I'm…I'm fine. Don't hold me like this. Someone will see us."

"I don't care. You're done for the night. Someone else can cover the coat check. I'm taking you back to the office so you can rest."

"No, Davison, I'm fine. Really."

"No arguments. Now, Allegra," he commands.

When I look at him, his jaw is fixed with an intense look in his eyes. As I let him lead me out, I glance over and could swear I see Ashton. He walks me back to the office and settles me on the couch, covering me with a blanket.

"Stay here until I come to get you," he orders, not welcoming any argument from me.

I nod and lie down on the worn leather, stretching out my tired limbs. I must have dozed off when I hear the door open, but it only swings open a crack. Then I hear low voices, Davison's and a woman's.

I step closer to the door to hear more clearly.

"What the hell was that?" the woman asks.

"What are you talking about?"

"You and that coat-check girl."

"It's none of your damn business, Ashton. You and I are done. What I do is no fucking concern of yours anymore."

I hear the click-click of stilettos fading as Davison steps into the room, shutting the door behind him. I don't bother running back to the couch to pretend I was sleeping.

His head rears back in surprise when he sees me standing up. I let my eyes bore into his so he'll know I'd heard everything.

"Why aren't you resting?" he asks, looking concerned, placing his hands on my shoulders.

"What was that about?" I demand.

"Nothing. It was Ashton being her usual self. Now, since you refuse to rest here, I'm going to walk out of this restaurant with my arm around you, put you in my car, then drive you home with you sitting in my lap with my arms around you. You're off tomorrow night, right?"

Once I nod, he continues, "Then you're going to have dinner with me at my house."

Something he just said scares me. It's one thing for me to be with him in private, but it's entirely something else for us to be seen in public together.

I grab his hands, shaking my head. "Wait, no, you can't walk out with me. Everyone will see."

Suddenly, his arms clasp around my neck, cupping my head. His lips find mine as I welcome his tongue into my mouth. We kiss so sweetly. I melt in his arms. It feels so comfortable with him. So easy.

"Davison…" I moan.

Suddenly, the heat builds between us. His lips still clamped to mine, he keeps one hand around my neck as the other moves down to grab my ass, kneading it tightly with his palm. My hands roam to his hair, holding the roots and pulling on them with my fingers, pushing him into me as far as he can possibly go.

I whimper in protest when he finally pulls his mouth away from mine. "And that, Venus," he pants, "is why I'm walking out with my arm around you. And if anyone has a problem with it, they can tell me to my face."

True to his word, when I leave Le Bistro that night, Davison's arm is gripped around my shoulders. I sense everyone's eyes on us, full of inquiry and curiosity. I don't want to think about the repercussions and questions to come tomorrow. All that I care about at this moment is the safety I feel when I'm with him.

* * *

The first surprise I have the next night, the night of my date with Davison, happens during the drive to his apartment. Charles picks me up, and as I check my face in my compact for the hundredth time, he turns south on FDR Drive instead of north.

"Aren't we going to the Upper East Side?" I shout up to Charles.

"No, Miss Orsini."

Members of the society circle that Davison's family belongs to tend to live uptown, either in a co-op on Fifth Avenue or a town house on Sutton Place. But in reality, as I find out, Davison lives in Battery Park City, the residential neighborhood on the southwest tip of Manhattan. It's unexpected and indicates that he likes to follow his own path. Something about that makes me smile.

Charles swerves the Maybach into a side street off Battery

Place, pulling in front of a tall glass building with THE APOGEE etched over the entrance.

I step into the marble lobby and announce myself to the concierge at the front desk.

"I'm here to see—"

"Yes, Mr. Berkeley is expecting you, Miss Orsini." He walks over to a lone elevator and retrieves a key from a chain hanging on his pants pocket. "Take this elevator. He has the top floor."

Once inside, I check myself in the mirrored elevator. I open my coat and straighten out the red jersey dress I'm wearing, making sure it hasn't gathered up on me in the car. My black knee-high stiletto boots haven't tracked anything in, and I apply one last coat of lip gloss.

When the elevator opens, Davison is standing right in front of me because he actually *does* have the entire top floor.

He is barefoot, wearing a long-sleeved black V-neck cashmere sweater with nothing underneath and khakis rolled up just past his ankles. The sleeves of his sweater are pushed up to his elbows, allowing me a view of the veins that cord his muscled forearms. His pants hang loose on him in a very casual, sexy manner.

While I love seeing him in the custom-fitted suits he wears for work, seeing him like this makes me want to curl up with him on a sofa, wrapped in his arms while we're watching a movie or just listening to music. He looks so different—a good kind of different. I'm so aroused already, my heart beating rapidly in my chest, my core already clenching with need.

"Allegra," he whispers, extending his hand to me. "Come in."

"Hi," I reply sheepishly as I take his hand and step into his apartment.

Still holding my hand, he kisses it, brushing his lips across my knuckles.

"Let me take your coat. Please make yourself at home."

As he puts my coat away, I look out across the large open space. The cream palette of the living room furniture contrasts against a black-stained wooden floor. A large Rothko hangs on one of the walls. Floor-to-ceiling windows line two sides of the living room. A female voice is singing bossa nova over hidden speakers.

I walk over to one set of windows, where the view takes my breath away. I can see the Statue of Liberty and Ellis Island from where I'm standing. Ships and ferries cross back and forth across the Hudson River.

"Davison, this is amazing," I tell him excitedly over my shoulder. "You're so lucky you can look at this view every night. Do you ever just stand here and just marvel at it all, the beauty of it?"

When he doesn't reply right away, I turn around. He is standing frozen in place, his eyes set on me like a laser.

Then he walks to me, his jaw tight. He pulls me into him, his lips prying mine open. It takes me less than a second to reciprocate as his tongue tangles with mine. I can sense how relaxed he is, taking his time to explore my mouth oh so slowly, so languorously. I sigh from the pure pleasure of being in his arms, melting into them. We kiss for a few minutes until he shifts to look into my eyes.

"Hi," he rasps.

I quietly laugh. "Hi yourself."

"You look gorgeous, baby."

I can feel my face redden. "Thank you. I feel overdressed actually."

"Are you hungry?"

"Starving. Whatever you ordered, it smells delicious."

Shock crosses his face. "'Ordered?' I cooked myself."

Now it's my turn to be shocked. "I don't believe you."

He raises his hand. "I swear. I hope you like filet mignon."

"What? No grass-fed Kobe beef?" I joke.

His face sinks. "Oh…umm…well, I can cook something else…"

I clamp my hand over my mouth. I can't believe it. I actually hurt his feelings. I feel horrible.

I cup his face in my hands. "Davison, I was only joking. I'm the daughter of a butcher. Of course I love filet mignon."

He smirks at me. "I'll get you for that, Orsini."

"Looking forward to it, Berkeley."

* * *

I'm now pleased to know something about him that the tabloids don't—he is a very skilled cook. The filet mignon is cooked to medium-rare perfection, accompanied by baked potatoes and French-cut green beans.

Now holding hands at one end of his long glass-top dining table, Davison and I are enjoying the last of the Bordeaux he served with dinner.

"You are quite a revelation," I tell him.

"How so?"

"I never expected you to be such an amazing cook."

He tightens my hand in his grip. "I'm glad I can keep you on your toes."

"You definitely have that going for you." I smile at him. "I'm surprised you live downtown and not on the Upper East Side."

"To be perfectly honest, our offices are down here, so I can walk to work if I want to. I like living in this area because I can be myself."

"Maybe that's why you chose this building—because of its name. An apogee is both the highest point of something and the farthest point of orbit for an object from Earth. I think that describes you to a tee."

He tilts his head curiously at me, silently indicating for me to continue.

"Well, because you're ambitious and you've achieved so much, but you live your life on your own terms."

He smiles slightly. "You know something? Nobody has ever made that observation before. Not even me. I never thought of that. You…"

"What?"

Davison brings my hand to his mouth, brushing his lips against it, and stands up from his chair. "I'll be right back."

He walks over to the coffee table in the living room and picks up a remote control. He aims it at his stereo system and presses a few buttons.

As he walks back to me, I can hear soft music begin to waft over the room. He reaches out to me with his right hand.

"Dance with me."

Pushing myself away from the table, I place my hand in his and let him lead me to his living room as Bryan Ferry's smooth voice begins to sing "Avalon."

Davison wraps his arms around me as we sway gently to the

music. I lay my head in the crook of his neck, shutting my eyes and taking in the scent of him, which is intoxicating me. When I pull my head back to see his face, he is looking right at me, his eyes soft, full of so much emotion.

"This song…it's how I felt when I first saw you, baby," he whispers. "I knew I was missing something in my life, and then when I saw your face…that was it. I was done. And now I'm happier than I've ever been in my life. Nobody has ever gotten me before like you have. I always want you with me."

I softly kiss his lips as his hands move to rest on the curve of my backside.

"I've never felt like this with anyone," I murmur. "It's so overwhelming that it scares me. But the thought of not being with you is…just…I can't even think about it."

He kisses my forehead. "I'm not going anywhere. Ever. You're mine."

As the last notes are played, he releases me from his grip, save for my left hand. He leads me down a long corridor, making a left at the first door.

A huge California King bed stands against the far wall, taking up a considerable portion of space in the room. The dark wood of the black headboard stands out against the white bedroom walls. The bed is flanked by two nightstands made from the same wood. One side of the room is all doors, hiding his closets and wardrobes.

Davison leaves me at the threshold, walking over to a black suede sofa in a corner of the room. He settles down on it, crossing his right ankle over his left knee.

"Come to me," he whispers.

I slowly stride in his direction when he suddenly calls out, "Stop."

As I wait for his next command, I'm not nervous. For once, I'm not in control. The relief of it excites me. I'm becoming wet from the anticipation.

"Take off your dress."

I do as he asks, letting it fall to the floor.

"Your bra."

I reach around and unhook it, removing each strap slowly. As the bra slips away from me, I softly run my thumbs over my nipples.

"Don't touch yourself. Leave your boots on and walk to me."

I cross to him, stopping within inches of his knees. He yanks me onto his lap, straddling his legs. He pulls me to him to kiss me, teasing my lower lip with his tongue, then entering my mouth as I feel his hot breath on me, tasting me again, taking his time.

Still kissing me, he begins to run his hands up my body from my waist to my chest. I shiver at his touch, sensitive in certain spots.

When he reaches my breasts, he caresses them from the bottom, swallowing them whole with his hands, kneading them with his fingers. I softly moan, dropping my head back, my eyes closed as I revel in his touch.

Suddenly, he retreats from my mouth, and I feel his lips on my right breast. He starts to suckle me, gently at first, then more insistently. I press his head to my chest, encouraging him further. He groans like a beast savoring his meal.

Without warning, Davison scoops me up with his arms and,

with a roar, shoots up from the couch and thunders over to the bed, holding on to me the entire time.

"I have to have you now, baby," he rasps lustily in my ear.

He sets me down on the edge and starts to quickly unzip one of my boots. I reach for the other one, but he stops my hand.

"No. I'm doing this," he insists.

He takes off my boots and pulls me up to take off my panties. Fully naked, I bring his face to mine and kiss him hard.

Then he rears his head back slightly. "Get on the bed, Venus."

I grin naughtily as I scurry up onto the delicious cotton sheets, lying back against the sham pillows.

I lick my lips with anticipation as I watch Davison take off his clothes. Once he's divested everything, my eyes widen and I snap my mouth shut once I realize it's dropped open.

His chest is hard and tanned, his nipples pebbled against his pecs. His abs are sculpted to perfection. He is bare but for the line of dark hair down his muscled torso, marking his happy trail.

And I want to travel that trail down to his…

Oh my God…

His cock, long and lengthened, is pointing upward, engorged and eager. I can already see a dot of pre-cum at its tip.

I swallow in my throat, nodding to his shaft. "Harvard, that thing is going to tear me apart."

He starts crawling onto the bed, his eyes boring into me, smirking mischievously. "It won't, trust me. But even if it did, I'm the one who's going to put you back together. Because you're mine."

He's on his knees now in front of me, close enough now for me to run my hands over his body. I stare at it in wonder, from his solid chest and hard nipples, down to his torso, running my fingers over his abs, feeling the crevices in between.

My hand travels to his cock. I take it in my hands, feeling its heat and smooth texture.

I look up into his hooded eyes. "You're beautiful, Davison."

Davison moans. "That feels so good, baby. Keep doing that."

I continue to let my hands roam over him. He reaches down with his right hand to my cheek, caressing it so softly.

"Oh, Allegra," he whispers. "Your hands feel amazing."

I glance up at him, and his head is lolled back, his mouth open in rapture.

I keep on stroking him when he says, "Lie down, baby."

I fall back and relax, watching as Davison moves over me on all fours while his eyes study me, hungry and hooded.

"Do you have any idea how exquisite you are?" he murmurs.

I shake my head.

"You take my fucking breath away," he growls.

My heartbeat starts to quicken at his words. "Davison, I want you inside me. Now."

He falls on top of me, his mouth traveling all over my body, sucking, biting, licking. He reaches down to my cleft, completely soaked, waiting for him.

I watch from the corner of my eye as he reaches over to the nightstand. I hear him open the drawer, slam it shut, then the tearing of foil.

I feel the mattress dip as he rushes back to me, his body over mine. He puts two fingers into my cleft. "You are so wet. So ready for me," he moans.

He takes out his fingers, and then plunges his hard cock into me. We both groan loudly at the feel of our bodies finally joining together. I clench around his shaft. As he fills me fully, my sex slowly adjusts to the size of him.

His face hangs over me. I can feel his hot breath on me. "Fuck, you are so tight. You feel so good."

With his hands clamped in mine, he starts to thrust his cock into me, again and again. The feel of him inside me is glorious. I want him so much. I coil my legs around his back, locking my ankles together. I look at him, and he is the image of a Greek god, his solid chest slick with sweat, his magnificent abs clenched together.

His cock pummels my sex. "Harder, Davison."

The sound of our fucking echoes throughout the room, the slapping of skin against skin and the primal moans that howl from our lungs. His hair is sticking from sweat to his forehead, his eyes open and burning into mine.

"Come for me, baby. I've fucking fantasized about this moment," he pants.

He takes his right hand, reaching down under him to my clit, rubbing it between his fingers.

"Yes, Davison. Please…" I beg.

Suddenly, I feel it. The wave is cresting, and I'm riding it so hard, it's about to overtake me…

It feels fucking incredible. My body shudders as my pussy clenches him, and I see bursts of light behind my closed eyes.

"Davison!" I shout from pure release.

He starts to pump into me even harder, his breathing rapid. "I'm so close, baby."

I'm still shaking when Davison cries out, "Allegra!" as he finishes coming. His cock still inside me, he collapses onto me, our panting breaths united in rhythm. I wrap my arms around him, my hands slipping down his back to his firm ass.

He turns his head to my ear. "Allegra," he whispers.

"Yeah?" I pant, wholly sated, smiling contentedly.

"I'm never letting you go."

Chapter Nine

I'm standing in front of Professor Waltz and the five members of my Wagner class, including Luciana. I clear my throat, take a deep breath, and begin to sing Brünnhilde's war cry from Act Two, Scene One in *Die Walküre*.

As Brünnhilde, I'm warning my father, Wotan, of the arrival of his wife, Fricka, in her ram-drawn chariot. I stand up straighter, and a sudden wave of confidence comes over me. I take deeper breaths from my diaphragm as I've been taught to do, my arms extended dramatically as if I actually were warning my own father of impending doom.

I sing the final line and look out at my audience. Because he's known for his stern demeanor, I'm shocked when a smile crosses over Professor Waltz's face.

He starts to clap. "*Brava! Brava*, Miss Orsini! I don't know what has caused this improvement in your performance, but whatever it is, keep it up! And on that note, class dismissed."

I walk back to my desk to get my bag and coat. Lucy strides over to me with a knowing look in her eyes.

"You can't fool me. I know what's caused the 'improvement.'"

I shrug on my coat. "Really? Do tell."

"You and Money Boy had sex!"

I pull her in closer to me. "Shit, Lucy, keep your voice down!"

"Calm down, will you?" She laughs. "Everyone's gone, and you're glowing. I've never seen you like this. I want details."

Just thinking of what had happened with Davison in his apartment two days ago makes me smile. It wasn't just the sex and mind-blowing orgasms he'd given me. We connected in a way that I never had with another man before. Davison is a primal creature, but he is also tender and loving, something that attracts him to me even more despite my attempts to fight it. And Lucy can see this written all over my face. "He cooked me dinner, we danced—"

"Whoa! Wait a sec! One of the richest men in Manhattan actually cooks?"

"Yeah, and he's pretty damn good at it too. In fact, he's pretty damn good at everything."

Lucy settles into a desk chair. "This is too much. Keep going."

I sit down across from her. "It was amazing. Actually, 'amazing' is too tame a word."

"Let me try. Wild, sensational, sheet-clawing…am I close?"

I smile, nodding my head.

She slaps the desk with her hand. "Oh my God! You're killing me, Alli! But I'm so excited for you."

"He's just…I can't put it into words. I just love being with him. But I'm scared."

Lucy reaches over to touch my arm. "Of what?"

"Like everything is happening too fast, and I'm starting to care too much for him when I know I probably shouldn't."

"Don't think like that, okay? Stop freaking out and just enjoy it, sweetie."

I smile in return. "I'll try," I tell her, trying to reassure myself as much as her.

* * *

Le Bistro is busy as usual that night. I barely have a minute to myself when I hear a chirp from my purse. A lull in customers gives me a chance to check my phone.

It's a text from Davison.

Baby, I'm stuck at the office. I probably won't make it to the restaurant tonight. Charles will drive you home. Call me before you go to sleep so I can tell you what I'd be doing to your wet pussy with my hard cock if you were lying next to me.

"Is that from Davis?"

A shrill voice causes me to raise my head. Ashton is standing at the coat-check door.

Since it's not any of her damn business, I simply shove the phone back into my purse and walk over to her. "Can I check something for you?"

"No, but I suggest you check your status on the society ladder, because you seem to be under the delusion that you're dating Davis."

Why do I suddenly have the feeling he hates being called that?

"I could say the same applies to you since he broke up with you."

"No, dear, he didn't break up with me. We're engaged. He's just stringing you along."

I make a point of looking down at her left hand. "If that's true, shouldn't you be wearing a ring?"

"The marriage has been arranged for years. Our families are old friends."

"That's funny. The last time I checked, we were living in twenty-first-century Manhattan, not nineteenth-century England."

"You poor thing. You really are deluded, aren't you? Check the top drawer of his desk at home the next time you're there. He just bought the ring for me at Cartier."

I stare back at her, my eyes not wavering for a moment. I refuse to let her see me fall apart in front of her as she delivers her final blow.

"You're just a distraction. Family comes first for him. Always has, always will. Enjoy the ride, because it won't last much longer."

She flips her hair over her shoulder as she slithers away, the lingering scent of her noxious perfume assaulting my nose.

I brace the door, gripping it with my hands as firmly as I can to control my breathing.

Hearsay. That's all it is. Hearsay.

* * *

Davison picks up before the second ring.

"Hi, baby. Everything okay? Where are you?"

"I'm in the car with Charles on the way home. I was afraid I'd fall asleep and forget to call you. I didn't want to worry you."

"How did it go tonight?"

"Fine," I reply too quickly.

"What happened?" he asks worriedly.

"Nothing."

"Allegra, I know you well enough by now to tell when something's wrong."

"I'm just tired. Really. I just wish you were here, that's all. I miss you."

"Then come over."

"Don't tempt me."

"I'm naked," he whispers.

The visual that pops into my head that second arouses me instantly as I moan in frustration. "Ugh. Stop torturing me, Harvard."

"Whatever it takes, Venus," he states confidently.

"Can we have dinner tomorrow? Your place?" I ask sheepishly.

"Of course. Hey, are you sure you're okay?"

I yawn to prolong the illusion. "Just tired."

He sighs. "All right. Anything special you'd like for tomorrow night?"

"The state you're in now will do just fine."

"Naked and horny?"

"Bingo."

"I think that can be arranged. Sleep well, baby. And one more thing…"

"Yeah?" I ask curiously.

"I miss you too."

* * *

After thanking Charles for the ride, I walk into the small foyer of my building. As my boots scrape against the floor, my right foot pushes something along the tiny square tiles. I look down, spotting a white business envelope sticking under the top of my boot.

I bend down to pick it up and turn it over. The name MIA ALLEGRA ROSSETTI is spelled out in small block letters, obviously printed out by computer.

My heart drops. Nobody has referred to me by that name in a very long time. Years. It was my name until I decided with my father to change it when I was a teenager. I've done so well keeping my identity hidden.

Until now.

I bite my lower lip to keep it from shaking, even as my hands are trembling, holding the featherlight envelope in my right one.

Holding my breath, I insert my quivering thumb into the seal and tear it open. I peek inside to find a folded piece of copy paper. Slowly, I pull it out.

Once it's fully spread out in my hands, my heart begins to beat faster. I lean against the door as my body begins to shake.

It's a photocopy of The Picture. The one that was plastered on the front page of every newspaper in New York City and broadcast for days on the nightly news nineteen years ago. Thankfully, the copy is black-and-white, so I can't see the dark brown irises of my widened eyes or the light blue of the shirt that the NYPD officer was wearing, which my five-year-old hands were fisting in their tight grip as I looked over the cop's shoulder when I was being carried to safety.

Below the picture, scrawled in black pen with a rough, uneven hand, are five words—

I KNOW WHO YOU ARE

I sink to the floor, my head bent down, my hands over my mouth trying to suppress my sobs so they won't echo throughout the entire building.

Oh God. No. Please. No. No. No.

Chapter Ten

The next morning, I realize the creaky wooden stairs that lead to the detective unit on the second floor of my local precinct haven't changed in nineteen years. Walking up them, images flash through my head, mostly of me at age five holding onto my father's hand as he took me to see Detective Leary every day after my mother's murder to check on the progress of their investigation, with my other hand tightly gripping the teddy bear that my mother had bought me at FAO Schwarz for Christmas. But this time, I'm walking up those stairs alone.

I step through the swinging double doors to the homicide detective squad room. The man I have come to see is not hard to miss. Detective Dermot Leary is holding court, surrounded by a group of young men and women. Since the last time I saw him, his hair has turned gray and he has a visible pouch around his midsection where his gun belt is struggling to hold on.

One of the young men yells out, "Can we help you?"

"Yes. I need to speak to Detective Leary," I announce.

Detective Leary turns around, a warm smile appearing across his face. He waddles over to me, enveloping me in a gentle hug. "Allegra! How are you?"

"I'm well, thank you, Detective," I reply. "I need to speak with you."

"Of course. I think interrogation room one is free. Cole, let's go," he orders in a gravelly voice, signaling to one of the young detectives, a tall, thin blond man who looks to be in his thirties. He walks over, outstretching his hand to me.

"I'm Josh Cole," he introduces himself to me. I shake his hand in return.

"He's new," Leary informs me. "I'm showing him the ropes. Is it okay if he sits in on this?"

I nod.

Leary and Cole escort me to the same room where I had been asked question after question about the night of my mother's murder. I stop before stepping through the door.

"Ah, shit, I'm sorry, Allegra," Leary says, recognizing the reason for my hesitation. "We can use another room."

I shake my head. "No, no. I'll be fine. I insist."

"Okay, if you're sure."

I walk through the door, indicating my answer.

The walls are the same putrid shade of green from nineteen years ago, except now the paint is chipping along the ceiling and baseboards. I sit down at the table, with Leary and the young detective on the other end.

"Now tell me how I can help," Leary says kindly.

I pull the envelope out of my purse. I slide it over to Dermot and Cole.

Leary picks it up and opens its contents, then shows it to Cole.

"When did you get this?" Cole asks.

"Last night. I found it on the floor of the lobby in my building."

The two detectives look at each other knowingly.

My heart starts to pound in my chest. "What? What is it?"

Leary clasps his hands together, leaning closer to me. "We've been investigating a sex-trafficking ring with origins in Europe. They've expanded here, setting up base as a fake talent agency, taking advantage of young women who want to become models or actresses, and then they're drugged and taken overseas to become sex slaves."

"How long has this been going on?"

"About five months. We're taking our time, building a solid case against everyone involved. We have someone on the inside."

I'm trying my best to keep calm. "Okay, but does this involve me in any way? The look you two gave each other made me panic there for a second."

"One of the cities where the ring's based is Naples," Cole informs me.

"Where Carlo and my mother were from," I finish his thought.

Leary nods. "We know this because one of the perps has a heavy Italian accent, and our language expert concluded that it was a Neapolitan dialect based on what she heard on the surveillance tapes. But whoever sent you this must've known Carlo somehow, maybe from when he came over all those years ago…"

"Before he killed my mother," I whisper. "Okay, but if this guy did know Carlo, why do this now?"

"Probably just to mess with your head," Cole deduces.

"Should I be worried?" I ask nervously.

"I would just be more careful when you're out in public, make sure nobody is following you, that kind of thing," Leary suggests. "And if you get any more of these letters, I want you to bring them in. Understood?"

"Yes, of course I will." I nod vehemently.

Leary stands up, walking over to my side of the table and sits in the chair next to me. "Allegra, why isn't Jimmy here with you?" he asks, referring to my father by his American nickname.

"Because I don't want him to know. I can handle this," I insist.

"He needs to know about this," he counters. "If you're feeling threatened, we can put surveillance outside your place just to make sure…"

"No." I cut him off. My hands clench into fists. "No, Papa doesn't need to know, and I don't need an officer to watch over me. Please," I beg, "I can take care of myself."

Cole shakes his head as Leary sighs. "Fine. Just promise me you'll tell your father. And anyone else important in your life. And you call me the second anything strange or out of the ordinary happens. Got it?"

I nod. *Papa—fine. Davison—absolutely not.*

"I assume if the lab dusts this envelope, they'll find your prints?" Cole asks.

"Yes. Is there anything else I should know?"

Leary rises from his chair, as does Cole. "No. That's it for now.

But you have to be careful from now on. You need to be hyper-aware of everything going on around you."

I stand up to face Leary. "I will be, Detective. I promise. I know how to protect myself."

He pats my shoulder reassuringly. "Don't worry, Allegra."

I smile slightly, giving them a grateful nod. "Thank you. Both of you."

Once I walk out of the station, I scan the street and look around for anything suspicious, just like Detective Leary told me to do.

I can do this. I can protect myself. I'm used to it by now.

* * *

Mamma told me to run and hide.

I'm running. Running as fast as I can. It's so dark. I need to find a place to hide.

I see an alley. I race down, looking…looking.

An open door. I run inside, down a damp hallway. Another open door.

It's so warm. There are big metal things making so much noise.

I lie down next to one. I'm so tired. I want to sleep. I close my eyes…

Then someone shakes me. A light in my eyes. "Mia? Mia Allegra Rossetti? Sweetheart, I'm a policeman. I'm going to take you to your daddy now."

He picks me up, carrying me outside. I hold tight to his blue shirt. More lights, all different colors. So bright…

I wake up with a start from my afternoon power nap, my body covered in sweat, shivering despite the wool blanket that covers me.

I reach for my water bottle. I pull my nightstand drawer open, then quickly slam it shut.

I don't need the pills. I can handle this. I can handle everything.

I know how to protect myself.

And I did. Nineteen years ago.

Chapter Eleven

When Davison waits for me at his private elevator in his apartment that night, he's barefoot in a rumpled white shirt and black pants, his shirttails pulled out of his waistband. Dark scruff covers his chiseled face. He's obviously just come home from the office. And he looks so fucking sexy.

"Hey, baby. Listen, I hope it's okay if we just order in. I was thinking—"

I rush to him as soon as I see him, slamming my lips over his. I know I need to start detaching myself from him in order to keep him safe from my past, but I need something more than that. I need his strength, his constancy. I need to be with someone who doesn't know anything about my past and thinks I had a normal childhood. I need *him*.

He doesn't hesitate in reciprocating. Within seconds, his

tongue is seeking mine. He pulls me into his arms, hauling me up with his hands as I wrap my legs around his waist. He moves us into the living room, his mouth attached to mine the entire way.

I can feel the plush cushions of the couch underneath me as we collapse onto it. We rip off each other's clothes, not saying a word to each other. It isn't necessary. Our eyes are saying everything that's needed between each other. The hunger in Davison's eyes makes them hooded, exciting me, moistening my core.

With his shirt gripped in my hands, I pull him closer as he settles himself over me, his hard cock nudging my belly. He descends on my breasts, sucking them like a beast feasting on his kill.

Our mutual moans echo in the wide-open space of his living room. He is driving me mad as I scratch my nails up and down his muscled back, writhing under him.

"Need you inside me, Davison. Now," I pant.

"Shit," he exclaims. "Need a condom."

"It's okay," I tell him hurriedly. "I'm safe. Go bare. Please."

Before I know what's happening, he sits up, pulling me with him, then lies back down with me on top of him.

"I want to see you when I make you come. I want your gorgeous body on top of me when I'm driving my cock inside you."

He tugs me to him, his lush lips clamping over mine, sucking my tongue into his hot mouth. His hands knead my ass, traveling up and down my back.

Coming up for air, I smile at him wickedly, then lean forward to dangle my breasts over his face. He smirks at me, raising one of his eyebrows at me.

"Such a tease, Venus," he murmurs.

I let my breasts hang over him, swiftly moving away when his mouth is inches from my nipple. Finally, with a roar, he tugs one nipple to his mouth, biting on it, then licking it to soften the pain.

My head lolls back as I revel in his ardor, but then I look down, and my eyes are locked on the image below me. Davison's eyes are shut, his face contorted in pure joy, as if he can't get enough of the taste of me.

Sated from the taste of my breasts, he sits me back onto his crotch.

"Ride me, Allegra," he commands.

I lean forward slightly until I settle his cock in my pussy, impaling me through my folds.

"Ah…there you are, baby. Now I can feel me inside your sweet pussy with nothing between us. Always so fucking wet for me," he whispers.

I begin moving on top of him, as his hips start to join mine in sync. I buck on top of him, my hands holding on to his for support.

"I need you, Davison. I need you to take it all."

He grunts as he meets me, thrust for thrust. I whimper, aching for more.

"Fuck, baby…you're so beautiful," I hear him pant.

He lets go of one of my hands, reaching down below me. I can feel his fingers on my clit as he begins to roll it between his fingers.

"Yes, Davison…yes!" I yell at the top of my lungs, arching my back, my head thrown back as my body shudders in release from the exquisite orgasm he just gave me.

I milk his cock again and again, opening my eyes in time to see the muscles in his neck straining, desperate for release. When he does come, his head rears back as he roars aloud, his body shaking under mine.

Davison gathers me in his arms, rolling me onto my side, now lying face-to-face with him. I take a deep breath, inhaling him and his sweat mixed in with his spicy aftershave and the scent of sex that permeates the room.

"Hmm. Maybe I should stay away from the restaurant more often," he coos in my ear.

I shake my head. "No. Bad idea, Harvard."

"If it causes these kinds of reactions from you…"

"For the record, you don't need to stay away from Le Bistro to get those reactions from me."

He cups my face with his hand, stroking my cheek with his fingertips, nodding his head. "I missed you," he whispers, his eyes soft and tender when he looks at me.

"I missed you too," I reply, putting my hand over his to keep it in place. I don't want him to move. My entire body warms from one single touch of his. I purr in contentment. I love being exactly where I am at this moment.

* * *

Not wanting to move, Davison pulls a cashmere blanket from an ottoman, cocooning us in the softest fabric, our bodies entwined, our limbs entangled in each other. We breathe softly, our eyes locked.

He tilts his head to my hair and breathes deeply. "Coconut?"

I smile. "Yup. Coconut shampoo, with a hint of brown sugar."

"Mmmm," he murmurs. "I like it. Very much. So, tell me something."

"What?"

"Am I your first?"

I look up at him, mouth dropped. "I'm not a virgin, Harvard."

He smirks at me. "Yeah, I kind of guessed that part. Allow me to rephrase. Am I your first serious relationship?"

I pause before I speak. "I suppose you are. I dated one guy on and off through college. Matteo. He lived in Queens. Italian like me. But in the end, when things started getting serious, he turned out to be a commitment-phobe, and we broke up."

He smiles. "His loss is my gain."

"I just haven't dated a lot, that's all," I snap at him, shutting my eyes when I realize I did for no reason.

He strokes my cheek. "You don't need to be defensive with me, baby. I don't care if you haven't been with a lot of guys. Honestly, I like that. You were just waiting for me."

I roll my eyes, softening at his attempt at levity. "Your arrogance knows no bounds, Berkeley."

"Just call them like I see them, Orsini." He cocks his head at me. "Don't you want to know about me?"

"Like I need to."

"What does that mean?"

"Please," I sigh. "I know your sexual history very well, thanks to every tabloid in this city. Which makes me wonder what the hell you're doing with me."

"Hey," he grunts, gripping my chin hard so he can look straight into my eyes. "Don't ever talk about yourself that way.

Those other women meant nothing to me. I never knew if they were with me because of my money—"

"Or your looks," I interject.

"Yeah, unfortunately," he sighs. "But they revealed their true intentions to me soon enough, and I just moved on to the next. And then there was Ashton, and when I met you, I just..."

I wait with bated breath.

"I just knew." He smiles so widely. "I looked into those gorgeous brown eyes of yours, and that was it. I didn't know what I wanted until I met you. Yes, I'll admit that you're different from the other women I've dated, but you're so easy to be with. You put me in my place. You're kind and sweet, and..."

He leans down and kisses me hard.

"Sexy as hell," he ends.

I hum in gratitude, burrowing my head into the crook of his neck.

I don't want to ruin the beauty of this moment, but something is bothering me, and after a few minutes, I take a deep breath.

"I need to tell you something."

"What's going on, baby?"

I exhale and take another breath. "I lied the last time I talked to you."

"I know you did."

My mouth drops. "How did you know?"

He smiles, raising his eyebrow at me, as if to say *Really?*

I smile back at him as he says, "Continue."

"Ashton stopped by the coat check to talk to me. More like intimidate me. She said that she was engaged to you, that the marriage had been arranged. It was all 'Davis this' and 'Davis that.'"

"I hate it when she calls me that." He grimaces.

I grin slightly. *I knew it.*

"Then she told me about the ring, that you bought it for her, and exactly where I could find it in your desk. I need to know if this is true."

He smiles at me. "I've never shown Ashton the ring. The only reason she probably knew it was in my desk was because she must have snooped herself during a party or some other event I had here."

"Are you serious?" I ask incredulously.

He nods. "That ring is an antique. I never bought it for her. It was my grandmother's. I just haven't had time to put it in my safe deposit box. Ashton and I are not engaged and we never will be. I don't love her and I never will."

"I think you need to tell her that."

"I agree. I've had enough of her shit, and now that she's bothering you, saying all of these hurtful things to you, she's crossed the line."

I smile and kiss him softly on the lips.

He caresses my cheek with his fingertips. "You can talk to me, baby. Always."

"Thank you, Davison."

"Hungry?" he asks.

"Starving."

"How about a pizza with the works, accompanied by a bottle of champagne?"

"Perfect."

We eat dinner that night sitting on his floor cushions naked, enjoying it all with Nina Simone's lush voice as our musical accompaniment.

* * *

I'm singing an aria from *Carmen* at the top of my lungs as I clean my bedroom the following afternoon. I love the music with its cheerful melody. I'm particularly upbeat as it is, thanks to the three orgasms Davison gave me before I left his apartment. He is a very generous man.

I don't hear my father knock on my door over the roar of the vacuum. He gives me a start when he waves his hand in front of my face.

My right hand flies to my chest as I shut off the Hoover. "Papa! I didn't hear you. Are you done for the day?"

"*Sì.* I need to speak to you about something. Do you have a minute?"

"*Certo.* What is it?"

I watch as my father pulls a white business envelope from his back pocket. He hands it to me as I sit down. It's identical to the one I found two nights ago in my building foyer, but this time it's addressed to him under his birth name, Giacomo Rossetti. I don't need to look inside to know what's there.

"Don't you want to know what's in it?"

I give in and nod, steeling myself.

My father takes the envelope from me, pulls out the copy paper, and unfolds it. It's the same picture of me, but this time the five words are I KNOW WHO SHE IS.

"We need to show this to Detective Leary," he announces.

"No, we don't."

"Why?"

I inhale deeply. "Because I found the same thing three days ago. And I already gave it to Detective Leary at the precinct."

My father's eyes widen in shock. "What? Allegra, why didn't you tell me?"

"Because I can handle it, Papa," I reassure him.

"What did Leary say?"

I'm not telling him about the perp being possibly connected to Carlo Morandi. He'll have me on permanent lockdown.

"He said he would look into it. Don't worry. I'll be fine."

"I don't accept that!" he shouts. "You are my daughter, *cara*! When I said good-bye to your mother, I promised her that I would keep you safe. I will do whatever it takes to make sure of that. Maybe I should tell your man—"

I jump to my feet. "No! Absolutely not! You are not going to tell Davison about this! Promise me, Papa. Please. I'm begging you."

"Don't you think he should know about this?"

Of course he should. Then I'll watch as he leaves me, humiliated and embarrassed for himself and his family. I know that is the inevitability of our relationship.

"I'll tell him when I'm ready."

My father shakes his head. "If you don't want to tell Davison, that is your business. But we are going to see Detective Leary together tomorrow. And I want you to call me once every hour whenever you leave the house. I need to know you're safe."

"Okay," I agree. "We'll go see Leary. And I'll make sure you always know where I am."

Papa looks at me worriedly. I can tell he's scared, and I am too, but I refuse to let this make me a prisoner again. Of course I'll be careful, but it won't stop me from living my life. It was enough that I changed my name to put this behind me. I've lived in a self-made box for nineteen years, and I refuse to crawl back into it.

My phone begins to chirp from my desk. I disentangle myself from my father and check the screen. It's a text from Davison. "Papa, I need to text him back."

He nods, placing a kiss on my forehead. "Fine. I'll see you for dinner, *cara*," he tells me with a clenched jaw.

Once my father shuts the door behind him, I sit down on my bed with my phone to read his message.

I need you, baby. I want you to come over tonight.

I want to see him more than anything. I crave his touch, but then I look over at the envelope that my father left behind.

Would it be okay if I take a rain check? I need to spend some time with my father.

A few seconds later…

All right. If it's for your father…I miss you. I'll call you later.

I text him back, *I miss you too, Harvard. Xoxo*

I fall back on my bed, dropping the phone next to me.

I know I need to tell Davison everything. And I have to do it soon before he finds out from someone else.

Chapter Twelve

What the hell am I thinking?

I'm standing in front of Davison's office building. The headquarters of Berkeley Holdings are housed in two turn-of-the-century brownstones on a narrow cobblestone street in the Financial District. I imagine horse-and-buggy carts on this street back in the day, gas lamps being lit at dusk to illuminate the sidewalks.

I'm here because I miss him. I can't get him out of my mind. I'm so drawn to him. His power. His body. The way he looks at me all combine to make a potent combination that makes me feel alive. No man has ever affected me this way. He allows me to forget my past. He makes me feel wanted and desired. When he texted me telling me he always wanted me with him, I knew exactly what he meant.

I don't have classes this morning. I texted him before I left, asking him nonchalantly what his day was going to be like, wishing him a good day. He didn't catch on, thank goodness.

Knowing that I was going to be seeing his office for the first time, I couldn't wear my sweats. Instead, I'm wearing the same clothes I had on for my interview at Le Bistro—a white silk blouse under the black Calvin Klein suit I bought on sale at Macy's, with black stockings and my black patent leather stilettos. My hair is tied back in the same style I wear at work, my long black winter coat cinched at the waist.

I step into the building, my heels echoing against the marble floor. A young blonde woman is sitting at a tall desk at the far end of the space. She raises an eyebrow at me as she gives me the once-over.

"May I help you?"

I clear my throat. "Yes, I'm here to see Mr. Davison Berkeley."

"Do you have an appointment?"

"No," I reply firmly. "Tell him Miss Orsini is here to see him."

She nods. "Very well. Just a moment."

The woman picks up her phone. "Eleanor, a Miss Orsini is here to see Mr. Berkeley…yes, I can wait…mmm-hmm…very well."

The blonde turns back to me, pointing to a narrow door on a side wall. "You can go up. Take the elevator to the fifth floor."

I smile at her. "Thank you."

Once I press "5" on the elevator panel, I quickly take my compact out of my purse and check my face and hair. I shove it back in just as the elevator comes to a stop.

The fifth floor is the top floor of the building, with a narrow hallway where an older woman, dressed in a pink suit with short chestnut hair, is sitting at a desk outside a set of polished double doors.

"Miss Orsini?" she addresses me.

"Yes, ma'am."

"You can go right in. Mr. Berkeley is waiting for you. Can I get you anything?"

I smile, knowing I'm about to hopefully get what I had come for. "No, thank you."

I turn the brass knob and walk through the doorway. What I see in front of me paralyzes me on the spot.

Dressed in a black pin-striped three-piece suit and a white shirt, his dark green tie matching his eyes, Davison is sitting in his black leather desk chair, leaning back into the headrest. I can tell his legs are crossed, his hands casually lying on the armrests of the chair. The power he exudes, the way he smolders at me makes me so damn wet, heightened by the sight of the sly grin on his lips. I'm breathless at the sight of him. My heart pounds against my chest, seeing a man of such magnetism and confidence. He can overwhelm me so easily, but I'm no longer frightened by him. He arouses me to the point where I cannot help myself, like a vulnerable moth to a burning flame.

"Forgive me," he says, "but my secretary doesn't recall making an appointment with you, Miss Orsini, is it?"

This is going to be fun.

"It must have slipped her mind."

"I don't think so. Eleanor is very good at what she does."

"So am I, Mr. Berkeley."

"I think I'll have to decide that for myself." He rises from his chair and slowly comes toward me. I stand still, dying from curiosity to see what he'll do next.

Davison stops a few inches from me. Taking the belt of my coat in his hands, he begins to undo it, then comes behind me and gently takes it off my shoulders, holding it in his hands.

Suddenly, I feel his hot breath in my ear. "Why don't you go try out my chair?"

As I walk to his desk, I hear the click of a door locking behind me. Once I sit down, I'm able to take in more of his office.

Modern and antique sensibilities clash, with antique furniture holding a large flat-screen television that shows a split screen of CNBC and CNN International. The windows provide a stunning view of the Brooklyn Bridge and East River. A round table sits in the far corner, accompanied by four high-back leather dining chairs. The sofas look comfortably weathered, as if they've been here for centuries. His Harvard degrees hang on a wall next to a portrait of a man who's probably the founder of the company. The entire office holds the air of a gentlemen's club, the kind where men drink Scotch from tumblers while smoking cigars and reading that day's copy of the *Wall Street Journal*. A computer sits on top of his desk, along with his cell phone and numerous files.

Davison remains standing at the door, watching me closely with a mischievous grin. "What do you think?"

"So, this is where you make billion-dollar deals and rule over the universe?"

"Something like that." He smirks. "I like it up here. It's quiet."

"Yes. You could probably hear a pin drop from outside."

He shakes his head. "It's soundproofed." He smiles wickedly. "The entire room, including the door."

I take a deep breath as I cross my legs to stop them from shaking.

Like a jaguar stalking its victim, Davison returns to the desk, never taking his eyes from mine, coming to a stop once he's standing next to me.

He gazes at me, the look of desire and hunger in his eyes as vivid as the one I know is mirrored in mine.

The rumble that I love in his voice comes to life. "Take your hair down."

I reach behind and pull the clip out, letting it fall to the floor.

"Unbutton your jacket, then pull up your skirt."

I take off my jacket altogether, then I sit up and hike up my skirt to reveal the only thing I'm wearing underneath it: a garter belt to hold up my stockings.

Davison lets out a growl and falls to his knees. He pulls the chair to him, the wheels squeaking loudly as they roll against the plastic cover that protects the wood floor.

Thank God for soundproofing.

He grabs my ass, yanking my crotch to his face, diving for my soaked cleft. His fingers hold the outer lips open while he shoves his hot tongue inside me. He is ravenous, pushing his tongue as far as it can go inside my drenched pussy. His lips cover my folds, sucking them into his mouth.

I can hear him moaning in delight at the taste of me on his tongue. I fold my legs over the armrests of the chair to give him more access. He grunts his approval as my hands go straight to his hair, running the soft, silky strands through my fingers, tightening on the roots as he thrusts his tongue into me again and again.

My body is turning into liquid. My limbs are loosening. Soft tears fall from the corners of my eyes from the pure joy I'm experiencing because of him. I am in ecstasy as he pleasures me with no end in sight. "Davison…don't stop…please…more."

Without warning, he takes my legs, hanging them over his shoulders. I cross my ankles, locking them as they rest against his back. He starts to suckle my clit, with two of his fingers now penetrating my pussy, impaling me with them over and over.

Oh God…

I'm teetering on the edge. My eyes shut when the wave of orgasm washes over me, bursts of light exploding behind my eyes. I scream his name in release. "Davison!"

When I finally look down, he is staring up at me, his mouth glistening with my cream on his lips. His eyes hold a crazed look, like that of a beast who hasn't yet reached the point of satisfaction.

Before I know what's happening, he grabs me and pulls me down to the floor with him as the chair goes flying behind me, crashing into the wall.

"I need you, Allegra," he rasps. "Need to be inside you now."

He falls back onto the floor as I sit atop him. I start to undo his belt buckle, his hands fumbling with mine to get it done faster. Our panting breaths are the only sounds in the room.

Once his belt is loosened, he pulls down his pants and boxers, exposing his beautiful hard cock. I settle myself onto him, my cleft wet with desire, greedy to finally take him. He is sheathed inside me. I grin at him, feeling triumphant at receiving what I'd come here for—surprising the man who needs to control everything in his life.

I'm ready to claim my prize. I start to move with him, anxious not to lose our rhythm.

"Take off your top. I want you to touch your tits, baby."

I tear off my blouse, flinging it over my head, followed by my bra. As Davison watches me, I touch my nipples, pinching them to elongate them. I lick my lips as I stroke my breasts, my eyes locked with his, telling him with one look how aroused and alive he makes me feel.

His hips begin to thrust upward, driving into me. He reaches for my clit, rubbing it between his fingers.

"Come, baby. Come with me," he whispers to me in a ragged breath.

I buck on top of him as another orgasm takes hold of me, again yelling his name when I come. My core tightens on his cock like a vise as I milk him to his own orgasm, the veins in his neck straining red, his eyes shut firmly as he roars in release.

I collapse on top of him, our rapid breaths matching each other's pace.

"Can I...just tell you..." he pants, "that you coming here...was...the sexiest thing...any woman...has ever done to me."

When I finally catch my breath, I manage to find my voice. "I aim to please, sir."

"I can't believe you did that."

"Neither can I." I laugh.

He laughs with me. "Now I want to do something for you."

"I'm listening."

"I'm taking you out for dinner tonight. In public."

A slight tremble shakes my body, but when I look into Davison's eyes, I know I'm not going to say no. After what had just happened, I'm not going to deny him anything.

"Just not on the Lower East Side. Is that all right?"

He tips his head at me curiously. "Of course. Any reason?"

"No," I reply as lightheartedly as I can. "I just don't like that area."

"Sure, baby," he quickly agrees. "Anything you want."

I rise from his body and start to put my clothes back on. I hear Davison zip up his pants behind me. I reach for my coat, but he takes it from me, helping me into it. I smile as he even ties the belt for me.

We stand and gaze at each other. He smiles so sweetly at me, his eyes softened. He reaches for my face, enveloping it, caressing my cheeks with his thumbs.

I don't want to go, and I wonder if he wants me to, because from the way he's looking at me and touching me, I think he wants me to stay.

"I should probably go," I tell him sheepishly.

"Yeah," he sighs. "But I'll pick you up at six thirty."

"It's a date, Harvard."

I watch him unlock the door. He clamps his hand over mine on the doorknob to kiss me softly on the lips before I walk out. I smile at him and leave.

As I step out of the elevator, I glance over at the blonde woman at the front desk again, her eyebrows raised at me suspiciously.

I grin widely at her, turning on my heel, my back ramrod straight as I listen to my shoes click against the marble floor. Once I'm outside, I raise my face to the sky, smiling into the sun.

* * *

I can't stop staring at Davison. This is a moment. I love the idea that nobody else has ever seen him like this, except maybe his mother or nanny when he was a child. I start rummaging around in my purse for my cell phone.

He looks up at me from his meal. "What are you looking for?"

"Just my phone. Want to check my messages."

He raises his eyebrow at me before diving back into his chicken curry. Now that he's occupied again, I turn on the camera.

"Davison?"

He raises his head. "Yeah?"

Click!

He starts talking with his mouth still full. "What the hell was that?"

I turn the phone around so he can see the picture I just snapped.

He's looking at himself dressed in a black button-down shirt, open at the collar, his green eyes ablaze, with a nickel-sized spot of curry sauce in the left corner of his mouth.

"I'm deleting this," he announces as he snatches the phone away from me.

In a flash, I reach over to grab it from his hands, but he fights me for it, lifting it high above my head.

"Give it to me, Davison!"

"No way! That has blackmail potential written all over it."

"If you don't give it to me—"

"You'll do what?"

"No sex for you tonight."

His arm shoots down from the air, gently placing the phone on the table in front of me. I now know something else about Davison Berkeley that nobody else does. Under the threat of withholding sex, he turns into pure mush.

We're sitting in a cozy back corner of Spice Market, a popular restaurant in the Meatpacking District. The trendy neighborhood around West Fourteenth Street is not familiar to me, but he wanted to take me somewhere fun for our first public date. He had made the right choice. I love the space, the dark wood accentuating the deep-colored draperies that contribute to its laid-back yet sultry Southeast Asian feel.

"I've never seen this evil side of you, Orsini."

"I have my moments." I smirk at him.

"Is the sauce still there?"

"Yes."

He grins wickedly at me. "Then maybe you should get rid of it."

Mirroring his smile on my own face, I reach over with my right thumb and begin rubbing it against the sauce.

"I think I got it."

"I don't think so. A bit more to the left."

As I move my thumb closer, he catches me by surprise, opening his mouth to take in my thumb, clamping his lips over it before I can get a chance to pull it out.

I start to breathe more heavily as he slowly runs his tongue around the pad of my thumb, licking off the curry sauce. My heart beats faster as he sucks in the rest of it, past the joint, coming to an end when he reaches my knuckle.

My panties grow wetter with each lick. Our eyes fix on each other, his darkening with lust, mine with desire, signaling that I'm his to do with as he wishes.

He finally releases my thumb from his mouth with a pop, but then he grabs my hands and runs his lips over my knuckles.

"I think I got it all, don't you?"

I nod silently as he twines my fingers through his, placing my hand under the table on top of the large bulge in the crotch of his black tailored pants.

He leaves my hand there as he reaches over to finish the last of his beer.

"Did you enjoy the steak?"

"Very much," I tell him as I begin massaging his hard cock through the wool material.

With my left hand, I pick up my mojito and take a long sip.

Davison starts to fidget slightly. "You don't want dessert, do you?" he asks with a small cough.

I continued rubbing his hard-on. "What do you think, Mr. Berkeley?"

With lightning speed, his right hand leaps in the air, giving our waiter the universal check-signing gesture.

Once he pays the bill, he grabs me by the hand, pulling me firmly behind him as I try to edge my way elegantly around the table without knocking anything over.

At the coat check, he hands over our claim tickets, rubbing the small of my back with his other hand. He leans over and whispers, "I hope our first public date wasn't too painful for you. I'm so glad you said yes."

"Me too. I had a wonderful time."

"I'll be expressing my gratitude to you when we get in the car."

I don't know how to tell Davison how much this evening has meant to me. For a few hours, I didn't think about the fiasco with Ashton and the ring, and the anonymous envelopes. I smile widely at him as he helps me into my coat before putting on his own.

As we walk out the door, he's holding me around the waist, his face in my hair, when a barrage of lights begins flashing in our faces.

"Over here, Davison!"

"What happened to Ashton?"

"Who's the girl? Are you fucking her?"

Suddenly, we're crushed against the wall of the restaurant. His grip around my waist tightens. The flashbulbs are blinding me. When I do open my eyes, I can see Davison raising his right hand up to hold off the paparazzi.

Oh God…

"Get the fuck back!" he yells. "I said back off!"

If not for Davison's arm around me, I would freeze in place. We seem to be walking slower with each step. I fist my right hand into his jacket, afraid that I'll lose him in the scrum. I burrow my face into his side to hide from the cameras. His left hand clamps over my head to keep me hidden from view. The way his body twists from side to side, Davison is fighting to get through the crowd, using his elbows, shoulders, and every other part of his body to clear a path for us.

"Fuck! Where the hell is Charles?" he shouts to himself above the photographers.

Don't leave me, Davison.

I can feel us moving faster, which probably means he spotted the Maybach. I peek out from under Davison's side and see an open car door. I sense the edge of the curb under my feet as Davison pushes me as far into the car as I can go, almost tumbling me into the door on the other side. The car door slams, and within seconds, we pull away, the tires screeching against the pavement.

Something is happening to me. I hear words being spoken, but it's as if I'm hearing them through a curtain of gauze.

"Damn it, Charles! Where the hell were you?"

"I'm so sorry, sir. They came from out of nowhere."

"Fucking vultures! Just get us home now!"

"Yes, sir."

The Maybach starts to speed down the street. I hear Davison sigh. "Someone must've called the paps when we were there," he mutters under his breath. "I'm so sorry—"

I know something is wrong when Davison starts shaking me and repeating my name again and again. I'm watching from outside my body what's happening to me, and I can't say anything.

"Baby, what's wrong?" I hear him shout. "Allegra! You're shaking like a fucking leaf! Charles, move! NOW!"

The car moves, gliding along the road. We are going so fast. I see lights whir past us. I'm on a carpet ride of some kind, I think. It feels amazing.

Suddenly, I'm being pulled out of the car and lifted into someone's arms.

He whispers in my ear, "It's okay. You're safe, baby. We're home."

I see the marble lobby of Davison's building, then the interior of the elevator. Before I know it, I'm lying on Davison's bed.

He is leaning over me. He presses the back of his hands against my face.

"You're freezing, baby. I'm going to get some blankets."

My shoes are being removed from my feet, my belt coming undone. Something soft falls over me, grazing my chin. I hear shoes dropping to the ground.

Davison's body envelops me, bringing me into a warm cocoon with his arms. I don't even know I'm speaking until he whispers in my ear.

"There's nothing to be sorry for, baby. I'm here. I'll never let anything happen to you."

His heartbeat against my back lulls me into darkness.

* * *

My eyes open to bright light streaming through Davison's bedroom windows. I adjust them by blinking a few times, trying to recall how I got there. Then I remember. I remember everything.

I stretch my body, feeling sore all over. I slowly move toward the edge of the bed, swinging my legs over. I moan from the aches as I rise to my feet, my body protesting against me.

I peek out into the hallway. I hear someone's fingers tapping on a keyboard.

"Davison?" I ask tentatively into the open space.

His beautiful face appears within a minute from his office. He quickly comes over, taking me into his arms. "Baby, what are you doing out of bed?"

"I have to go. I have class."

He shakes his head. "No way. You're staying here with me today."

"I can't miss school."

"Are you allowed any absences?"

I nod. "One. Unexcused."

"Then today you're taking it. And I'll call William and get him to get a temp to cover your shift tonight."

"No, I can't miss work. I'm telling you, I'm perfectly capable of going to school and work. I need to do this," I insist.

"Lucky for you, I know the boss. And after last night, I want you to take it easy."

I shut my eyes, recalling last night's events. "About that. I'm really sorry. I can't believe I just lost it like that. I don't know what happened…"

He grabs my shoulders. "Stop it. Those pap scumbags are what happened. They're vicious when they want something. None of it is your fault. You're staying with me today. Case closed, Allegra."

I know better than to argue with him when he's in this protective mode. I stare at my wrinkled clothes. "Fine. I'm too tired to fight. Any chance I can take a shower?"

He takes me by the hand, leading me back through his bedroom into the adjoining bathroom. "There are fresh towels laid out for you, a new toothbrush on the counter, and a bathrobe hanging on the back of the door. Do you need me to stay?"

Suddenly, I panic. "Are you leaving?"

He cups my face with his hands. "I'm not going anywhere today. Anyway, I can't exactly go to the office dressed like this."

I smile at his Harvard sweatshirt and torn jeans. A thought strikes me. "Where's my purse?"

"In the kitchen. I'll leave it on the bed for you. Oh, and I called your father and told him you stayed over last night because you weren't feeling well."

I soften at everything he's done for me in the past twelve hours. I'm most grateful for the fact that he hasn't pushed me for answers. "Thank you, Harvard. For everything."

He leans in, gently kissing me on the lips. "Anything for you, beautiful. Take as long as you need."

I walk into the bathroom, where I brush my teeth with the toothbrush Davison left for me. I turn on the shower, letting the water run until it reaches the right temperature. I step in, allowing the water to sluice over me down my front and back. It feels amazing, cleansing myself, feeling whole again. I spot a bottle of coconut shampoo on the built-in marble shower shelf.

I shake my head and smile to myself.

That man.

Once I finish in the shower, I wrap myself into the bathrobe that feels like heaven against my body. I get my phone from my purse to check my messages. One voice mail from my father, and nine texts from Lucy, all telling me to check out that day's Page Six.

I open the browser on my phone and search for the website.

When it pops up, I'm staring back at my face hidden in Davison's coat, his arm outstretched to protect me from the paparazzi. The headline reads, "Who's Davison's New Mystery Girl?"

Fuck!

"DAVISON!"

Footsteps pound outside in the hallway. Half-crazed, he appears at my side in seconds. "What happened? What is it?"

I show him the picture on my phone screen. "We're on Page Six!"

He exhales in relief. "Christ, Allegra, is that all?"

"What do you mean 'is that all?' Everyone knows now."

"So?"

Shit. Shit. Shit. I have to go. This isn't going to work.

I spot my clothes on the bed. I walk over, take off the robe, and start getting dressed.

"What the hell are you doing?"

"I'm sorry, but I have to go," I tell him as firmly as I can over my shoulder.

"You're not going anywhere."

"I have to," I repeat as I'm bending over and putting on my shoes.

Before I can stop him, he walks over to me and yanks me up-right so he can look at me.

"What is with you? It's just Page Six, for crying out loud! This shit happens to me all the time."

"Exactly, and that's why I have to go."

"Fuck, Allegra, I don't get it. Just tell me what's wrong," he pleads, shaking me slightly by the shoulders.

Tell him. How? How do I tell him? How do I tell him that I was the subject of a two-day police search when I was five after I saw my mother murdered?

"I'll have to quit my job," I decide aloud.

"What are you talking about? Of course you won't. And if anyone gives you a hard time, you'll tell me."

My heart is pounding in my chest. I stare at him. This man. This man who has been nothing but kind, warm, and thoughtful to me, and now I just want to walk away because of what might not even happen?

I sit down on the bed, confused as ever, and Davison joins me, taking my hand in his.

"Baby, I think you're just tired from last night. That's why I want you to stay here: so I can take care of you."

The fabric of the policeman's shirt is rough under my hands. He is running with me, holding me tightly in his arms. I can't see anything because my eyes are being blinded by all of the lights. The flashing lights that won't stop going off.

"Almost there, Mia. You'll see your daddy in a minute."

He takes a step up into a truck. It's an ambulance. He sets me down.

"Mia!"

I hear Papa's voice. When the policeman backs away, I see him. His eyes are all red and puffy. His hands shake as he reaches for me, holding me, kissing my hair over and over.

I start to cry out, "Papa! I want Mamma! I want Mamma!"

He cries into my hair. "She's gone, cara. She's gone. I'm so sorry."

"Allegra? Are you all right?"

Davison shakes my arm. I turn to him, a worried look reflecting in his emerald eyes.

"Yes, I'm fine," I reassure him as best I can. "Would it be…Could we just stay in the next few weeks?"

"Why?" His demeanor changes when he looks into my eyes. "Never mind, stupid question. I get it."

"You do?" I ask nervously.

"Last night really freaked you out, and you're not used to that kind of attention."

If you only knew.

"Yes," I murmur.

"I'm okay with that," he replies, caressing my face with the tips of his fingers. "We'll be hermits. I'm loving the sound of that, actually."

He stands up and walks over to one of the closets. He returns with a Harvard wardrobe consisting of sweatpants, a T-shirt, and a hoodie.

"You can wear these. When you're ready, come to the kitchen. There's a feast waiting for you."

"Davison, about last night…Did I say anything?"

He shakes his head. "Nothing of consequence. You just kept saying you were sorry about something. I held you until you fell asleep."

"Thank you."

"I told you I'm not going to let anyone hurt you." He pulls me to my feet. "Now get changed and come eat." He kisses me on the forehead and walks out.

Once he's gone, I take in a deep breath and release the air from my lungs.

Fuck. This is not good. Not one damn bit.

* * *

I'm sitting at Davison's dining table, surrounded by a glass pitcher of fresh-squeezed orange juice, a platter of fruit, a basket of warm croissants, butter, jam, and a French press full of coffee. It is pure bliss being taken care of like this, something I'm not used to in my life.

I hear Davison on the phone when a *ding* from his private elevator sounds, signaling that someone has entered the apartment. Not sure if he heard it, I get up from the table and walk to the foyer.

An older woman in a mink coat is standing in front of me. The collar of a quilted suit jacket pokes through the top of her fur, with black patent pumps on her feet and a black alligator bag with a round bamboo handle in her right hand. Her light gray hair is pulled into a bun on the back of her head. There is something about the woman's face that seems familiar.

"Hello. May I help you?"

"I'm Mona Cabot Berkeley, Davison's mother. You must be Allegra."

My throat goes dry. I cough slightly to get my voice back. "Umm, yes, that's me, Mrs. Berkeley. Allegra Orsini."

Great first impression. I'm dressed in Davison's clothes and I sound like an idiot in front of his mother. Well done.

"Baby, who was—"

Davison stops suddenly when he sees his mother standing in his foyer. "Mom, what are you doing here?" he asks with a smile, stepping closer to her to give her a hug.

She pecks him on the cheek. "Just checking up on you, darling. I saw you this morning in the paper and wanted to make sure you were all right. Those photographers are such beasts." She turns to me out of her son's embrace. "Are you all right, dear?" she asks, placing a hand on my shoulder.

Totally caught off guard by her concern, I stutter again. "Umm, yes...thank you. I'm just glad your son was with me."

He smiles sweetly at me, then turns to his mother. "Was there anything else, Mom?"

"My goodness, Davison, I never taught you to be so rude, did I? As a matter of fact, I wanted to invite Allegra to dinner with you, your father, and myself at our house. Perhaps next week? I want to get to know her better."

Her last words make me shiver. But this is Davison's mother. I need to get over the fear of the unknown.

"I would like that very much. Thank you."

She nods at me with a smile. "Wonderful. I'll look forward to it. I'll be on my way, then. I have an appointment."

Mrs. Berkeley extends her hand to me, which I take in mine. "Lovely to meet you, Allegra."

"Thank you. You too, ma'am."

She turns to her son, giving him a brief embrace and another peck on the cheek. "I'll be in touch, darling."

"Okay, Mom. Have a good day."

We watch as the elevator door shuts, a cloud of Chanel No. 5 still hanging in the air. It was my mother's favorite perfume as well.

Before I know it, I'm in his arms. "You okay?"

"Barely." I laugh nervously. "I hope I passed."

"Why would you say that?" he asks, tilting his head at me. "She obviously saw the paper and wanted to make sure we were okay."

"Yeah, but maybe she was just making sure that I was good enough for you."

Davison shakes his head. "First of all, my mother isn't like that. She's not one of those snooty society types. I know she might dress like one of them, but she has a good heart. And second, you should know something else."

"What?"

"In my whole life, she's never done anything like that before. I mean, I've been photographed with other women, but she's never shown up at my apartment to check up on me to make sure I was okay. That means that she thinks you're somebody important in my life."

"And the fact that I was here? That doesn't look bad?"

"We're adults, baby. And I think she knows I have sex. I am thirty-one years old, you know," he says smiling, obviously trying to lighten the mood.

I smile in return. "I just wish I weren't wearing these the first time I meet your mother," I reply, glancing down at his Harvard sweats.

"You're beautiful in anything you wear," he says to me, cupping my face. "Or don't wear, for that matter. Speaking of which, when I'm done with my calls, I'm meeting you in the bedroom."

"Let me finish my breakfast first. I'll need the sustenance."

He swats me on my ass before going back to his office.

Calm down, I tell myself. *It's just meeting the parents. What could possibly go wrong?*

Chapter Thirteen

Despite the fact that I'm a native New Yorker, there are still many sections of my beloved city that I have never encountered before. Davison's family home is in one of them.

In the Sutton Place neighborhood of Manhattan at the end of East Fifty-Eighth Street sits a cluster of elegant town houses, known as Sutton Square. Across the street from them is a house, a true honest-to-goodness detached brick house, something that I rarely see in the city. As I discovered when the Maybach pulled up to it, it was the home of the Berkeley family.

For the dinner with his parents, I'm wearing a cream silk tea-length dress, accentuated by a black lace Peter Pan collar and a thin black belt around my waist. With my black patent kitten heels, I step onto the black-and-white tiled floor of his family's foyer.

The space itself takes my breath away. A huge crystal chandelier hangs from the ceiling, with two long staircases that wind their way along the curved wall to the landing at the top.

A man's voice snaps me back to the present. "Good evening, sir."

I glance over to see a tall, thin white-haired man dressed in a black suit and tie with a white shirt hovering over Davison and me as we stand in the entryway. "Ames, for once and for all, you can call me Davison."

"Not in this lifetime, young man."

Davison smiles. "Fine. This is my girlfriend, Allegra Orsini."

Ames bows in my direction. "A pleasure, Miss Orsini. May I take your coat? Your parents are in the living room, sir."

Hanging on to my mother's clutch and Davison's hand like two lifelines, Davison steers me toward the next room, but stops suddenly.

"Christ, Allegra, I'm going to need hand surgery," he says, looking down at our interlocked fingers. "Please relax. I'll be with you the entire time. Everything will be fine."

"Sorry," I whisper sheepishly.

I loosen my grip on his hand. He leans over and kisses me on the cheek. "You look beautiful, Venus."

I smile. "Okay, let's do this."

When we walk in, I take in the elegance of the room, from the marble fireplace to the furniture upholstered in an understated chintz print. Mrs. Berkeley is sitting on one of the sofas, flipping through an issue of *Town & Country*. An elegant man whose gray hair matches his gray pin-striped suit is standing with his back to us at a window, talking into a cell phone. They don't even notice our presence until Davison clears his throat.

"We did get the correct night, didn't we?"

His mother looks up from her magazine. "Oh, of course, darling. Forgive my rudeness, Allegra." She shouts to the man, "Hart, they're here. Get off that damn phone already!"

The man ends his call and walks toward Davison and me. He extends his hand in my direction, giving me a nod while simultaneously taking in my appearance. "Hartwell Berkeley, Davison's father. You're Miss Orsini," he says in a way that makes me feel awkward. Not creeped out, but more like he's checking me out to make sure I'm suitable.

I shake his hand in return, while he addresses his son with a quick nod, "Davison."

"Dad," he replies in acknowledgment.

I silently take note of the lack of emotion between father and son.

"It's so lovely to see you again, Allegra. Please sit down," Mrs. Berkeley says as an invitation.

Mr. and Mrs. Berkeley sit on opposite ends of the sofa, while Davison pulls me toward the love seat. Ames enters a few seconds later.

"Ah, yes, Ames. A G and T for me, and a Glenlivet neat for my husband. Davison and Allegra?" his mother asks.

"Same as my dad for me, Ames, and a white wine for Allegra," he says, looking over at me for confirmation.

I nod absentmindedly at him because I can't take my eyes off the painting over the mantel. It's a Canaletto depicting the Rialto Bridge in Venice. My parents took me there when I was a little girl, and on my bookshelf at home, I have a photo of us standing on it. I've never seen a Canaletto outside a museum before, but then again, I've never known anyone who can afford to own a Canaletto.

"You're admiring the Canaletto, aren't you?" his father inquires.

"Yes, sir. I've been to Venice."

"Recently, dear?" Mrs. Berkeley adds.

"Um, no, ma'am. When I was a little girl. My parents took me."

"I adore Venice," she says. "We always stay at the Danieli. Your family is Italian, correct?"

"Yes. My father is from Milan, and my mother was from Naples."

His father makes a *Hmm* noise that sounds like a *Really? Interesting* acknowledgement of my statement. "Is your mother deceased, Miss Orsini?"

"Dad," Davison cautions him.

"Yes, sir. She died when I was five," I reply quickly.

Even though she's sitting across the room from me, when Mrs. Berkeley leans forward in her seat, I sense she is going to express a sincere thought. "My dear, I'm so sorry."

I don't realize my knees are shaking until Davison places his right hand on my left knee and begins rubbing it to calm me down. I give him a quick nod in gratitude.

Oh God, please don't ask me how she died.

At that minute, a miracle is delivered in the form of Ames carrying a tray of drinks. He distributes them, Davison's mother leading us in a toast after he leaves the room. Before we can take a second sip, Ames returns to announce dinner is served.

***

As we make our way through our bowls of lobster bisque and entrees of grilled salmon, new potatoes, and a green salad with champagne dressing, there is a coldness in the room despite the central heat. It is palpable. His parents are sitting at either end of the long oval dining table, while Davison and I are in the middle across from each other. No one is speaking. It's such an unnatural feeling for me. Whenever I'm with my relatives in New York City or in Italy, you have to shout to be heard over the laughter and yelling.

At one point, I look across at Davison, who glances up from his food. He gives me a quick smile and a shrug of his shoulders, as if he's saying *Welcome to my family*, and then goes back to eating his fish. I just want to cry. This is breaking my heart.

Someone finally says something, thank goodness.

"So, Allegra," Mrs. Berkeley directs to me, "Davison tells me you're an opera singer."

I take a swallow of my wine. "Yes, ma'am. I'm in my last year at the Gotham Conservatory."

"Did you try for Juilliard?" his father cuts in.

"Oh, for God's sake, Dad!" Davison admonishes him.

"It's okay," I reassure him, even though I'm also seething inside. "I auditioned and I was accepted, but I couldn't afford the tuition, even with scholarships."

"I see," Mr. Berkeley replies, returning to his Scotch.

"You should come with us one night to the Met, my dear. We have our own box," his mother announces.

I look at Davison, who suddenly seems fascinated by the pattern engraved on his Limoges dinner plate.

I feign surprise at the news about their seats. "Oh, thank you so much, Mrs. Berkeley. I would love that. You're so lucky."

She taps her index finger to her lips. "Hmm. You know, we do so much for the Met that I think we should do something for your school as well. I adore opera, especially anything Italian."

I smile. "As do I, ma'am."

"What do you think about having a benefit for the Gotham Conservatory, Hart? Here at the house," she asks her husband.

My eyes nearly pop out of my head. This is completely unexpected.

"Whatever you want, Mona," he mumbles under his breath.

Davison speaks up, "That's very generous of you, Mom. Allegra, what do you think?"

I smiled widely. "I'm overwhelmed. That is so kind of you, Mrs. Berkeley. But only if you're sure it wouldn't be too much trouble."

She waves her hand dismissively at me. "Nonsense. We have these small soirees for our favorite charities all the time. As long as you promise to sing for us."

Oh God. How can I possibly say no to her?

"Oh, Mrs. Berkeley, I don't think I should. I can help you organize it, but I don't think it would be a good idea for me to sing."

For the first time that night, Davison appears to be genuinely happy and interested in something. "Of course you should sing. I haven't heard you sing yet. Please, Allegra. For me."

I look at him and at his mother. Both of them are staring at me with such expectant faces.

Okay, what could possibly happen? The people who come to these things are Upper East Side society types. I doubt any of them would know who I am. And I want to do this for both of them. And I am an aspiring opera singer after all, who, God willing, will perform one day in front of hundreds of people, so I need to get over this, and this will definitely help.

"All right," I give in. "I'll sing something Italian for your mother."

She claps her hands together. "Excellent! I'll call your director in the morning."

The sound of an antique chair creaking as it's pushed back breaks our reverie. Davison's father is standing at his seat.

"Davison, would you join me in my study? I have some papers to review with you."

"Can it wait, Dad? We—"

"Now!"

Davison looks across at me with a slight smile, mouthing *Be right back* to me.

Mrs. Berkeley sighs, watching her husband and son walk out of the dining room. "Oh dear. Goodness knows how long they'll be. I should go tell the kitchen to wait until I tell them to serve dessert. I hate to leave you alone at the table."

"Please, go ahead. Don't worry about me," I reassure her.

Once she leaves the room, I stay in my chair for a few minutes. Finding the silence in the room too oppressive, I grab my clutch and go in search of the nearest bathroom. I turn in the corridor, hoping I can find the toilet without having to ask someone. I walk past a door when loud voices sound from behind it.

"I won't tolerate this insubordinate behavior, Davison."

"Christ, Dad! *'Insubordinate'?* I'm not a damn private under your command. I'm your son."

"That's right, and you seem to be forgetting that little fact. We have an image to protect. This has gotten too serious. I won't have the heir to my family's company tarnished by you gallivanting around Manhattan with some baker's daughter."

"Her father is a *butcher*," he counters furiously.

"I don't give a fuck! Why are you doing this? Seeing what it's like dating beneath you just to piss me off? Slumming it just for a piece of tail?"

"Don't you *dare* talk about Allegra like that! If you ever—"

I can hear laughter. "As if you could ever scare me with your threats. I'm warning you, Davison. End this now. Take Ashton back. Or else I'll have the board remove you as CEO of Berkeley Holdings."

"You don't have the votes."

"Watch me."

"You know what, Dad? I don't give a shit. Remove me. I have my own goddamn money. I don't need yours."

The sound of a door closing somewhere in the house snaps me back to my current position: eavesdropping on Davison and his father. I rush to the nearest door and step into the room, which turns out to be a guest toilet by the looks of it.

I stand at the sink, gripping the counter tightly. My legs shake as I keep standing. Unable to keep myself upright, I sit down on the toilet lid, clenching my fists while taking deep breaths.

Someone raps on the door.

"Allegra, dear, are you ill?" his mother asks worriedly.

I exhale the breath I was holding on to. "No, ma'am. I'm fine."

"Dessert is about to be served."

"Thank you. I'll be right there."

I stand up and step to the sink. I splash some cold water on my face to calm myself down and reapply my makeup, praying that this evening won't last much longer.

* * *

I watch the East Side of Manhattan fly past us as the Maybach speeds down FDR Drive back to my apartment. Davison hasn't said a word to me since we got in the car, but neither have I. He hasn't even reached for my hand.

I can't even imagine how lonely his childhood was. He grew up in a huge, cold mansion, he has no siblings, he was shipped off to boarding school probably when he was still a little boy, and worst of all, he has a total asshole for a father.

He's told me why he likes being with me, that I'm different, that I don't want anything from him. But I think there's more to it. I think I bring him warmth and compassion and the ability for him to be himself.

I love how he defended me to his father, and then when he told him off and stood up for himself, it showed me how strong and sure of himself he truly is. And it makes me think that I actually am an important part of his life now. That thought still frightens me because of his public persona and my reluctance to be thrust into the public eye again, but just for now, at this moment, he needs me more.

I glance over at him. He's still quiet, now looking out the window.

I put my clutch aside and slide over to his side of the backseat. I startle him at first, but then when he realizes what I want to do, he smiles slightly and lets me settle into his lap.

"Hey," I whisper.

"Hey, yourself, beautiful," he murmurs, still smiling at me.

"What are you thinking about in that handsome head of yours?"

He runs his index finger down my cheek before he replies. "I was thinking how my father is a complete prick. I was thinking how glad I am my mother is a kind person with a good heart. And finally, I was thinking how grateful I am that you were the one working the coat check at Le Bistro the night I came to get my glove, because since that night, I've never been happier in my life."

I smile back at him, then I reach for the back of his neck and bring his mouth to mine. We kiss each other gently, but I need more. After the tumult of the night, I need to know that he really is mine. I need to claim him.

I drop to my knees, the skirt of my dress gathered around my waist.

"Umm, baby, is there a reason you're on the floor of my car right now?" he asks amusedly.

I reach for his belt and start to unbuckle it. "Shhh. Just sit back and relax."

"You really don't have to—"

"Shut up, Harvard. Just do as I say."

"Yes, Miss Orsini." He grins mischievously.

I smile slyly at him, then he leans back, his head tilted toward the ceiling, still grinning.

After I unzip his trousers, he raises himself so I can pull them down without having to even ask him, followed by his briefs. His beautiful cock is lying against his belly, ready to be taken. I sit forward, caressing it, stroking it back and forth, back and forth.

Davison begins humming in pleasure. "You're so gentle, Allegra. Your hands are so soft. Feels so good," he moans.

Once I see the pre-cum appear at the tip, I lick it clean. The taste of it with Davison's powerful male scent intoxicates me. My eyes are closed. I want to pleasure him so much.

I take more of his cock into my mouth, swirling my tongue around it. His hands tangle in my hair, his moaning becoming even louder. "So good. God, that's so good."

I curl my lips over my teeth, clamping them like a vise over his penis. I go faster, moving my mouth up and down, swallowing his cock as far as I can into my mouth without gagging.

Once I know my limit, I speed up as his grunts become louder. With a few more strokes, his body begins to shudder, his legs stiffening and his hips thrust forward as if he's feeding me his cock.

A loud roar escapes Davison's throat as a flood of cum spurts into my mouth. I swallow as quickly as I can, the warm liquid spilling down my throat. When it finally stops, I slowly slide his cock from my mouth and lick my lips clean. I sit back on my calves, catching my breath.

Davison can only manage monosyllabic words through his panting. "You. Up here. Now."

I laugh quietly to myself. Placing my hands on his knees, I push myself off the floor and once again sit in his lap. I turn so that I can lay my head down on his chest, his arms tight around me.

"That was…I can't…" he stammers. "You didn't have to do that. Not that I'm complaining."

"I wanted to, Davison."

"Why?"

"Because I wanted to make you come. I wanted to know that I can do that to you."

He takes a deep breath, then he pulls my head back so he can look into my eyes. "Baby, you can do that to me anytime. But you have the same effect on me just by being with me. By saying my name. By letting me hold your hand. By your laugh when I say something stupid. By your smile when you first see me after we're apart."

I tilt my head so I can see his eyes, which are staring back at me so tenderly. I reach up to run my hand along his strong, chiseled jaw.

"Wow," I exclaim.

"What?" he asks, his eyebrows furrowed.

"You are such a romantic, Davison Berkeley."

"I have my moments." He smiles sweetly, cupping his cheek into the palm of my hand, as he tries to reach over and kiss it. I laugh watching him contort his lips, and he just manages to catch the edge of my hand with his lips.

Still laughing, I lay my head back down in the crook of his shoulder when I hear him say, "Oh my God, you make me act like such a dork. I love it. I l—"

I pretend not to hear that he caught himself and didn't finish that sentence. I just keep on laughing.

Chapter Fourteen

The next day, I'm waiting for Luciana in the conservatory's café sipping a cup of hot tea with lemon when I see her enter. A long black velvet cape covers most of her body from her neck to her knees, which means only one thing. She's in diva mode.

I roll my eyes when she waves one end of the cape with dramatic flair before she sits down. "I forgot." I sigh. "This is part of your process."

"How could you possibly forget? I'm very disappointed in you, Alli. Yes, I'm singing an aria from *Tristan und Isolde* today. I have to prepare."

"Well, before you do, could I beg one moment of your time?"

She waves her hand at me. "Please proceed."

"Oh, well, thank you," I reply, not disguising the sarcasm

in my voice. "Last night at dinner with Davison's parents—"

"Whoa! Stop right there! I want details about dinner first."

"Okay. Let's put it this way. I totally understand now why Davison wants to be with me, more like needs to be. Their house is gorgeous, of course: a Canaletto over the mantel, everything is perfect and in its place. But there's no warmth. At dinner, nobody spoke a word. It was like being in a mausoleum. You could've heard a pin drop."

"God, that sounds horrible."

"It was. Davison felt so miserable afterward."

"For what?"

"It doesn't really matter. His dad said a few things—"

"Like what?"

"Nothing. But then his mother really surprised me. She wants to have a benefit for the conservatory at her house."

Lucy's eyes widen. "You're kidding! Any reason why she wants to do this?"

"She said she loves opera, especially the Italian ones. She asked me to find students who would want to participate, and I was hoping you'd do it with me."

"Of course. Any chance to perform in front of a live crowd."

I smile. "Thanks. I was thinking I could sing some Puccini and maybe we could duet on Delibes's 'Flower Duet.' I think the crowd would like that since everyone knows it from that British Airways commercial."

"Good idea. The more popular arias will probably bring in more money. We don't want to sing something obscure. We need to get a tenor too, you know. Someone who could do a great 'O sole mio' and 'Nessun dorma.'"

I point to the tall blond man sitting at a corner table eating a sandwich and reading a Milan Kundera novel. "And I know the perfect tenor to complete our trio."

Lucy glances over her shoulder and shakes her head. "No! Allegra, no!"

I ignore Lucy's protests as I rise from my chair and make my way over to Tomas Novotny. He's Czech, with blue eyes, broad chest and shoulders, and a mad crush on Lucy.

He looks up at me from his paperback. "*Hallo*, Allegra. How are you?"

"Very well, thank you. And you?"

"Good. Why didn't Luciana come with you?" he asks, casting an eye over at our table.

I don't understand why Lucy wouldn't give Tomas a chance. The way her name rolls off his tongue is very seductive.

"She's shy."

He laughs out loud. "That is something Luciana definitely is not. Was there something you needed?"

"Actually, yes. My boyfriend's mother wants to have a benefit for the school at her house, and I was wondering if you'd be interested in performing. Definitely 'Nessun dorma,' and maybe something from *Pagliacci*?"

"Is Luciana going to sing?"

"As a matter of fact, yes, she is."

"Then how do you say, count me out?"

I cringe, hoping I'm right. "Do you mean 'Count me in'?"

He nods. "Yes, that's it. Count me in."

"Excellent. Thank you so much. I'll be in touch with the details."

As I get up, Tomas adds, with a glint in his eye, "Please tell Luciana she doesn't have to be shy with me."

The second I return to Lucy, she starts peppering me with questions. "What did he say? He didn't ask about me, did he? Oh God, I hope not."

"Wow. For someone who doesn't seem to be interested in him, you sure aren't acting like it. Yes, he said he'd do it. And yes, he asked about you. Furthermore, he told me to tell you that you don't need to be shy with him."

Her eyebrows furrow. "What the hell does that mean?"

"Guess you'll just have to ask him." I smirk.

She goes silent for a minute.

"Are you figuring out what to say to him?"

Lucy shakes her head at me. "No. I was just wondering about something. Did Davison's mother come up with the idea for the benefit after his dad made those comments that you won't tell me about?"

"No. Why?"

"It's just…"

"What?"

"I just hope she's doing this for the right reasons, that's all. I don't want to see you get hurt."

"Why would she want to do that? Believe me, if Davison thought she was plotting something against me, he would totally call her on it. He would protect me."

"Okay, if you're sure."

"Positive."

Lucy looks at her watch. "We'd better get to class."

Halfway through Signora Pavoni's lecture on the popularity of

Puccini's operas, a thought strikes me. I told Tomas that Davison is my boyfriend. And I didn't hesitate when I said it either. It came naturally to me.

For the rest of the class period, I can't wipe the smile off my face.

* * *

The next morning, I'm at my kitchen table, enjoying a cappuccino and buttered toast when my father's voice rings out.

"Who is that beautiful young woman sitting at my kitchen table? It couldn't possibly be my daughter, Allegra Orsini, because I don't think she lives here anymore."

He bends over to place a kiss on the top of my head.

"Ha. Very funny. Sarcasm does not become you, Papa."

He sits down across from me, a small porcelain espresso cup in his hand. "It does when it's true. I never see you anymore. You're always with your *ragazzo*."

"I know. I'm sorry. *Mi dispiace*. But I promise we'll do something this weekend."

He takes a sip of his coffee. "*Bene*. I feel better."

I take another bite of my toast as I watch a concerned look cross his face. "What's wrong?"

"Have you received any more of those letters?"

"You mean the pictures."

He nods.

"No. Thank God."

My father exhales. "That's good. And no more bad dreams?"

I shake my head. Even though it technically wasn't a bad

dream, I decide not to tell him about my episode at Davison's after the paparazzi incident.

He puts his hand over mine. "I just worry about you so much, *cara*. If anything ever happened to you..."

"I know. Don't worry. Nothing will happen to me, especially with you to protect me, *sì*?"

I rise from my chair to embrace my father, who now has tears in his eyes. "*Sì. Sì, Allegra mia.*"

Chapter Fifteen

The night I arrive with Davison for the benefit at his parents' house, the end of East Fifty-Eighth Street is lined with luxury cars, from town cars to BMWs, even a Bentley convertible.

Davison keeps a firm grip on my left hand, while I can't resist touching the necklace that hangs around my neck. It's his Christmas gift to me. I melted when he presented it to me, pulling out the robin's-egg-blue Tiffany box that he had been hiding in the breast pocket of his jacket. It's a small diamond pendant of a hummingbird on a silver chain. It took my breath away, a reminder of what I was doing when we first met: humming an aria while I was working. He remembered. The smile on his face when he saw my reaction made my cry, and he took his time putting it on me as I held up my hair, making sure none of it got caught, stroking my neck and shoulders when he'd finished, then directing me to the mirror so we could both share the look of it around my neck. The kiss I gave him in gratitude led us to his bedroom within a matter of seconds.

In return, I gave him an iPod with my favorite opera recordings, ranging from Maria Callas to Luciano Pavarotti. I made it a point to include the arias that were going to be sung tonight. Listening to him sing along when he plugged in his earbuds was an experience. Even though I cringed when he did it, I couldn't help but laugh when he added dramatic gestures while he sang, his arms flailing in the air. This was a side of Davison Berkeley only I got to see, and I treasured it.

His hand squeezes mine. "Christ, Allegra, will you please stop fidgeting with your necklace? You're going to be amazing. Don't be nervous."

"So speaks the man who doesn't have to sing in front of a group of strangers! I'm singing in front of my boyfriend's parents!"

Suddenly, he takes my face in his hands and kisses me full on the mouth.

"Not that I'm complaining, Harvard," I remark when he pulls away, "but what was that for?"

"You know why." He smirks.

"To calm me down?"

"And because I love it when I hear you call me your boyfriend." He grins at me from ear to ear, his eyes sparkling.

In his tuxedo and with his hair slicked back, he tempts me to climb into his lap and kiss him senseless, but with the car coming to a stop in the driveway, I have to settle for giving him a smile.

As is now his custom, I wait until Davison comes around to my end to open the door for me.

I look down at my dress to make sure it hasn't wrinkled too much from the car ride. I'm wearing a strapless royal-blue silk A-line gown and kitten heels on my feet, since I'll be standing most of the night. With my tote bag that holds my makeup, I walk into the Berkeley home.

The noise of the party guests echoes throughout the house. Servers go back and forth holding trays of glasses and canapés in their hands. Davison's parents are standing in the foyer, welcoming the guests with the president of the conservatory, Carter Morgan.

The face of Davison's mother lights up when she sees us. "Finally! The stars have arrived!"

I can feel myself turn red as she leans in to hug me after embracing her son. "Good evening, Mr. and Mrs. Berkeley."

Davison's father grunts, "I need a drink," and walks away.

His mother turns to President Morgan. "Carter, this is my son, Davison, and, of course, you know Allegra."

My boyfriend and my school president exchange handshakes, then Morgan addresses me. "Allegra, a pleasure to see you, as always. I know you'll do the conservatory proud."

Davison brings his arm around my waist. "Of course she will, sir."

Mrs. Berkeley says to Davison, "Darling, Luciana and Tomas are in the upstairs living room getting ready. Could you show her the way?"

"I'd love to."

With my hand in his, he leads me up one of the staircases to the second floor. He heads straight across to the double doors, where we find Lucy and Tomas standing close together with their backs to us looking out the window, his lips whispering something into her ear.

I clear my throat to announce our presence. "Ahem."

They pivot in our direction, guilty looks plastered on their faces.

"Are we interrupting?" Davison wonders aloud.

"*Ne*…no," Tomas stutters. "You have a lovely home, Mr. Berkeley."

"Thank you, Tomas." Davison looks over at me. "I'm going to go. Can I get you anything?"

"No, I'll be fine. I need to warm up with them, if you don't mind."

He smiles and kisses me softly on the lips. "Of course not. I'll see you soon." He brushes his fingers across my cheek, closing the door behind him when he leaves.

"Alli, let me tell you, if your boyfriend weren't taken…"

I glance over at Tomas, who suddenly finds something of interest on the floor.

Damn it, Lucy.

I need to quickly shift the vibe in the room. Thankfully, a face familiar to the three of us walks in.

"Who's ready to rock the house?"

The three of us laugh. It's Derek Fisher, our favorite accompanist, who has been practicing with us for tonight, a tall, older gentleman with salt-and-pepper hair. His eyes practically pop out of his head at the sight of the Steinway in the corner.

"God, I love people with beaucoup bucks," he declares as he

saunters over to the piano, running his fingers over the polished ebony wood. "There's a matching one in the ballroom that I just tried out. Perfectly tuned, of course. All right, kids. Let's play some scales."

We warm up our voices, then take our turns with the arias we're going to be performing.

A knock at the door interrupts us. Mrs. Berkeley pokes her head in. "Twenty minutes, everyone. If you need the restroom, there's one right next door."

"Thank you, ma'am," Lucy replies. "We'll be ready."

I grab my bag and head for the bathroom. I apply another coat of mascara and lip gloss, then check my hair, pulled back in a low chignon at the nape of my neck. Thankfully, it has held, but I put on a layer of hairspray just to be sure.

When I come out of the bathroom, I see the entrance to a large room to the right of me. I take a few steps to peek in.

The ballroom is spectacular, the crystals of the chandeliers bouncing light off the mirrored side walls and waxed floor. Gilt party chairs form two sections, with a piano in the far corner and a microphone in the center at the front of the room. I can see the lights from the street coming in through the windows. A huge screen is set up just to the side by the piano, the logo of the Gotham Conservatory already project-ing from it.

I jump when a set of arms comes around my waist.

"I can't wait to hear you sing for me," Davison rasps in my ear.

"You and what looks like the entire community of Sutton Place," I reply nervously.

"As far as I'm concerned, I'm the only one you're singing to."

I exhale, turning around to face him. "Just sit as close to the front as you can, okay?"

He leans in and gently kisses my lips. "Front row center, baby. Always."

I smile, wiping a smudge of lip gloss from his mouth before I leave him to return to the living room. "Gotta go."

"Break a leg, Venus," he shouts after me.

* * *

Lucy, Tomas, and I stand to the right of Mrs. Berkeley in front of the ballroom, which is filled to capacity.

In a deep purple gown, diamonds sparkling from her ears and wrists, she clears her throat and tries to speak, but the audience doesn't stop talking. Thankfully, Derek helps her out by pounding out the opening notes of Beethoven's Symphony No. 5.

Dun, dun, dun, dun…

Everyone laughs as Mrs. Berkeley turns to Derek and nods in gratitude.

"Good evening, ladies and gentlemen. My friends, Hartwell and I have invited you here this evening for a wonderful cause. All of you know how much I love the opera. I recently realized how vital it is not only to support the great houses like the Met, but also the schools that bring us the new talent in the opera world. One of those schools is the Gotham Conservatory, and I'm pleased to introduce its president, Carter Morgan. Mr. Morgan, if you would…"

As Mr. Morgan addresses the crowd, I glance over to see Davison in the front row. His eyes sear into mine, then he winks at me and smiles, which instantly dismisses the butterflies in my stomach.

Davison's mother returns to the microphone. "Tonight, we have the honor of hearing three wonderful voices who are now in their final year at the conservatory. Our first performer is Miss Allegra Orsini, who will be singing 'Sì, mi chiamano Mimì' from *La Bohème*. Please welcome her to the microphone."

I step forward, bowing my head to acknowledge the applause. I look back at Derek, giving him the signal that I'm ready. I dare myself to look at Davison quickly, who's beaming from his chair front and center, just like he promised.

I take a breath and enter my world—the world that has provided me comfort and solace since I lost my mother so many years ago. I become Mimì, a seamstress living in 1830s Paris, introducing herself to Rodolfo, a poet, for the first time. *Yes, they call me Mimì*, I sing to them in Italian, the title of the aria.

When I finish, I shut my eyes and smile, opening them to see a standing ovation, led by Davison yelling the traditional "*Brava!*" I bow humbly, my hand over my heart.

I raise my head once more and notice a woman in an aisle seat, barely pressing her hands together as if she were pretending to clap, a scowl on her face. When she leans over to the center, she comes into full view.

Ashton.

I give another quick bow, then quickly walk off to the side and out of the ballroom. I head straight for the living room, where Lucy, Tomas, and I left our belongings.

I shut the door and drop onto one of the sofas. I throw my head back onto the cushions, taking deep breaths.

The door creaks open as Davison appears.

"Did you know Ash—"

Before I know it, he grabs my hands and jerks me up to my feet. His lips crash into mine, impaling my mouth with his hot tongue.

His breath caresses my face. He is hungry for me. It's infectious. Once I have a taste of him, I always want more.

He rears his head back. "Come with me," he commands.

He tugs me behind him into the hallway, coming to a door that opens to reveal a narrow stairway.

"Davison, we don't have long. Tomas is only singing two arias."

He ignores my comment as we alight on the third floor. We hurry to the left and into the first door.

He has brought me to what looks like his childhood room. It's painted blue with a matching rug, a twin bed in the corner. One side of the room is covered in posters of various players from the Yankees and Rangers, while the other is decorated in Harvard pennants and memorabilia.

With the door shut behind us, he pushes me against it, my arms wrapped in his grip.

He starts to kiss me, sucking on the spot between my neck and collarbone. "A hot girl in my room while my parents are downstairs without a clue. This is my teenage fantasy come true."

"Mmm. Boys will be boys, huh? Not that I'm complaining."

"Stop talking, baby. We don't have long and I need to fuck you now," he grunts, his voice rough, his emerald eyes hungry with lust.

He hikes up my dress, searching for my panties under the silk to pull them down, while I quickly unbuckle his pants and lower his briefs. Once he hitches one of my legs around his hip, he shoves his cock into me. I'm already soaked and ready for him.

In a blur, Davison picks me up, holding my ass in his hands, my back against the wall for stability. His cock pistons me again and again. I open my eyes to look at him. In his tuxedo with his hair tousled, his chin tightly clenched, the muscles on his neck ready to burst from the strain, I know I've never wanted him more than at this moment.

"Don't stop, Davison. Fuck me hard," I plead.

"Oh, baby," he says breathlessly.

A few more pumps, and we come together, our breaths reflecting the other. He releases me to the floor. I lean against the door for support as Davison nestles his head into the crook of my neck. I can't stop smiling, feeling so giddy for doing this so stealthily. I actually feel naughty.

Before I can say anything, he turns me around roughly, his cock still sheathed inside me, my front pressed up against the door.

"Davison, we can't! As much as I want to, we don't have enough time," I plead.

"Like hell we don't. You didn't honestly think we were done, did you?" he whispers into my ear, his breath hot on my neck.

"Silly me," I murmur, smiling wickedly to myself.

He reaches around with his right hand to rub my clit, sucking on my throat. Once he finds it, it doesn't take me long to get wet again.

"Come on, Harvard. Give it to me good. You know you want to," I tease him.

"I'm going to fuck the wiseass right out of you, baby. Get ready," he warns me.

I gasp at his first thrust combined with his fingers pressing on my clit. It's a heady mixture that sends me reeling, desperate for more.

"That's it," I moan. "Don't stop."

"Never will, Venus. Never," he rasps huskily.

I extend my arms out against the door, offering my backside to him for easier access.

It works, because now I'm pushing myself into the wood as both of his hands grab my hips, his fingers digging into my skin. He pumps into me hard, flesh smacking against flesh. The sound of our rough grunts echoes through the room.

His hard cock fills me completely. My blood is surging through my veins, hot and fast. I'm on the verge of erupting. "Yes…fuck yes," I pant.

"I love fucking you," he growls into my ear. "So. Fucking. Hot."

A few more thrusts, and I explode, shouting from the exquisite release. He comes right after me, roaring in ecstasy.

He collapses against my back as we struggle for breath. "Thank you for making my fantasy come true," he pants.

"You're welcome." I laugh.

A knock against the door jolts us. "Sir, it's almost time for Miss Orsini's duet," Ames informs us.

"Thank you. We'll be right down," Davison answers him.

He turns me around to face him. I can feel my face redden. "God, that's so embarrassing."

"Don't worry, baby. He's very discreet."

We fix our clothes and head back downstairs. We stop in the

living room so I can check my makeup and get a drink of water.

I need to know something before I join Lucy for the duet.

"Did you know Ashton was going to be here?"

"I had a feeling she would be"—he sighs—"but please don't let that ruin the rest of the night."

I smile at him. "No worries. She's on my turf now. Well, the opera turf anyway."

I start to walk to the door when he stops me.

"Before we go back, I just wanted to say that you…you were incredible," he tells me, my face in his hands as he stares at me with a look of reverence in his eyes. "I can't explain…your voice is angelic. I had no idea. I…you…you're just so beautiful, Allegra."

I try to stop the tears that start falling from my eyes, giving him a smile, then a quick peck on his lips. "Thank you for that, but don't start, Harvard. My mascara isn't waterproof."

* * *

"And now, ladies and gentlemen, a special treat for you. The 'Flower Duet' from the opera *Lakmé*, as sung by Miss Orsini and Miss Luciana Gibbons," Mrs. Berkeley announces to the audience in her brief introduction.

Standing with Lucy at the second microphone that had been set up alongside its twin, I sneak a peek at Davison, who gives me another encouraging wink.

Derek starts on the piano, and Lucy opens with the first line as Lakmé, the high priest's daughter. I'm singing the role of Mallika, her servant.

My first line complete, I connect with Lucy. We are in total sync. It sounds so beautiful, so lyrical…

Why is Lucy looking at me like that?

I glance over at Davison, who is now sitting up straight in his chair with his head tilted, alternating between looking at something behind me and then me again.

When it's my turn again to sing solo, I notice the entire audience's focus is not on me, but something over my shoulder.

Still singing, I finally turn my head to see what's behind me.

I'm on the screen where the school's logo had been.

Oh, look. There I am with my mother.

The picture changes. My mom by herself.

Another slide. A newspaper headline. "Little Italy Mother Murdered. Five-Year-Old Daughter Missing."

Wait. That's…

"Little Girl Lost. The Search Continues for Mia Rossetti."

Me.

"Little Girl Found. Mia Safe."

Oh my God.

I clamp my hands over my mouth.

What's going on?

Then, The Picture appears. The one a photographer took when the policeman brought me out after finding me hiding in an abandoned basement: the cop carrying me to safety, the blue of his shirt in my tiny fist contrasting against the cocoa brown of my frightened eyes.

My knees turn into rubber. I can't stop shaking. I start crying, my body starting to shudder from the wracking sobs.

I don't look at Davison. I run as fast as I can down the aisle and into the living room.

I need my things.

What did I bring?

Coat. Coat. I need my coat.

Okay, I've got my coat on.

God, my bag. Where the fuck is my bag?

Just as I'm about to flee to safety, the door is thrown open.

Davison flies to me. He grabs my shoulders, forcing me to look in his direction.

"Allegra, what the fuck was that?"

"Leave me alone, Davison."

"The hell I will! Talk to me! I don't understand. Was that you? Was that what happened to your mother?"

Oh God, get me out of here, please, please, please.

I try to wrestle my body from his grip, but every time I move, he only holds on harder.

"Damn it, just talk to me," he insists roughly.

I look him straight in the face, my voice clipped and monotone. "We're done. I never want to see you again."

With the impact of those words, he finally lets me go and I run out the door.

I reach the top of the stairs when he wrenches my arm back.

"Goddamn it, Allegra! Just stop already!"

I fight him, desperately trying to pull away, shaking him off me. "No!"

Suddenly, my footing gives way. Before I can do anything, I'm falling...falling...falling.

I hear Davison's voice. "ALLEGRA!"

I put my hand out to grab the banister, but somehow I turn on my belly, my chin scraping against the carpeted stairs. I push my feet down hard, pressing my toes in to bring myself to a stop.

Everything aches. It hurts. It hurts so much.

I hear Luciana's voice screaming, "Oh my God!"

Davison is at my side alongside her. "Don't move, baby."

"Get away from her!" Lucy yells at him. "Can you move, Allegra?"

I moan, trying to see if any of my limbs are broken. "I don't know."

Using my elbows, I slowly turn myself onto my back, my body protesting the entire time. I start feeling woozy, hearing loud voices surrounding me in a daze.

"I don't think you broke anything. But I'm taking you to the hospital right now," Davison declares.

"No way in hell! I'm going with her," Lucy shouts.

"Lucy," I whisper. "Get me out of here. Please."

"You heard her, Davison."

"I don't care!" he yells at her.

The ground disappears from under me as I feel Davison pick me up in his arms.

My head falls against his broad chest. "No, Davison," I beg with a whisper. "Let me go."

The rumble of his voice vibrates in his chest against my body. "Never."

His scent assaults my nose. The spicy, woodsy cologne that I love mixed with his body sweat intoxicates me, as I'm dying inside knowing this will probably be the last time I'll be able to enjoy this small pleasure that he had always afforded me. I will probably never see him again.

"Charles! New York Presbyterian! Now!" he shouts.

I feel myself being carefully slid onto the backseat of the May-bach, with Davison coming in after me, cushioning my head in his lap.

I shut my eyes, the emotional weight of the past hour finally taking its toll on me as I start to sob again.

Davison's hand starts to stroke my hair, then wipes my tears away with his thumb.

"Please don't cry, baby. Everything's going to be okay," he says softly.

I turn my head away from him, hopefully to deter him from touching me. But he continues to caress me as I shut my eyes, cringing from his touch, knowing that I have to start detaching myself from him now because it's over.

I can hear a female voice in the front seat. Lucy's.

"Mr. Orsini, it's Luciana. Something's happened to Allegra...I'm taking her to New York Presbyterian now...and...someone exposed her past tonight...everyone knows...I don't know...yes, I'll be with her...we're almost there...okay...okay."

The car stops. Then the ground goes away again. Hands are lifting me like Papa used to do when I was little. I look up and see Davison's face, his eyes determined, his jaw locked.

"I've got you, baby."

We're going inside a building. Lucy and Davison are talking loudly. Everyone is shouting. He gently puts me down on a gurney, and I'm whisked away.

I'm looking outside myself, the doctor poking me, checking to make sure I haven't broken any bones. But all I can think about is Davison's face, the shock in his eyes when I told him I didn't want to see him anymore.

The doctor examining me is of medium height, older, with curly brown hair. "Allegra, I'm Dr. Jonathan Berg. I'm going to send you upstairs for an X-ray and an MRI to make sure there's no serious damage anywhere. They're a bit backed up, so you might have to wait awhile."

I look into the man's deep blue eyes through his glasses. He's old enough to be someone's father. I nod my consent.

Lucy appears at my side, handing me a tissue.

"Where did Davison go?" I ask her nervously.

"Who the fuck cares," she spits out. "Probably to push his weight around with the staff."

I hear my father's voice. He's right next to me now, kissing me on the forehead. "*Cara mia*, are you okay? Who did this to you?"

I start to cry softly. "I don't know. And they showed the pictures. Everyone saw me, Papa. Davison knows. Oh God, his mother. I humiliated them. They must hate me so much now. The scandal I brought to their house. It's all my fault."

"You didn't get a chance to tell him, did you?" Lucy asks.

I shake my head.

"And you were planning to, right?"

I nod.

"Don't worry, Alli. I'm here."

My father reaches his arms over and holds me tight. "*Ti amo, cara.* Don't worry. Your papa is here now."

"Someone did this to you on purpose," Lucy says, anger raging in her voice. "We'll find out who it was and make sure they regret it."

Suddenly, the hooks on the curtain rod screech against metal as the curtain is yanked back. It reveals Davison with his white tuxedo shirt undone, his tie missing, his eyes sunken, his face pale.

"Allegra," he whispers. "Please don't turn me away. I need to talk to you."

"Not now, Mr. Berkeley," my father protests. "My daughter needs rest."

"Davison," Lucy says firmly, "this is not the time."

Suddenly, he becomes enraged. "I'm not leaving, Luciana!"

"*Basta!*" my father shouts. "That's enough, Mr. Berkeley. Please go."

Davison's eyes shift to me, pleading with his face. "Allegra, the pictures. What happened…the newspapers…I…I want to understand."

I turn my eyes away from him. "I don't want to see you."

I hear him inhale from shock. "Don't do this, baby," he begs. "Please."

"You need to go, Davison," I manage, barely above a whisper.

My father steps closer to him. "You heard my daughter, sir."

I hear the curtain rustle. When I look over, Davison is gone. Probably for good.

Papa and Lucy are staring at me with faces of anger mixed with pity and sadness. I can't stand it anymore.

"I'm going to close my eyes for a bit. I'm really tired. Would you mind?"

They nod, with Papa leaning over to kiss me on the head. "We'll wait outside, *cara*."

* * *

I'm dreaming. I don't see anything, but I hear Davison's voice.

"Allegra, can you hear me? It's Davison. Or Harvard, as you call me in that sweet voice of yours. I'm here. Do you know what I thought the first second I saw you? I thought you were the most beautiful thing I'd ever seen in my life. And when you showed up at my office, I'd never wanted a woman more in my life. I'm so sorry. Please don't leave me. I can't lose you now. You mean everything to me, baby."

The voice drifts away.

It feels so real to me. The pressure on my hand, someone's lips softly kissing mine.

And I sleep.

* * *

"Miss Orsini? I'm here to take you for your tests." A young orderly is standing over me with a sheet of paper in his hand.

I rub my eyes. I feel so out of it. "How long have I been out?"

"For about an hour," I hear my father's voice announce. "I made Lucy go home. But she said she'll see you tomorrow."

Davison. No, he couldn't have…

"Okay," I sigh. "Let's get this over with."

The orderly unlocks the wheels on my gurney and whisks me away.

* * *

Finally, I'm back in the ER. Dr. Berg has given me the all clear, and I'm waiting to be released, lying on the gurney.

"Papa?"

"*Sí?*"

"Did anyone come to see me while I was asleep?"

"I don't think so. Lucy went home, and I only walked away for a minute when I had to fill out more paperwork."

"Oh, I thought…"

"What?"

"Nothing, it was just a dream."

It was. Just a dream. It had to be.

"Let's go home, Papa."

Chapter Sixteen

I'm still sore the next morning, my muscles aching. My mouth hurts when I move it, thanks to the bruise on my chin. I glance over at the clock, which reads eleven fifteen a.m. I need to call the restaurant to let them get a temp for tonight.

My stomach growls just at the moment Papa walks in with a steaming cappuccino and a fresh cannoli.

"*Buongiorno, cara.* How are you feeling?"

"Like I fell down a flight of stairs." I grimace.

"That's not funny, Allegra," my father admonishes me. "You need to eat."

"*Grazie, Papa.* It's exactly what I want," I thank him, taking a gentle sip of my coffee, inhaling its robust scent.

The doorbell rings just when Papa hands me the cannoli.

"I'll be right back," he says, going out to see who's at our door.

I bite into the cannoli just as Luciana appears in the doorway, and with Tomas of all people.

"What are you doing here?" I ask with my mouth full.

"Ugh. Manners, Alli," Lucy admonishes me, staring at my mouth full of cream and pastry. "How are you feeling?"

I sigh. "I think I'll just hang a sign around my neck. 'I'm in pain.' Next question."

Then Lucy and Tomas exchange knowing glances, which totally throws me.

"Okay, what's going on with you two? Spill it," I order.

A solemn look crosses Lucy's face. "We know who was behind what happened last night."

"How do you know?" I whisper.

Lucy looks at Tomas in awe and smiles. "Because this genius got it all on video."

"What are you talking about?"

Tomas clears his throat. "After you ran out of the room, it got so crazy. People were about to leave, and I wanted to help. So I ran up to Derek and told him to play 'La donna e mobile.' I started singing and everyone calmed down."

"Oh, that was so nice of you. Thank you, Tomas," I say quietly, overwhelmed by his kindness.

"But that's not the end of it!" Lucy says excitedly. She grabs Tomas's arm. "Show her what else you did."

I look curiously at my best friend. Yesterday she was drooling over my boyfriend, or whatever he was. And now she's beaming from ear to ear with pride at Tomas.

"How long have I been out?" I ask jokingly.

Lucy looks at me confusedly, and I shift my eyes to Tomas, who's digging through his pockets for his phone.

Not now, she mouths at me.

Tomas finally pulls out his cell phone, touches a few buttons, and hands it to me. My father steps over, leaning over to watch with me as I press the "play" button.

The video shows what looks like the hallway outside the ballroom in the Berkeley house. From the angle Tomas shot it, he was hiding around the corner from the two people who were on-screen—Davison and Ashton.

He was yelling at her.

"You did this, didn't you, Ashton? You and my father!"

"Did what?"

"Don't even attempt to play coy with me! I don't know who you bribed to put that up on the screen, because God knows you'll throw money at anything or anyone to get what you want, but this was all you. You made damn sure that Allegra was humiliated tonight, and for what reason?"

"To show you what you're getting into with her! I love you, Davis! We're perfect together. You know we are. And I did it all by myself. Your father had nothing to do with it."

Ashton was crying, mascara running down her face. She actually loves him. I almost feel bad for her. Almost.

"'Davison,' Ashton! My name is Davison." He reared back in shock. "Oh my God, you hired some PI to investigate her, didn't you?"

"Of course I did! I can't believe you never checked her out before you got involved with her! You needed to see the shame and embarrassment she would've brought to your family."

A sharp voice rang out, "The only one who brought shame and embarrassment to my family was you, Ashton, you bloody shrew."

Ashton's mouth dropped as Mrs. Berkeley stepped into the hallway from the ballroom. She was seething. "You little bitch! Not only did you make that poor girl suffer, but you committed something just as heinous—you ruined one of my social events!"

"Mrs. Berkeley, I…I—" Ashton stammered.

Davison's mother stepped closer to Ashton, pointing her index finger right in her face. "Nobody does something like that to me and gets away with it. I'll make sure that you're blackballed from every charity board and club in this town. I don't care how long our families have been friends. You're done. Now get your skinny, bottle-blonde ass out of my house!"

Ashton started to walk away, then turned back one last time. "You have no idea who you just messed with. You'll be sorry," she screeched.

"No, dear, you're the one who'll be sorry," Mrs. Berkeley said calmly in a cool voice, almost as if she were stating a foregone conclusion.

Once Ashton stepped out of the screen, Mrs. Berkeley walked up to her son, placing her hands on his. "Darling," she whispered.

I can see his chest rising and falling rapidly, his face red and heated. In a flash, he spun around and punched the wall, a load roar bellowing from his mouth.

"Davison!" his mother shouted.

Then the screen went black.

I look up at my father, Lucy, and Tomas. Lucy pulls a tissue out of the box that sits next to my bed and hands it to me.

"*Cara*, he obviously cares about you very much," my father observes.

I nod, knowing Papa is right.

"But I sent him away," I cry, talking through my tears. "He'll never speak to me again. And his mother…God, I totally embarrassed them."

"Umm, Alli, were you watching the same video we were?" Lucy asks. "Because it sure as hell looked like she was defending you to that skank."

"I know, but…"

"No 'buts.' He really cares about you. Can't you see that?"

This is too much. I need to think.

"I love you both for doing this for me, but would it be all right—"

"Say no more, sweetie," Lucy stops me, the palm of her hand facing me. "You need your rest. Come on, Tomas."

I had to smile at them. She's bossing him around already, and I don't think he minds, because he's got the brightest glint in his eyes.

Tomas walks out, but Lucy gives me a hug before she follows him. "Just promise me you'll think about everything and then talk to him. Don't do anything rash."

"I promise. And thanks. Both of you. And I'm still waiting for details."

"You're welcome," she replies. "Soon, I promise."

Once they're gone, I call my manager at the restaurant to tell him I am sick.

"It's fine, Allegra. We know," William tells me. "Davison said you weren't feeling well, so we already have a temp for the dinner shift."

I'm too tired to decide if I should be grateful to Davison for being so thoughtful or royally pissed at his possessive alpha ways.

"Oh. Did he say anything else?" I ask nervously.

"No, why?"

"It's nothing. Never mind. I should be better tomorrow," I reassure him.

"Don't worry. Just get better."

After I talk to William, I take an aspirin and settle under the covers.

I check my messages. Nothing from Davison.

Just as well. Do I really want to drag him into all this? And now that he knows, the tabloids will pick up on it and I'll be in the public eye again, something I've managed to avoid for the past nineteen years. And what I did all those years ago, when I changed my name thinking I could stay out of said public eye, is now totally gone to shit.

* * *

The next day, I walk into Le Bistro for my shift. I'm wearing my standard uniform, but on my face, I'm wearing more makeup than usual. Concealer hides the bruise that turned yellow overnight. The scrape on my chin is healing, but it's still visible.

I haven't heard from Davison in forty-eight hours, since he left me in the ER. I quickly scan the room for him, but I don't see him anywhere.

"Allegra, I'm so glad you're all right," William greets me at the hostess stand. "You're sure you're ready for tonight?"

"I'm fine. I want to work," I tell him assuredly.

"I'm pleased to hear that. It shouldn't be a busy night, if that helps."

"It's okay. I'm ready."

"Good. Just let me know if you need anything."

"Thank you," I reply, grateful for his kindness.

I make my way to the coat check, hanging up my coat and bag. I take inventory of what's already been checked. I'm pulling down the box with the claim numbers when I hear his deep voice.

"Hi."

I turn to the door. He's wearing a black suit accentuated by a white shirt and red tie. Davison's green eyes sear into mine, but they're missing the confidence and glint that arouse me to my core.

"Hi."

"How are you feeling?" he asks, concern etched on his face.

"I'm better. Not as sore," I reply.

"Please come closer," he commands.

Taking a deep breath, I step up to the counter. I look anywhere but his face as he studies me. I hear him inhale deeply, no doubt seeing through the thick layer of makeup.

"I'm going to take you home tonight. We'll talk," he declares firmly, not welcoming debate.

I look into his eyes. They're blazing into mine now, fiery and powerful.

"Okay," I agree, completely pointless to argue.

"Good," he replies, giving me a quick smile and a nod before walking away.

He smiled.

So far, so good.

*   *   *

When I finish work, Davison is waiting for me, his hand on my lower back as he steers me outside to the Maybach.

Charles is standing at the passenger door, his back ramrod straight and hands clasped, awaiting our arrival.

"Sir," he nods to Davison. "Miss Orsini, I'm pleased to see you. I hope you're well," he says with a gentle smile.

"Thank you, Charles. I'm better."

I climb into the car with Davison directly behind me.

The engine comes to life and we move into traffic, heading downtown to Little Italy. Davison isn't looking at me, only straight ahead. My heart beats in my throat as I wait for him to say something.

"I can see it, Allegra. Under the makeup. The bruise," his voice rumbles.

"Don't worry. It's getting better," I try to reassure him.

"It's my fault," he rasps.

I finally turn to him. "No, Davison, it was an accident. I fell. That's all. Please look at me."

I see his beautiful face, the guilt reflected in his eyes.

I lean over and take his hand. "I didn't call you because I needed time to think. I know what you and your mom said to Ashton after the accident. And I saw you punch the wall."

"What the...how?" he asks, his eyes widened.

"It doesn't matter. But now you know why I reacted the way I did when I saw us on Page Six, why I tried to pull away."

"When I got home after the accident, I went on the Internet."

I swallow in my throat.

"I did my research. And what happened to you is horrific. See-ing your mother…" He trails off. "But I want to know. I want you to tell me everything. And I'll listen to it all, baby. Every single word."

"I can't. Not here." I ask in a low voice, even though I know Charles can't hear us. I'm practically begging.

"I know. Come over to my place for a late supper tomorrow af-ter work."

I exhale. "That works for me." I nod.

Suddenly, Davison picks me up under my backside and my knees, bringing me over to him, placing me gently in his lap. He curls one arm around my waist and, with his other hand, carefully lifts my chin to look into my eyes.

"Tomorrow," he whispers.

"Tomorrow," I repeat, placing my head on his shoulder. He wraps his other arm around me. We don't say a word to each other for the rest of the trip, only listening to each other's breath-ing.

* * *

Late the next night, I walk into Davison's apartment, allowing him to take off my coat.

"Go sit on the couch. We'll eat there," he asks of me in a low voice.

I do as he says, settling into the comfortable cushions, remov-ing my shoes, and tucking my feet under my legs.

I hear a cork pop in the kitchen. Within a few minutes, he's approaching with a tray of food and two glasses of white wine.

There's hummus, pita bread, a wedge of Brie, and a small bunch of green grapes.

He hands me one glass, and we clink glasses without a toast.

"I hope this is all right," he says, gesturing toward the food.

"It's perfect. I'm starving," I tell him, which puts a smile on his face.

We dig in and silently eat our meal rather quickly, realizing he's probably as nervous as I am, him waiting to hear my story, maybe worried it'll be too painful, and me to tell it for that reason.

I take a long sip of my wine and ease back into the couch. He turns to face me, one leg resting on his other knee. I inhale a deep breath and begin.

"My mother's name was Concetta Laterza. She left Naples when she was eighteen. She loved her family, but she wanted to see America. She also wanted to get away from a man who was infatuated with her. Carlo Morandi was his name. He had known my mother since they were kids, but she was never interested in him. He became obsessed with her, to the point where he started hounding her friends, asking them what she liked so he could know her better. My mother loved opera, so he began listening to opera too, standing under her window and serenading her in a really horrible voice. She was terrified of him.

"My grandparents finally gave their permission and let her leave for America because they saw how much Morandi scared her. When she got to New York, she stayed in a boardinghouse on the Lower East Side and found work as a seamstress. On the weekends, she would explore the city. One day, she got lost in Little Italy, and bumped into my father when she was looking up at the street signs. It was definitely one of those 'meet cute' things, and the rest was history."

"Kind of like us, except in our case, it was a lost glove," he remarks.

I tilt my head. "Hmm…I never thought of it like that."

"Go on," he insists.

"From the day I was born until the day my mother died, my childhood was idyllic. Mamma stayed at home with me, walking me back and forth to school every day while Papa worked in the shop. I loved seeing my parents together, always laughing and hugging each other. We visited my relatives in Italy every summer. We were so happy."

I breathe deeply as Davison takes my hands in his, holding them tightly.

"When I was five, Mamma made me take ballet classes on the Lower East Side in a building on Rivington Street. I loved it. The leotard, the tutu, the ballet slippers. I carried a special bag, shaped like a box that had a special slot for my slippers on the bottom. I was so proud carrying that bag to class after school twice a week, holding Mamma's hand.

"At the end of the year, my class had a recital. We rehearsed so hard for it. Papa couldn't come at the last minute because the refrigerators in the shop broke down. Mamma was so mad at him, and she yelled at him for not coming with us.

"The recital was so much fun. Mamma cheered so loudly for me. We all got little tiaras from my teacher as rewards for our performances. I felt like a princess with my tiara and tutu. When we left, it was late, about nine o'clock."

I close my eyes, bracing myself.

"It was quiet as we walked home, and then suddenly someone pulled my mother into an alley. A man had his hand over Mamma's mouth. I stood frozen, not knowing what to do. I saw something shiny in his other hand. He was a short man, fat, balding. He was talking to her in Italian, saying, 'I've missed you, Concetta. Have you missed me?' Then he lifted the shiny thing, which was a knife. And he said, 'If I can't have you, nobody will.'"

I start to cry as I continue. "Then he started stabbing her. She yelled to me to run, but I started screaming, telling him not to hurt her. He just kept stabbing, and she still kept telling me to run. 'Run, Mia.' Again and again. When she fell to the ground, Carlo looked at me, and that's when I finally ran."

Davison releases my hands to reach for a napkin so I can blow my nose and wipe my eyes. "Oh, baby. You don't have to keep going."

I shake my head. "No, you need to know this. I ran down the street and ducked into another alley. I found a door that was unlocked, so I ran in and hid in the basement of some building. It was the boiler room. It was warm in there, so I just fell asleep in my tutu and tiara."

"When did they find you?"

"Two days later. I was so scared to leave because I didn't want him to find me. The police did a sweep of the neighborhood, canvassing all of the basements, roofs, anyplace where a five-year-old could hide. That picture of me in the cop's arms was taken right after he'd found me in the basement. He said to me that he would take me to my daddy. I wouldn't go with him at first because I was in shock, but something about him made me trust him. When he carried me out, the photographers swarmed us, and that picture of me hit the wires in a flash. I made national news. The tabloids here had a field day. 'Little Girl Lost' and 'Little Girl Found.'"

"Allegra…" his voice coos, stroking my face.

"My grandparents wanted her buried in Naples, and my father agreed. The last time I saw her grave was when they put her in the ground a month after she was murdered."

"I'm so sorry," he tells me in a gentle voice.

"This might sound like an odd question, but how did you not figure out who I was?"

"I was away at boarding school in New Hampshire when you were five. I was twelve then. I had no idea what was going on back here. Is that why you changed your name?"

"Yes," I whisper. "I didn't want to be known as Mia Rossetti, Little Girl Lost, for the rest of my life. Papa and I talked about it when I was a teenager, and I decided I didn't want to be Mia anymore. And the press wouldn't stop hounding me, giving updates on me every year on the day she was killed, waiting outside our building for one fucking shot of me. He changed his name too so people wouldn't ask why we had different surnames. But it still says 'Mia Allegra Rossetti' on my birth certificate."

He nods. "I understand now. I just wish you had told me all this sooner. So, what happened to Morandi?"

"The police tracked him down by Pier 17, where he was hiding. They shot him and he fell into the river."

"Did you have to testify against him?" he asks curiously.

"No." I pause. "Because they never found his body."

"Thank God for small favors," he mutters.

"But there's something else you need to know."

"What?" he asks, his voice raised in worry.

"A few weeks ago, Papa and I received two anonymous letters. They were both of the picture of me being carried out by the cop the night they found me. We gave them to the detective who worked on my mother's case."

"Do the cops know yet who sent them?" he demands.

"No."

Suddenly, Davison is on his feet, his hands clenched into fists. He's looking at me with a frenzied glare in his eyes.

"That's it. I'm getting you a bodyguard. And I'm going to see that detective to get him to tell me everything."

"Are you crazy?" I yell, jumping up to face him. "He's not going to tell you anything because there's nothing to tell. And you can forget about the bodyguard. I can handle it. I'm not a damn wallflower."

"I know you're not, but for crying out loud, Allegra, I want you safe, especially if you don't know who sent them to you."

"Then you can have Charles drive me everywhere, or hire another driver. I don't care. But no bodyguard, Davison. I mean it. I want my life to remain as normal as possible," I insist.

He sighs at me in exasperation, running his hands through his hair. "Fine, whatever you want."

I watch as he steps closer to me, taking me in his arms. I look up into his beautiful face and his emerald eyes.

He smiles. "You're one stubborn woman, you know that?"

"You're just learning that now, Harvard?" I grin at him.

He looks at me solemnly. "I've missed you calling me that."

"Hmm," I wonder aloud. "Did you…"

"What?"

I shake my head. "It's nothing. When I was in the hospital, I was sleeping at one point and I could've sworn I heard you talking to me."

"You did, huh?" His eyebrows rise suspiciously. "What was I saying?"

"Oh, nothing important."

"Really?" He presses his lips together, smirking. "That's too bad."

I smile knowingly, then let out a loud yawn. "I think I should get some rest. I'll get my coat."

I start to walk away, but he tugs my hand, pulling me back to him. I look into his eyes, full of expectation.

"I want you to stay with me tonight. We won't do anything, as much as it'll kill me not to. I just want you next to me so I can hold you. I've missed having you in my bed."

"How can I turn down such a tempting invitation?" I tease him.

"You can't," he says, scooping me up into his arms as I gasp in surprise, allowing myself to laugh for the first time in days.

"Davison?"

"Yes, baby?"

"I'm glad you know everything."

He kisses me gently on the lips. "Me too, Venus. Me too. Just promise me something."

"What?"

"Promise me you'll never leave me again."

I smile, then kiss him again. "I promise, Harvard."

Chapter Seventeen

When I turn around in Davison's bed the next morning, I come face-to-face with quite a sight.

He's lying on his stomach, his dark hair tousled, his mouth open and audibly snoring.

Perfect blackmail material.

But I won't get my phone. I'm just enjoying the view of his muscled back, and his chiseled biceps holding tightly on to his pillow. His tanned body contrasts against the creamy white of his Egyptian cotton sheets.

I climb onto him, straddling his lower back. I start stroking his skin with my fingernails, slowly, up and down, following the curves of his muscles.

"Wake up, sleepyhead," I whisper, leaning down to plant soft kisses on him.

I hear Davison mumble. "Why would I want to do that when I have a gorgeous creature sitting on top of me and making me all hot thanks to her skilled mouth?"

"Because we have something important to do this morning."

"What's that?"

"We need to have make-up sex."

He turns his head as far as he can to look back at me. He's got that glint in his eyes, the one that says he's about to take me and fuck me until I scream.

"I love the way you think," he growls.

I quickly disentangle myself from his hips, allowing him to flip over. He pulls me back onto him so I'm stretched out over his long, hard body. He tugs me down, his lips on mine, prying them open. I instantly accept his tongue, needing to taste it so desperately. I suck him into me as deeply as I can. I wrap my arms around his neck, pressing into him. We're both mewling loudly with desire. In a flash, he sits up, positioning me onto his lap. His engorged cock bumps against my belly.

"Ride me, baby. Hard," he commands with a raw grunt.

"Oh, fuck yes…I want you so much," I groan, dying to have him inside me.

I feel his fingers searching for my slit, holding my lips open to get inside me. His cock enters my wet pussy, so easily, so smoothly.

We moan at the same time from the feel of our bodies joining. I look into his eyes, dark and hooded. Our eyes bore into each other's, sensing just how aroused we are. I cup his face with my hands, inserting my right thumb into his hot mouth. Our gazes remain fixed as he sucks on it, making my pussy even wetter. My heart is pounding in my chest, reveling in the feel of my breasts pushing up against his sculpted chest.

Oh God, how I want him.

I can't keep still. I start riding him, his throbbing cock clenched tightly by my sex. It feels glorious having him inside me again after so long. Once we find our rhythm, my curvy hips meeting his deep thrusts, I buck on top of him. I'm riding him hard, just as he demanded of me. Davison, a raw, primal beast with dark hair and green eyes whose desire for me makes me breathless, pushes me to the edge.

"Fuck, baby. You are so beautiful like this," he rasps, his eyes widened in awe.

My head lolls back in ecstasy, groaning, "Yes, Davison...I love your beautiful cock inside me."

I feel his lips on my breast, biting, then licking my nipple. Shivers run up and down my body.

"Please don't stop! Don't stop!" I beg.

He shifts and angles his penis so it rubs against my clit, sending me spiraling as I move with him.

I'm getting so close...closer and closer...my body begins to shudder violently.

I scream out Davison's name as I come, milking his pulsing cock. His cum spurts into me as he explodes, a deep growl of release roaring from his mouth.

Sated, we fall back together onto the bed. We stretch out, languorously facing each other. Davison strokes my hair, smiling at me. I wrap my arm around his waist.

He kisses me softly. "Mmmm. I wouldn't mind spending all my

mornings doing that with you. My girlfriend comes up with the best ideas," he purrs.

"I have my moments." I smile. "Do you have to go into work soon?"

"Nope. It pays to be the boss on days like this. How are you feeling?"

"Sore."

His eyebrows furrow. "Oh God! Did I hurt you?"

I run my hand over the rough stubble on his cheek. "No, baby. It's a good sore. Like post-coital sore."

"Oh, really? So I did that to you." He smirks, his eyes blazing with pride.

I roll my eyes. "God, that's such a guy reaction. And just for that, Mr. Berkeley, you're going to prepare appropriate sustenance for your woman while she's in the shower."

"At your service, Venus."

We both rise from the bed. Davison pulls out the sweats I wore last time so I have something to wear. I start to head for the bathroom when he calls out to me. "Oh, and Miss Orsini…"

I turn to look at my sexy boyfriend.

He smolders at me. "When you're done with those, don't put them in the hamper. I want to be able to smell you when I put those on again."

* * *

For the next two weeks, I attempt to get my life back to normal as much as I can. The only obstacles I face in this task are the two people I love the most—my father and my boyfriend. They are driving me insane. I'm being treated like an invalid, and I'm losing my mind.

The one person who doesn't treat me with kid gloves is Luciana, bless her. She knows what not being able to practice one's passion does to a person. If I can't sing, then I'm not a whole person. She comes over and rehearses with me. She plays the upright piano in my living room, first practicing the scales, then singing arias that aren't too heavy. But we don't sing the "Flower Duet." That's still too painful for me.

I also find comfort at school. All of my professors were informed about the accident, and they cut me some slack, which I appreciate. But I'm determined to build up my strength, so I have some private tutorials with Signora Pavoni and Professor Waltz, who are incredibly patient as we work together to get my vocals back to perfect condition—as perfect as they can be, that is.

Work also serves as a distraction from the other parts of my life. When I'm home, Papa hovers over me. Davison watches me like a hawk at work, whenever we're at his apartment, or when we go out. I know they're acting like this because they care for me, but it stifles me at times. I envision bringing them together in some sort of intervention, basically telling them to back the hell off me, but I know that their counterargument would be exactly that—that they're doing this because they need to know I'm safe. So I let them hover.

One evening, in the middle of the dinner rush, I'm hanging up a coat when I hear an audible gasp from the patrons in the front room. I rush to the counter and see Elias Crawford, the face of Le Bistro, walk into the restaurant, his head held high, a wide grin on his face. I'd heard his recovery was going well, but

I didn't know he was expected back so soon. He looks impeccable as always, with his hair neatly groomed, his Armani suit and tie freshly pressed. Everyone starts applauding his entrance as he walks straight up to the hostess and kisses her twice on her cheeks, shaking William's hand, moving on to Henry, our new bartender. I love that he greets his staff first.

As I wait my turn, I notice how thin he's become. The heart attack must have taken a lot out of him. His suit doesn't hang on him, probably because he's had it taken in. But even though his eyes still have that same spark in them, his face is more gaunt, and one can tell he's just gone through some sort of health crisis.

I'm clapping along with everyone else when a strong hand attached to an arm wrapped in light gray flannel clasps my arm.

"Hi, baby."

I look up into Davison's eyes. His smile warms my entire body.

"Did you know about this?" I ask.

"William said there was a possibility he'd be stopping by tonight. He said Elias is eager to get back into his old routine."

"I know the feeling."

I glance at him again, and I know without a doubt that the resigned look on my face reflects his. It means that Davison's time as acting co-manager of Le Bistro will soon be coming to an end.

"Yeah," he murmurs his reply to my nonverbalized question. "But I'm still going to have Charles drive you home every night."

"Davison, you don't—"

His jaw clenches. "Yes, I do. It's nonnegotiable, Allegra. End of discussion."

When he has that look on his face, I know arguing with him is pointless.

"Okay," I whisper.

Before I can say something else, Elias appears in front of us. He wraps Davison in a huge bear hug.

"Davison, I can't thank you enough for taking care of my home away from home while I was gone."

"Happy to do it, Elias," he says, smiling.

Mr. Crawford turns to me, taking my hand and leaning over the open space to give me a peck on the cheek. "Allegra, I heard you had an unfortunate accident. I hope you're right as rain now."

"Yes, thank you, sir. I am. I'm very glad to be back."

"Excellent. And as for the two of you," he says, pointing at Davison and me, "don't think anything got past me while I was laid up like some old fart."

My stomach sinks. "Sir, I…"

He pats my hand. "I'm teasing, my dear. I'm just glad to see my godson so happy. Davison, join William and me in the office in a few minutes, would you? We need to talk business."

"Certainly. I'll be there shortly," Davison replies with a nod.

I breathe a sigh of relief after Mr. Crawford walks away, acknowledging more customers as he makes his way to the back of the room.

"I think I stopped breathing there for a second," I admit.

"You worry too much, baby." He caresses my cheek. "I knew he'd be okay with us. I'm his godson, after all."

"Yeah, nice of you not sharing that with me, by the way," I say, pinching his arm.

"Ow!" he winces. "It's not a big deal."

"Anything else you're keeping from me? What famous New Yorker is your godmother? Lady Liberty?"

"Ha-ha. What a funny girlfriend I have." He kisses me quickly but firmly on the lips. "Gotta go. Can't keep my godfather waiting."

I watch as Davison makes his way to the office. I shake my head and smile when I notice a man staring at me from the bar. He's sitting where the brass railing curls around to the side, his knees tucked under it, but his face is set on me. His large hands are too big for the crystal tumbler he's holding containing an amber liquid, probably whiskey. I'm used to getting looks from customers sometimes, a smile here and there. As long as they don't touch me, I don't mind if someone looks at me.

But this man is different. He isn't smiling. He's not even leering. His eyes are cold. He has a shaved head and resembles a bodybuilder, the type of man who doesn't look like he has a neck. He's wearing a leather jacket and jeans, the jacket much too small for his body. And he won't stop staring at me.

A wave of chills shakes my body. I step back into my space to get my sweater, buttoning it almost to the top. I can't get warm fast enough. When I come back, the man is gone.

Marcus, the sommelier, just happens to pass by me at that moment, heading down to the wine cellar.

"Hey, Marcus!"

He stops, his brows furrowed.

"What's wrong, sweetie? You look like something just scared the crap out of you."

"I'm okay. Could you do me a favor and ask Henry who the guy was in the leather jacket at the bar?"

"Uh-oh. I'm going to tell Davison on you," he teases me.

"No, no, it's not like that. Please, Marcus," I ask with a more serious tone.

Marcus puts his hand over mine. "Hey, are you really okay?"

"Yes, I swear. Could you just…"

"Of course. That couple with the attitude can wait for their damn Dom Pérignon. Anything for you."

Marcus steps over to the bar and gets Henry's attention. I see them glance in my direction, then back to each other as they engage in discussion. After a few minutes, Marcus heads back to me.

"Okay, the guy paid cash for his drink, so Henry didn't get a name. He spoke in a rough accent, definitely from the city. He didn't say anything to Henry except when he ordered his drink and paid for it."

I nod. "Okay. Thanks, Marcus."

"Anytime, doll. Now I'll get that Dom for those snots."

Despite the sweater I'm wearing, I rub my arms with my hands, desperate for warmth to make the lingering chill dissipate from my body.

Chapter Eighteen

I have always loved the aria "O mio babbino caro" from Puccini's *Gianni Schicchi.* The character Lauretta sings to her father about her love for Rinuccio and the tensions it has caused between their families. She wants to buy her wedding ring and then threatens to throw herself off the Ponte Vecchio bridge in Florence into the Arno River.

It's a popular aria, featured in one of my favorite films, *A Room with a View,* sung by Dame Kiri Te Kanawa, which I saw ages ago. But it resounds with me now more than ever. I think of my parents who come from different backgrounds in Italy, northern and southern Italy being different in every sense from dialect to economy. My father's parents objected to his marriage to my mother, even more than his decision to immigrate to America. As a result,

I have never been close to them, which my parents and I always regretted.

And now that I'm with Davison, it's as if art has truly imitated life and come full circle, not just because it's the aria I was humming when we first met. Granted, his mother liked me from the start. His father is still indifferent to me, but I don't let it bother me. At the other end of the spectrum, my father worries about me being involved with Davison because he's afraid I will somehow get hurt. I never told Davison that my father wanted me to break up with him after my fall. However, when Papa sees how much he cares for me, thankfully he doesn't bring that up anymore.

I'm singing the aria now in one of the rehearsal rooms at school with Derek, the man who served as the accompanist at Mrs. Berkeley's event. I practice as often as I can in preparation for our graduation recital. I've decided on this aria, but I still need one more. Lucy is singing Wagner, of course.

As I bring the aria to a close, Derek smiles. "*Brava*, darlin'. That was amazing."

I give him a slight bow. "Thank you. I don't want to embarrass myself."

"Not a chance in hell," he reassures me.

I laugh at his blunt compliment when the door opens, and Lucy pokes her head in, her blonde hair in a messy topknot. We're all dressing casually these days for school with rehearsals now starting for the final-year students, and booking time in a rehearsal room has practically become a blood sport.

"Hey, guys. You finished?" she asks.

"Yup, that's all for today," Derek replies as I drink from my water bottle.

"Good. I'm starving. Let's get a bite."

"Sounds good," I say as I gather my things. On the way out, I give Derek a firm hug.

"Same time next week?"

"Works for me, darlin'. See you then."

Lucy and I step out onto the street and walk to Gramercy Park North, the unseasonably warm air for March hitting us in the face with a soft breeze.

"This weather rocks. How about that veggie café on Irving Place?" she suggests.

"Perfect."

I take in the beauty of the park, noticing how the flower buds are raising their heads above the soil, dying to blossom already. A mother is watching as her baby boy takes hesitant steps on the pebbled ground.

"So, how's Money Boy?" Lucy asks, interrupting my reverie.

I sigh. "I really wish you wouldn't call him that. But since you asked, he's just fine. Being more overprotective with each passing day."

"It's just because he loves you, idiot."

I knew it. The counterargument raises its rational head.

"I'm not some scared little waif," I insist. "I'm a New Yorker. I know how to take care of myself." I sigh. "Oh, never mind. How are things with Tomas?"

"Oh my God, Alli! I don't know what I was so afraid of."

I smile. "I told you so."

"Yeah, yeah, I know. And that accent…"

Lucy goes on and on about Tomas. As we're about to cross Gramercy Park South to Irving Place, I suddenly glance over to my right when I see him again. The bald man from that night at Le Bistro a few weeks ago. He's standing at the other end of the park looking at me through the tall black metal bars of the fence, wearing the same jacket and jeans, with the same cold stare in his eyes.

Lucy's hand tugs on my arm. "Hey, Alli! It'd be nice if you paid the same attention to me when I talk to you about my love interest."

I pivot my head to hers as I grip her hand. "Do you see that man over there?"

"What man?"

"At the other end of the park in the leather jacket."

"Honey, there's nobody there."

I turn back to look. She's right. He's gone.

She starts to shake my arm. "Hey, are you okay?"

I pat her hand and offer a smile. "Yeah, I just thought I saw him somewhere before. Come on, let's go eat."

"Stop," she insists, pulling me back on the sidewalk. "Talk to me. Is there something you're not telling me? Has someone been following you?"

"What? No. I just thought he looked familiar, that's all," I tell her as dismissively as I can.

"I'm telling Davison about this," she declares, pulling out her cell phone.

"No!" I hiss. "Please, Luciana. If you tell him, he's going to put me on twenty-four/seven lockdown. It was just a case of mistaken identity. I'm begging you. Don't make a big case out of this. I can take care of myself."

"Fine," she says, giving in. She shoves her phone back in her purse. "But if you see him again, I want you to tell someone, got it?"

"I promise."

* * *

Thankfully, that strange man disappears from my life as quickly as he invaded it. Everyone eases off on their overprotection of me. Davison and I are now closer than ever. Along with the toe-curling, sheet-clawing sex we always have, I love just lying on his couch with him, watching an old movie, laughing with him at something silly we see on the street, or walking with him along the Esplanade by his apartment on the Hudson River, holding hands. We even have Sunday brunch now and then at his parents' house. His mother is still as warm and friendly to me as ever, which is a constant surprise to me, but it makes me happy because I see how happy it makes Davison.

Before I know it, the night of my graduation recital arrives. Davison texts me from the car when he arrives outside my building. Along with my classmates, I'm going to get dressed at school.

When I come downstairs carrying my gown in one hand and a tote bag with the other, I freeze on the sidewalk. Davison is leaning against the Maybach, wearing the same tuxedo he wore the night of my fall. I don't stop because of that. I'm paralyzed because he looks so damn hot in it, with every strand of his silky dark hair in place, his emerald eyes searing into me. I still have trouble wrapping my head around the fact that this man, this gorgeous man, the head of an international financial house, one of the most famous society bachelors in Manhattan, chooses to be with me, a curvy Italian-American girl of medium height, the daughter of a Little Italy butcher.

The wide smile on his face instantly arouses me, warming my entire body. "Hi, baby."

I step forward to adjust his tie. "You look so handsome, Harvard."

"Thank you. It's going to be an amazing night. Why don't I take these for you while you get into the car?" he offers.

"Thanks." I smile, kissing him quickly on the lips.

As I set one foot into the car, I realize I can't sit in my usual spot because lying in my seat is an exquisite bouquet of twelve pale apricot roses, wrapped in clear cellophane with a bow the color of champagne tying them together.

"Davison…" I whisper in awe.

"You like to wear pale apricot lip gloss, so I thought you'd like these. Go on," he insists, giving me a gentle tap on my lower back to get me into the car.

I pick up the roses, sitting down in my seat once I have a secure hold on them. I bring them to my nose to inhale their intoxicating scent, holding them close to me. I want to cry because he noticed something about me, something that I do with regular occurrence. I feel myself softening from his kind and attentive heart.

"Mmmm, they're so beautiful." I turn to my boyfriend. "Thank you, baby."

He swiftly pulls me onto his lap while I'm still holding on to my roses, clamping his mouth over mine. We luxuriate in the taste of each other for a few minutes until we have to come up for air.

"I'm so proud of you, Allegra," he murmurs, stroking my cheek.

I stare into his exquisite eyes. I think about everything that he's done for me, how thoughtful he is, how he's always interested in what's going on with me, how he worries about me. We're always touching each other when we're near one another. As strong and independent as I am, I always feel like something is missing when I'm not with him.

And the way we look at each other…

This man is it for me.

We're silent for the short ride to the conservatory until we get closer to Gramercy Park.

"When is your father coming?" he asks.

"He was just finishing up in the shop. But he has his ticket, so he'll be there soon."

"You know my mother is coming tonight."

My head pops up from the crook of his shoulder when I hear those words.

"Davison! I'm nervous enough as it is! You couldn't have told me this, oh, I don't know, after the recital?"

"Calm down, baby," he pleads. "I just wanted you to know how much support you were going to have tonight, that's all."

I can see a slight look of hurt in his face. He's just trying to be nice, and I've cut him down.

"I'm sorry. Of course I'm glad she'll be there," I reassure him with a kiss. "Please thank her for me when you see her."

"I will," he says with a smile. "So, what color is your gown?"

"Black."

"Text me a picture of you in it before you come out onstage," he requests.

I bite my lower lip. "I don't know if I'll have time. I need to warm up, and my nerves—"

He strokes my face with his index finger. "It's fine. I totally understand. It'll just be a surprise for me, right?"

"Right," I agree, kissing him again on the lips, something I never get tired of.

The car stops and double-parks in front of the school. I wait as usual for Davison to open the door for me, with Charles holding my gown and bag.

"Break a leg, Miss Orsini," he says.

I give him a grateful smile. "Thank you, Charles. I'll do my best."

With our hands linked together, Davison and I walk into the main entrance of the conservatory. I have to part ways with him here to go backstage to get ready.

He holds me tightly before we separate.

"You know where to look for me, right?" he checks with me.

"Yup. Front row center as always," I reply knowingly.

He kisses me softly on the lips before I walk away. I look back one more time, giving him a quick wave and a smile, then turn the corner in the lobby to get to the backstage area of the auditorium. Two rooms are cordoned off as dressing areas for the male and female grads.

I pass Tomas outside the men's dressing room, decked out in a tux with a white tie and tails.

"Wow! Tomas, you look great! Lucy is going to lose it when she sees you."

"That is what I hope for," he replies with a twinkle in his eye. "Break a foot, Allegra."

I smile, deciding it's sweet and not necessary to correct him. "Thanks, Tomas. You too."

Luciana is already dressed when I walk in, her jade-green gown a perfect complement to her blonde hair. She's putting the finishing touches on her makeup when she sees me, practicing her scales as she gives herself one last brush of powder.

"You look amazing, Lucy!"

"Hey! There you are! Thanks, sweetie!" she says, glancing at me. "About time you got here. Money Boy give you a lift?"

"Yeah. And just to add to my nerves, he told me his mom is going to be here."

"How thoughtful," she jokes.

"By the way, prepare yourself, because Tomas looks very handsome in his tux."

"Really?" she says, rubbing her two hands together like a mad scientist. "I think I'll have to go investigate."

I laugh, then quickly change into my gown, a floor-length strapless A-line of silk and organza, tucking my hair into a low chignon at the nape of my neck as I usually do. I slip into my favorite black patent kitten heels.

I go through my usual warm-up routine as I make up my face—singing the scales like Lucy did, flapping my lips while exhaling, humming the opening notes of the arias I'm going to sing.

As I apply my apricot gloss to my lips, a voice comes over the backstage PA system. "Good evening, ladies and gentlemen. This is your five-minute warning. Five minutes, please."

Lucy reappears with Tomas at her side. "Come on, Alli. It's time!"

I give myself one last look in the mirror, taking in a deep breath.

This is it. I can do this. Davison is waiting.

"*Andiamo!* Let's go!" I declare.

Both dressing areas empty as we join the other grads lining up behind the curtain for our introductions.

Suddenly, I start to feel guilty for giving Davison a hard time about his mother coming tonight. I want to make it up to him.

I tug Lucy by the elbow. "I'll be right back."

"Where are you going? Are you going to be sick?"

"Don't worry. I'm fine," I reassure her. "Back in a sec."

I rush back to the empty dressing room and dig for my cell phone in my bag. I hum excitedly at the thought of surprising Davison after all with a shot of me in my gown, even though I told him I wouldn't have time. I turn on my camera app and switch the lens to face me.

When I lift the phone to my face and smile widely, someone else is in the shot with me. It's the man with the evil eyes and no neck, the man who's been following me.

Suddenly, a piece of cold metal is pressing to my neck, and a large hand smelling of onions and cigarettes clamps over my mouth.

"If you make a sound, I'll fucking kill you," he whispers roughly into my ear as he pushes the knife harder against my skin, the blade threatening my carotid artery.

I nod quickly before he throws a sack over my head and darkness envelops me.

Chapter Nineteen

Cold. I'm so cold.

I open my eyes, my teeth chattering, and see nothing but gray concrete walls.

Where am I?

The room smells of damp. Pipes crisscross overhead. This has to be a basement. A window high above on the wall next to me is boarded over with a sheet of plywood, but through a sliver between the wall and the window, I can detect a faint light, possibly from an alley.

I want to warm myself up by rubbing my arms together, but I can't. My hands are tied in front of me, and my bare feet are bound at the ankles. The ropes cut into my skin. A gag is shoved into my mouth as I lie on a thick, musty mattress, a wire poking through the top, with no pillow or blanket.

My heart starts to palpitate. I quickly start recalling everything in my mind, desperate to remember. It was the recital, and I was about to go onstage when I went back to take a photo for Davison.

Davison…

And then I saw that man with no neck who'd been following me standing behind me.

Oh my God.

Soft tears start falling down my face.

Suddenly, a metal door against the far wall screeches against the concrete floor. I push myself up so I can see what's happening.

My stalker appears in the doorway.

"Good. You're up," he croaks. "Yo, Carlo, she's awake."

No. It can't be. How can he be alive? Oh God.

As if I were five years old again, the stout form of Carlo Morandi fills the door frame. My stomach begins to spasm from the harsh sobs that escape my mouth as I scoot as far back as I can on the mattress.

He slowly walks toward me. I turn my head into the wall and lift my bound hands to my face so I don't have to look at him.

"Hello, Mia," my mother's killer coos to me in a stomach-churning voice. "It's so lovely to see you again. I've missed you. You've grown into such a beautiful woman. *Una bella donna.*"

He roughly turns my head so he can look me in the eyes.

"Don't cry, *bella*. You have nothing to be afraid of."

I start talking to him, but the rag in my mouth muffles my words.

"Do you want to say something?"

I nod.

"I'll take this off if you promise not to scream."

I nod again, shutting my eyes as he leans in to untie the kerchief from my mouth, cringing as his noxious body odor invades my nose.

I start coughing so I can take in fresh oxygen. I watch as Carlo walks out of the room, returning with a bottle of water. He lets it spill into my mouth. The water cascades down my throat as I try to drink as much as I can. I start choking when I've had enough.

Once my breathing normalizes, I remain sitting up, staring right at him. He's not going to scare me.

"How could you have survived…How can you be here?" I stammer in shock.

"I'm a survivor, Mia. It's not that easy to get rid of me."

"You'll never get away with this."

"I will, with Tony's help. He's an idiot, but he gets the job done."

"The pig who stalked me?"

"I needed to keep tabs on you, *cara*—"

"Don't call me that!"

Without warning, his right hand slaps me across the face. I fall back onto the mattress from the force of the hit. "You should learn now what happens when you speak to me like that. Only your sweet papa calls you that, right? I can't wait to take away the last thing from him that he loved. I got rid of Concetta, and now it's your turn."

Swallowing in my throat, I quickly sit back up to ask the question I've wanted the answer to for nineteen years. "Why did you kill my mother? If you loved her, why did you hurt her?"

"Because I wasn't good enough for that *puttana* you had for a mother. I was so nice to her before she left Italy. I brought her flowers, so many presents. I learned about opera because she loved it. But she wanted more. She wanted to see America, as if Napoli was too small for her. *I* was too small. Just because I was a mechanic's son. All she wanted was a rich man. And your father took her from me."

"Finally, the truth, as warped as it is," I tell him right to his face. "And here is my mother's truth. She was afraid of you. She thought you were mentally unbalanced, bordering on sociopathic. All that attention you paid to her terrified her. That's the reason she didn't like you. The reason she left for America. And then she met my father, who isn't rich. He's just a butcher. But he is kind and warm, something you never were to her. That's the truth, you asshole. *La verità.*"

Morandi's jaw begins to tighten as his eyes blaze in fury. This time I see his open fist coming, but I stay upright. My eyes widen from the shock of the slap as my head twists from the impact. I spit out the blood that pools in my mouth onto the concrete floor.

I smile, steeling myself with determination to look at him, straight into his bloodshot eyes. "You truly are a sociopath if you think the cops won't track you down. I know people are already looking for me."

"I highly doubt it. And that rich *bastardo* you hooked up with? Forget him. You're a *puttana* just like your mother. Once I'm done with you, he'll never want to be with you again, that is if you're ever stupid enough to escape. You'll be worse than garbage left on the street."

My brows furrow in confusion as I start to shake from the threatening tone in his voice. My defenses are crumbling.

"What do you mean?"

"When we're back in Napoli, I'm going to let all my friends enjoy you for a price. I'm getting hard just thinking about watching it happen."

I gasp, but then I quickly collect myself.

Fuck him. I'm not going to let him do this to me.

Carlo steps over to me, patting my head in some perverted form of comfort.

"Don't worry, Mia. We'll have so much fun. Trust me."

He takes my hands into his, sensing the feel of cold metal against them. I watch, afraid of what he's going to do next. In one swipe, he cuts the rope from around my wrists.

"I'm not completely heartless," he says, watching me rub my hands together, then running them down my arms to get their circulation back. "I'll get you a blanket and some food. I need to keep you healthy, after all."

He pats me again on my hair. "Don't worry, *bella*. I'll take care of you. I'm your family now."

The impact of his words hits me as if he'd physically struck me again. My hands clench into fists. I punch the mattress, releasing a loud yell of frustration. I lie back down, utterly exhausted. But his words, ominous and disturbing, remain in my head, fearful what he'll do to me if I fall asleep. I sit up, take deep breaths, leaning my head against the wall, pressing my cheek into the cold concrete to keep me awake.

* * *

The sliver of light is now gone. I must have fallen asleep. I can't let that happen again.

My head is heavy with pain, but I sit up.

That's when I spot a full bottle of water and a package wrapped in parchment paper lying near me. The paper is like the kind we use at the shop to wrap meat.

I lean over, reaching for the food in the parchment. I unwrap the paper, revealing a pepperoni stick. There is no way I'm eating anything he's left for me. I throw the meat and the water across the small space.

That's when I notice the writing on the paper.

Papa!

My father is the only person I know who writes numbers like that with a grease pencil.

I wrap my arms around my waist, smiling with this newfound knowledge.

I must be so close to home.

I feel energized. I'm determined to find a way to escape.

Morandi can go fuck himself.

I'm going to see Papa again.

And Davison…I will hold him again, kiss him again, laugh with him again. No matter what it takes, I will make that happen.

The metal door again screeches against the floor. Carlo appears with a plastic bag, packed full.

"*Buona sera*, Mia," he rasps at me. He bends down and unbinds my feet with a flick of his knife. I'm stretching out my legs to get the circulation going when he throws down the bag next to me on the mattress.

He glares at me noticing that I've tossed his food away. I stare him straight in the eye refusing to cower away from his gaze. "You need to change into these. That gown will catch someone's attention."

My heart sinks. "Are we going somewhere? What time is it?"

"You're a curious little whore, aren't you? It's late. That's all you need to know. Once you change, we're leaving. Now hurry the fuck up!" he shouts.

He drops the bag to the floor and slams the door behind him.

This is it. I need to do something.

Something flashes in my head. A daytime talk show I watched once. I can't remember which show it was, but it was an episode with a security expert who said that if you're ever kidnapped, you should do everything you can not to be taken to a second location, probably to make it easier to find you.

Once I put on the sweats and hoodie that are in the bag, I sit down on the mattress. I smooth out my gown, my beautiful black gown, which everyone gushed over at the recital.

It's then that I know what I need to do. The only ammunition I have at my disposal.

The door opens again, with Tony trudging toward me, and Carlo right behind him.

"Is she ready?" Carlo demands of his accomplice.

"Yeah," Tony barks, throwing the hood over my head.

"*Aspetta, per favore*," I quietly ask, cringing internally as I look Carlo directly in the eyes.

"We don't have time to wait, bitch!" Tony yells at me.

I can tell Carlo is intrigued. Hearing the Italian language come from my mouth must have disconcerted him. "What is it?"

I swallow. "May I sing for you? A beautiful Puccini aria, one I'm sure you'll know."

"Are you fucking nuts?" Tony shouts, shaking me by the shoulder.

"Why do you want to sing, *cara*?"

I take a deep breath.

He wants me to be his slave? Fuck that! I know what I have to do.

Praying like hell that Carlo will buy my fake sincerity, I soften my eyes and give him a wide smile. "Well," I say in a gentle voice, "since we're starting this new life together, I want to do it on a positive note."

It's obvious Carlo is seriously considering what I said.

Please. Oh God. Please.

Finally, Carlo nods his head. "*Si.* I would like that. Sing as if you were singing only to me."

"You lost your damn mind, Carlo?" Tony yells.

"Shut up, *stupido*. She wants to sing to me. And we have time. It's only midnight. Go make sure the car is ready."

"Goddamn it!" Tony curses as he goes out the door, slamming it behind him.

Carlo walks to me, lifting his hand to my hair, patting my head as he brushes my cheek with his lips. I grit my teeth, fisting my hands to keep me from pushing him away. I have to endure this. My father's handwriting on that paper was a sign. Even if the police are nowhere close to finding me, at least I'll know that I tried.

My mother's murderer whispers into my ear, "Finally. You understand, don't you?"

I silently nod.

Carlo stands with his back to the door, taking a few steps back. "Go on, *bella. Cantala per me.*"

I nod. I vocalize the scales and shake my hands to release the tension. I clear my throat and open my mouth, singing with as much strength as my body allows.

The opening lyrics of "Sì, mi chiamano Mimì" echo from my mouth. I stare at Morandi full-on, keeping his attention. I act out the lyrics, imagining I'm onstage at the Met in my debut role, the house is sold out, and Davison is sitting in his family's box, admiring me from afar.

I use every muscle in my body to make sure I'm singing as loudly as I can, praying that someone hears me.

But with the last lines of the aria, I try to think of something else I can do. Anything to keep me here.

Carlo starts clapping after I finish. He steps closer to me, touching my face with his fingers. My stomach turns from the feel of his filthy hands on my skin, but I hide the disgust from my face. His hands travel down to my throat, his thumbs pressing tightly into my trachea.

"*Brava*, Mia. So beautiful," he says, his putrid breath exhaling on my face. "Too bad you'll never be able to perform at La Scala in Milano. Your voice is such a gift. I'm so lucky you'll be singing to me from now on. And if you ever disobey me, I'll crush your lovely neck so that you'll never sing again. Do you understand?"

Before I can comprehend what's happening, the metal door is being kicked in. A loud male voice shouts, "POLICE!" Gunshots ring out, and as Carlo's hands release me and his body collapses to the floor, it knocks me down and I feel myself falling back. My head hits the edge of the mattress, cushioning it, but my body slams into the concrete floor, making me cry out in pain.

A series of coughs shakes my body as I take in large gulps of oxygen. My entire neck is stinging from the pain of Carlo's hands. When I look up, I'm staring into the eyes of Detective Dermot Leary, his upper body covered in a Kevlar vest with NYPD boldly printed across it in blinding white letters.

He picks me up in his burly arms, running out of the building. "It's okay. I got you, Allegra. It's over. You're safe now," he pants.

My eyes widen when I see what's waiting outside for me. Camera flashes go off as a cordon of policemen surrounds Leary and me. "Get back!" he roars to the horde of reporters and paparazzi.

He lays me down swiftly onto a waiting gurney. "I'll see you at the hospital with your dad. Get her out of here!" he shouts to the EMS paramedics who are hovering over me. They quickly strap me in, lifting me into the waiting ambulance. When they lock the gurney in place, I glance to my left and burst into tears.

Davison is sitting next to me, wearing the Harvard sweatshirt I always wear at his apartment. His eyes are wet with unshed tears, but his face turns fiery red when he sees me.

"Allegra..." he says in a rough voice, taking my hand in his, kissing the back of it, my palm, my fingers, his eyes never leaving mine. "I'm here, baby. And I'm going to kill that son of a bitch myself."

I fall into wracking sobs, my entire body shaking. "He's dead. He's dead. I sang for him, and I...I just..." I sputter. "Don't leave me, Davison."

"Baby, calm down. Please," he begs, holding my hand in one of his while stroking my hair with the other. "I'm never leaving you. It's over. You're safe now. I'm here."

I can't stop crying. I'm losing my breath, panting for oxygen.

Oh my God. Just like Papa was waiting for me in the ambulance so long ago…

One of the paramedics shoves a needle into my arm and a mask over my nose. "We need to calm her down, Mr. Berkeley. She's going into shock."

A wave of warmth begins coursing through my veins. As I fade away, I hear Davison's soothing voice repeating, "I'm here, baby. You're safe. I'll never leave you. Never."

Chapter Twenty

W hen I open my eyes again, the brilliant light of the morning sun floods the room I'm in, accentuated by the crisp shade of white that surrounds me—white walls, white bed sheets, white hospital gown. The overload on my senses is blinding. It takes some time for my eyes to adjust to my new environment after what I've just been through. Even the temperature of the room is unnerving. The heat from the sun warms my small hospital room, and despite lying under a thick blanket, shivers still shake my body, goose bumps popping up all over my arms.

I glance to both sides of my bed, finding the two men I love asleep—my father on a metal cot, and Davison in a chair, wearing the same clothes he had on in the ambulance, his head lolling back and dark scruff on his face. I'm desperate to see his brilliant emerald eyes again, and his lush lips reflecting the smile in his eyes when I make him laugh over something silly we both share.

My throat is parched. A water pitcher and a plastic cup sit on a side table. I reach for them with my right arm, but with the IV sticking in the crook of my elbow, I can't reach them fully and the cup goes flying to the floor, waking up Davison in the process.

He snorts once, shaking his head to get his bearings. When he sees me, he jumps to his feet, leaning over to take me in his arms.

"Allegra, thank God," he murmurs, kissing me softly on the lips. "Are you in pain? I can get the nurse."

"No, no, I'm fine. Where am I?"

"Beth Israel. Do you need something?" he asks worriedly.

"I'm really thirsty."

"Hang on, I'll get some water for you."

I watch as he picks up the cup from the floor, taking it into the bathroom.

"No, Davison, it's okay. I'm sure it's clean."

"I'm not taking any chances," he shouts over his shoulder.

I sigh in exasperation as I hear the water running, then him returning and pouring the cup full from the pitcher, poking a straw into the cup to make it easier for me to drink.

As I sip the cool liquid, rehydrating my body, my father stirs on the cot. He sits up, placing his feet on the floor and running his hands over his eyes and hair. When he sees me awake, he stands and moves closer to me.

"*Cara, ma stai bene?* Are you all right? We were so scared…" he cries, tears forming in his eyes. He hugs me, kissing me on the top of my head.

"I'm okay, Papa," I whisper, my voice still raw. "How did you find me?"

Davison looks directly at me. "When you didn't come out for the group introduction, I knew something was wrong. I went backstage and found your phone on the floor in the dressing room. I guess you had gone back to take a picture of yourself for me and that's when Tony grabbed you?"

I nod in reply.

Papa pats my hand. "Then Davison came to tell me what happened, and I called Dermot. The recital went on because we didn't want to alarm anyone."

"I sent my mom home," Davison continues, "and we set up command central in your house, hoping someone would call with a ransom demand, but nobody did. You won't believe this, baby, but you actually managed to get half of the pig's face in the shot, so Detective Leary was able to track him down faster than he would have without it."

A deep voice booms, "It's true, Allegra. That picture helped save your life. *You* saved your own life."

We all turn our heads as Detective Dermot Leary walks into the room.

Leary steps forward to me. "We studied all of the CCTV feeds and found him on the Lower East Side. You were being held in the basement of the same building on Rivington Street where you took ballet lessons when you…"

I cover my mouth with my hands. "Oh my God…"

Davison and my father come closer to comfort me, with Papa using soothing words and Davison placing soft kisses on my hair.

"How are you feeling?" Leary asks me.

"Tired and sore, but better than I was."

"Good. You don't have to worry. Carlo is dead—"

"Yeah, I was there," I say under my breath.

"And Tony Greco is in custody."

A worried look crosses my father's face. "She won't have to testify against him, will she?"

Leary shakes his head. "I doubt there will be a trial. It's an open-and-shut case. He'll probably make some kind of deal with the DA."

"Will she still be in danger?" Davison asks, taking his hand in mine.

"No," he assures us. "With Morandi dead, Tony knows better than to mess with Allegra anymore. It was personal for Carlo, but he was just his accomplice. And if I have to, I'll remind him what will happen to him if he does decide to contact her again because it's personal for me."

"It's personal for all of us, Detective," Davison corrects him. He leans down and kisses my hair. "Be right back, baby."

I watch him step into the bathroom. When I hear the door lock, I turn to Detective Leary.

"Before he comes back, I want to tell you something," I announce hurriedly.

"What is it?" he asks with complete focus.

"Carlo's plan was to take me to Naples and make me his sex slave," I tell him as quietly as I can. "He was going to pass me around to his friends."

Papa takes my hand. *"Cara mia!"* With tears in his eyes, he leans over and embraces me. "Thank God we found you in time."

"I know, Papa. Just don't tell Davison," I plead with him. "It would devastate him."

"I won't," my father reassures me.

"Same goes for me," Leary adds in. "And that Italian in the trafficking ring wasn't connected to Morandi; Carlo was working on his own."

"I understand. But I hope you can bust them soon and save all those girls."

"Don't worry, Allegra. We're making solid progress."

I hear the lock releasing in the bathroom. Davison steps out, an odd smile on his face, which disconcerts me.

My heart starts beating nervously. "Is something wrong?"

"Of course not," he answers somewhat quickly. "You're here, safe and sound with us."

"Okay." I accept his answer, but something about it still bothers me.

A thought strikes me unexpectedly. "Did...Tony..." I gulp. "Did he come to the shop?"

"How did you know?" Papa asks.

"Because I saw your handwriting on the paper," I tell my father with tears in my eyes. "I took that as a sign that I couldn't give up, that I was somewhere close to you. And I was right."

Davison squeezes my hand when he hears that. I look into his eyes and smile as widely as I can, my face still bruised from Carlo's hits.

"I showed the picture to Luigi," Papa confirms. "I wasn't working because I was upstairs with Davison and the police waiting for a ransom call. Pietro was in the shop then too, and Luigi had him run upstairs to tell us to come down right away, and that's when Luigi told us."

"From then, it was just a matter of tracking him, watching his every move, and eventually, he led us to you," Leary reveals.

"We moved in when we saw him packing the getaway car, which meant Carlo was probably getting ready to leave the city with you."

Thankfully at that moment, a tall man with blond hair wearing a white coat comes through the door. "Good morning, Miss Orsini. I'm Dr. Andrew Scott. How are you feeling this morning?"

I roll my eyes, but refrain from making a snide comment about the frequency that question had been asked of me in the last two hours. "I'm fine. Just sore and tired."

He picks up a chart that hangs attached to the foot of my bed. "Well, everything looks good. All of your test results came back negative, but I still want to run some more to make sure you're completely out of the woods."

"When can I go home?"

"You'll go home when the doctor says you can," Davison declares with a *Don't even think about it* look on his face. And with Papa nodding in agreement, I know I'm outnumbered.

"And you're going to have a twenty-four-hour police guard outside your door until you leave," Leary adds.

I start to shiver again. "But why? You said I wasn't in danger anymore."

Davison and Papa take my hands in theirs to calm me down.

"It's not Tony, Allegra," Leary reassures me. "It's the press. They're swarming outside."

"Great," I mutter under my breath.

"Don't worry, baby," Davison says. "Nobody is coming in here uninvited. We'll make sure of it."

An orderly comes in with a wheelchair. "Time for those tests,

Miss Orsini," Dr. Scott announces. "These will take a while. If you need to, go get something to eat," he suggests to Davison and my father.

I slowly sit up, with both of them rushing to help me. "I've got this," I tell them, even as Davison picks me up to put me in the wheelchair himself. "Watch the IV, Harvard," I warn him.

"I got you, baby," he says to me with that confident tone in his voice that I have missed so much.

My father comes around from the other side of the bed. He kisses my cheek. "I'm going to go home and change. I'll be back as soon as I can."

"Take your time, Papa. And tell Luigi *grazie* for me and that I can't wait to tell him that myself."

"I will, *cara. Ti amo*."

"Ti amo anch'io."

Leary steps over, placing his hand on my shoulder. "I'm so glad you're okay, Allegra. Come by the precinct when you're feeling better so you can give an official statement. I'll see you soon."

I put my hand over his. "Thank you, Detective. For everything."

He nods, then slaps my father's back. "Come on, Jimmy, I'll give you a ride home."

Davison and I watch as everyone leaves the room. I'm alone with him for the first time. He crouches down to look at me at eye level.

"You should go home too, Davison. Take a shower, change clothes."

He shakes his head. "Not a chance. I'm going to be here when you get back."

"What about work?"

"It's a good thing I hire smart people to work for me. And I have everything I need here," he says, pointing out a large carryall. "My mom brought it over for me. She's so relieved you're okay. She wants to see you too."

I smile at his mother's thoughtfulness. "Tell her thank you for that."

Mindful of the doctor and orderly waiting outside, I pull Davison closer to me, placing a warm kiss on his mouth until the pain from the pressure forces me to stop.

"On second thought, don't shave," I whisper. "That scruff does something to me. Now, roll me out of here, Harvard."

"Yes, Venus. At your service." He grins at me wickedly.

Chapter Twenty-One

Thankfully, I was released from the hospital the following day. I went home and recuperated with two overprotective male nurses seeing to my recovery—Papa and Davison. Once I felt stronger, I started going stir crazy and insisted on leaving the apartment. But some photographers were still lurking outside, waiting to get a shot of me. So I had to wait another week until I could escape.

Now I'm sitting in my favorite place in the world—on the floor cushions in Davison's living room eating dinner, both of us in Harvard sweats. I'm watching him dunk his spicy tuna roll into a dipping bowl of soy sauce. As thoughtful as ever, he's also ordered my favorite sushi rolls—mango shrimp and salmon avocado.

Once we finish, I swallow the last of my Sapporo beer and

climb into Davison's lap. I gently run my fingertips over his stubbled cheeks. "Hi, Harvard."

"Hey." That's all he says, accompanied by a quick smile, without that glint in his eyes that usually signals the start of a sexy night.

Moving my hands around to the nape of his neck, I lean in and start to suck on it, breathing on his hot skin as I repeat, "Hi, Harvard," but this time in a lusty whisper.

Nothing is happening. I pull back. "Okay, something is obviously bothering you and I want you to tell me what's wrong," I demand.

"I'm really angry with you," he murmurs under his breath.

I rear back in surprise. "For what?"

"For not telling me about Tony stalking you before Carlo took you."

I pull myself off his lap and take a few steps from him, attempting to absorb what he just told me.

"I didn't want to worry you. I thought I could handle it."

"Well, you thought wrong!" he shouts.

"Jesus, Davison, what is your fucking problem?" A thought crosses my mind that makes me grow livid. "Wait, were you this pissed at me when I was gone? Did you think this was my fault?"

Davison shoots up from the couch, his eyes ablaze, his jaw clenched. "Of course not! What kind of person do you think I am? Christ, Allegra, you know me better than that! And now that I know what that fucking bastard was going to do to you..." His eyes blaze with a fury I never thought possible. "I failed you! I wasn't there to protect you! Goddamn it!"

My heart stops, my eyes widening in shock at his revelation.

He heard me? Oh my God!

Fuck. Shit. Fuck.

"You heard me tell Leary? Why didn't you—"

Before I can finish my thought, I watch frozen as a shattering howl of pain roars from Davison's mouth. He grabs the crystal vase sitting on the coffee table and hurls it across the room, hitting the wall and shattering into a million tiny pieces.

He sinks to his knees, his hands covering his face as his body shudders in anguish. I run to him and fall onto the carpet next to him. He latches onto me with his hands. I hold on to him as tightly as I can.

"I'm here, Davison. I'm here. I'm safe," I swear to him, tears streaming down my face. I never wanted him to know. I never wanted to see him in pain. And I never want to see him like this again.

"I thought I'd lost you forever," he breathes into my neck, his voice deep and raw. "I felt so helpless. I just wanted you back."

"Baby," I tell him softly. "The only thing that kept me going was the thought of seeing you once more. Of you holding me in your arms."

Davison finally looks up at me, his eyes glistening with unshed tears. He straightens his back and takes a deep breath, cupping my face in his hands. "I love you, Allegra. I love you so damn much."

In this moment, with those words, I have never felt more safe or alive in my life.

I look directly into his eyes. "I love you too, Davison. More than I ever thought possible."

I can see both need and something primal blazing back at me

in his beautiful green eyes. He brings his lips to mine, and I open my mouth, ready to welcome the familiar taste of his tongue. I suck on it like it's my source of life. We kiss each other fiercely, holding each other's heads, desperate to plunge our tongues in as far as they can go. He pushes me back onto the floor, still attached to my mouth. Then he pulls back, and I watch as he strips off his sweatshirt in one swoop, flinging it to the side. With his help, he yanks me up and removes all my clothes in a frenzy.

I lie back down, boring my eyes into his.

"Touch me, Davison."

He covers his body with mine and starts to move over me, his lips licking my flesh, his nose taking in my scent. He takes an erect nipple in his mouth, sucking on it gently at first, then more insistently. I hear him murmuring, "I adore you. I need you. Need you so much," as he moves to my other breast to continue his ministrations.

I run my hands through his silky hair, mewling my pleasure, reveling in his ardor. "Don't stop," I whisper.

"Never, baby. Never," he vows to me.

He travels down to my belly, leaving a trail of kisses. He reaches the apex between my thighs, spreading my legs farther apart. As he reaches inside my slit with his fingers, I hear him moan.

"Ahhh. So wet. You're ready for me, aren't you, baby?"

"I'm always ready for you. I need you inside me. Now," I beg.

"Just one thing first, my love."

My back arches as I feel his tongue inside my pussy, then on my clit when he starts to lick it. He plunges his fingers inside me again, moving them in and out, over and over.

I'm on the precipice about to come apart for him, but I want it to be with his hard, beautiful cock inside me, not his tongue.

Moving my hands down his body, I reach underneath the waistband of his sweatpants and squeeze his rock-hard ass.

"This…you…" I pant. "Now, Davison. Fuck me now."

I hear him grunt as he pulls his mouth away from my sex, lifting himself up and sliding his long, solid, sculpted body over me until he's covering me completely.

I pull down his sweats as he lets out a growl, impaling me in one quick thrust.

"Ahhhh, God, yes!" I yell. "Do it, Davison! Fuck me hard!"

My body moves with his as we start to build a mutual rhythm, the hard carpet underneath my back burning my skin. The heat from the burn radiates around my flesh, our bodies growing slick with sweat. He moves faster inside me, with my hands gripping his ass, pushing him, demanding him. I want everything from him. Every grunt, every thrust, every drop of his cum.

My orgasm crests and I scream Davison's name in release, milking his cock with my cleft. His entire body shakes as he comes right after me with a ferocious grunt, collapsing onto my chest. Our breaths pant at the same rate. He raises his head to look at me. I flash him a wide smile as he gives me one in return. He lays his head down in the crook of my neck as our heartbeats cool in tandem, my hands around his waist and his cradling my head.

* * *

The feel of Egyptian cotton sheets tickling my chin wakes me up the next morning. I open my eyes, finding myself lying in Davison's bed with him next to me, smiling from ear to ear with that glint in his eyes that I've been so desperate to see.

He won't stop staring at me. "Morning, beautiful."

I smile. "Morning, Harvard. Got a question for you."

"Which would be?"

"How did we get here? The last thing I recall is lying on that very uncomfortable carpet with you in your living room."

"Around midnight. I carried you in here," he informs me.

"Thank you."

"You're welcome."

I feel so alive, so grateful for this man. My heart is practically leaping out of my chest cavity. "I need to ask you something now."

He raises his eyebrows in curiosity. "What?"

"I'm going to start seeing my therapist again. I'll have solo sessions, of course, but would you consider having joint sessions with me? Dr. Turner is amazing, and she's—"

"Okay."

My eyes widen at his quick answer. "Really?"

He nods. "We need to heal from this, and I want us to do it together. If she's good enough for you, that's all I need to know."

I lean in and kiss him. "Thank you, my love."

"But do you think we could wait to make an appointment with her until after?"

A wave of chills sweeps over me. "After what?"

With my hands still in his grip, he sits up and pulls me to him, a sly smile now plastered on his face. "It's your turn, Venus. I want you to do something for me."

I narrow my eyes, wrinkling my nose. "Hmm, you're smiling, so I'm thinking whatever it is, my answer is going to be 'yes.'"

"I've been thinking about this all morning. I want us to go away. We need a break, and—"

I jump into his lap. "Yes!"

He laughs as I cover his face in kisses. "I haven't even told you where I want us to go."

"Doesn't matter," I tell him breathlessly. "I'll go anywhere with you."

He suddenly pulls back, his hands on my shoulders. His eyes hold a concerned look. My heart drops at the sight of how serious he's become. "I just realized something. Maybe it's too soon after everything that's happened. The paparazzi might still hound us, especially if someone tips them off. The paps in Europe are just as nasty as they are here. I can find someplace more private—"

I clamp my hand over his mouth. "Stop talking. I have something to say."

He nods, his eyes now anxious.

I drop my hand. "I've been to hell and back twice, first when my mother was murdered in front of me, then for twenty-four hours with the scum who killed her. I compartmentalized my entire life into this box where I kept myself hidden, afraid to step outside it because of the potential for more pain and sorrow the world might hold for me."

Davison keeps focused on me as I continue, my heart soaring knowing what I'm about to tell him.

"But I'm not afraid anymore, and that's because of you, Davison. I was so scared to even consider the possibility of being with you, and then I realized that I didn't need that box anymore. You've been so patient with me, so caring, so tender. I never thought I would meet a man like you, who wants to be with me in spite of all of my baggage."

He reaches out to stroke my face. "I do, Allegra. I do want to be with you. And your past makes you who you are. You understand that, right?"

My eyes moisten as I nod my head. "I do. I finally do. And the media and the paps can go fuck themselves. They won't keep me from you anymore. You're worth the risk, Harvard."

He cups my face and leans in, kissing me firmly. "I love you so much, baby."

My eyes and heart soften from both his touch and his words. "I love you too. I am yours, and you are mine."

Davison leans his forehead on mine. "We're shatterproof, Orsini. You and me. Now and always."

He falls back with me onto the mattress, both of us still kissing each other and holding on to one another tightly as we begin to make love, releasing the pain and anger that have been holding us captive for far too long.

Chapter Twenty-Two

A wind of salty air whips through my hair as the private water taxi Davison and I are sitting in speeds down the Grand Canal. I turn up the collar of my red trench coat and press my capri-clad legs together to keep myself warm, even though the heat from his body pressing into mine is doing a sufficient job of it already. Wearing a black suede jacket, a charcoal-gray long-sleeved V-neck sweater, jeans, and black driving shoes, he smiles widely, his black aviator sunglasses hiding what I know is a glint in his eyes. I nestle closer into him, his grip around my shoulders tightening. I feel his lips curve in a smile as he presses his lips to my hair and kisses me.

When he first mentioned he wanted to take me to Venice, he hesitated because he didn't know how I would react with everything that had happened to me, knowing Italy was where Carlo was going to take me. But Italy is my motherland, and just the fact that he was concerned enough not to book anything until I consented proves to me how kind a man he is.

Once I agreed, he made all of the arrangements. His private jet flew us into Aeroporto Marco Polo, where the boat he'd hired for us was waiting for our arrival.

The greatest surprise came when he told me where we would be staying. The only time I'd ever been to Venice was when I was a child, and my parents and I stayed at a *pensione* in the Dorsoduro district of the city. But this time, I would be spending my vacation in Venice at a fifteenth-century *palazzo* on the Grand Canal, thanks to my generous boyfriend. I had expected us to stay in one of the luxury hotels like the Danieli or the Cipriani. I even told him that he didn't need to rent an entire building; just an apartment would have sufficed for me. But he insisted, telling me he wanted to make our trip as magical as possible.

The boat starts to decrease in speed, pulling up to a dock in front of a building, its copper walls glistening in the morning sun. There are balconies on every floor, covered in dark green awnings.

"*Ecco Il Palazzo degli Innamorati,*" the driver announces.

I raise my eyebrows, turning to Davison. "Ahem..."

"What?" he asks, playing the total innocent.

"The Palace of Lovers? Really?"

"What about it?"

"How the hell did you find a building on the Grand Canal with a name like that?"

"I have connections," he smirks.

"I'll bet you do," I reply, rolling my eyes.

I watch as our driver removes our suitcases from the boat and places them on the dock. An older man with white hair dressed in a black suit stands by the luggage, holding out his hand to me.

"*Buongiorno, Signorina Orsini.* Allow me."

"*Grazie.*"

The man then does the same for Davison, addressing him as "*Signor Berkeley.*"

With the both of us now on the dock, the man formally greets us with a slight bow. "Welcome to Venezia. I am Vincenzo Santarno, the concierge for the Palazzo. We are so pleased to have you with us. Please allow me to show you inside."

Davison links his hand with mine, and we walk inside. My breath escapes me as soon as I enter, my hand tightening in his. I have never seen such a beautiful building before in my life. This magnificent structure and every object it holds must have so much history, so many secrets attached to them, and I yearn to know more.

The high ceilings make me feel so small. Chandeliers made from the finest Murano glass hang from above. The furnishings, everything from the carpets to the cabinets, look antique and precious. I recognize the work of the Italian masters in the paintings that adorn the walls—Canaletto, Botticelli, Titian. I feel as if I've been transported to a different time. It is overwhelming.

After meeting the staff who will be with us during our stay, Vincenzo leads us to a marble staircase, leading the way to the second floor where the master suite is waiting for us. He opens the double doors, allowing us to walk in first.

I take a few steps inside and freeze on the Persian carpet. The room is just as sumptuous as the downstairs. Our bed is covered in crimson red Fortuny silk fabric. The bed itself is so tall that it has a small step ladder on either side in order to get into it. Another Murano chandelier, this one dripping in red crystals, hangs from the ceiling.

A small sculpture of an intertwined couple kissing in each other's embrace sits on a credenza against the far wall. In fact, as I look around the room, I notice that most of the art in the room is erotic in nature, from a painting of a naked woman lounging on a chaise to the sculpture of the couple that I first spotted.

"Umm, am I missing something?" I wonder aloud. "There seems to be a theme to this room. Not that I'm complaining, mind you."

"*Mi scusi*," Vincenzo says. "I thought you knew about the *Signora*."

"The *Signora*?"

Davison comes up behind me and holds me around the shoulders. "Vincenzo, if it's all right with you, I'd like to be the one to explain the history of the *palazzo* to Miss Orsini."

He nods. "*Certamente.* I'll have some food brought up for you. If you need anything at all, please do not hesitate to ring the gong for the staff."

"*Grazie*, Vincenzo," Davison thanks him.

Once the door is shut, Davison grabs me and slams his mouth over mine. I hold on to him with my hands fisting his jacket.

"What was that for, Harvard?" I ask as my breath pants.

"Nothing gets past you, baby, and that makes me hard."

I laugh huskily. "Good to know. What was that about the *Signora*?"

"Come with me."

Taking my hand, he leads me onto one of the balconies that

overlooks the Grand Canal. My eyes widen at our view, spotting the spire of the bell tower, the Campanile, of St. Mark's Basilica, which marks the location of Piazza San Marco in the distance.

Davison embraces me by the waist. "What do you think?"

"It's so beautiful, Davison. I…I'm so happy."

Hearing the catch in my voice, he turns me, spotting the tears in my eyes. I run my fingertips down his cheeks.

His eyes soften at my touch. "*You* make me happy, Allegra," he whispers. "I can't imagine what my life would be like now if I'd never lost that glove."

A knock at our door interrupts the moment. Davison goes back inside while I wait, watching the vaporettos and other water traffic move up and down the Canal.

Davison returns, holding two flutes of Bellinis, the traditional Venetian cocktail of prosecco and white peach puree.

"Perfect choice, Harvard," I smile.

"What else would we drink to toast our arrival?" he winks.

We clink glasses. "To my *bellissima* in Serenissima."

I take a sip before correcting him. Even though he knew the nickname of Venice, "the most serene," he neglected one part of grammar.

"La Serenissima. You forgot the article, baby," I tell him, biting my lower lip.

He takes a long sip of his Bellini, his eyes never leaving mine. "Hmm, I think I'm going to need your services as my personal Italian language tutor."

I lean in, tasting the Bellini on his tongue as I suck on it. "That can definitely be arranged, *bellissimo*," I inform him when I pull back. "Now, what were you going to tell me about this mysterious *Signora*?"

"Oh, right. Well, the name for the *palazzo* originates from the woman who lived here in the sixteenth century, Alessandra della Costa."

"Who was she?" I ask, taking a sip of my Bellini.

"A famous courtesan."

I choke on the liquid that's going down my throat, coughing to get air back into my lungs.

"Didn't see that coming, did you?" He laughs, patting me on the back. "You okay, baby?"

"Yes." I nod with a smile. "Tell me more."

"She managed to evade the Inquisition using the protection of her 'patrons,' shall we say? She took in young girls who needed help and protected them, teaching them basic skills like reading and writing. If they wished to become courtesans as well, she took them under her wing and educated them in the art of seduction and erotic arts."

I narrow my eyebrows. "Exactly how much research did you do about this place?"

"Enough to show you what I learned," he smiles at me slyly, leaning in closer to nuzzle my throat.

"Looks like I have something to learn as well."

The Palace of Lovers indeed.

* * *

Sunlight streams through the two open sets of glass balcony doors in our suite. A light breeze wafts through white gauze curtains. The outside sounds of morning water traffic carry through the wide space, the sound of church bells pealing in the distance.

A warm, heavy arm is wrapped around my waist where we lie in bed under the white linen Pratesi sheets. I feel Davison's hot breath on my neck. I shift my head to glance at him. He snores quietly. I smile, tracing his lips with the pads of my fingers.

His breathing catches, his mouth curving under my touch. "*Buongiorno*, bellissima."

"Your Italian is improving, sleepyhead. I'm giving you a gold star."

"Thank you, Miss Orsini," he says into my ear, his voice rough and husky, instantly arousing me.

"So, do you think maybe for a change of pace we should actually leave this room today?"

His arms tighten around me as his mouth nuzzles my neck. "I think I'm good here, thanks."

"Davison." I sigh. "It's been two days. We're mostly over the jet lag. And we're in one of the most romantic cities in the world. I'd like to see more than the view from our balcony."

"I prefer this view," he says, opening his eyes, running his fingers over my cheeks.

"You're incorrigible," I smile.

"Okay, okay. We'll go out. But before then, we need to clean ourselves up."

"I'll go hop in the shower."

I sit up to go to the bathroom, but a strong arm pulls me back. "Where are you going?"

"To the room that has the bathing facilities."

"Not without me."

Mouth agape, I watch as he jumps out of bed, then I squeal when he snatches me up with him. I laugh as he spanks my bottom. "Get in there, woman."

"Bath or shower?" I ask, pointing at the gleaming white marble tub.

"Shower," he quickly answers.

He notices my pout. "Don't worry, baby." He assuages me with a sly smile. "We're going to take advantage of that when we come back. Trust me."

* * *

For the next few hours, we make up for the hermit-like existence we've been living the past two days. We start in Piazza San Marco, from there exploring the city by foot, traversing Venice's alleys and bridges. Davison takes me to see Teatro La Fenice, the historic opera house of Venice that had been restored to its former glory after it was destroyed by fire in 1996. We stand on the Rialto Bridge, where Davison snaps a photo of me, twenty years after I posed with my parents in the same spot. After that, the Peggy Guggenheim Museum is our next stop, and from there, we have a long, leisurely lunch at Harry's Bar, quenching our thirst with Bellinis at the place where the famous cocktail was created.

Now we are slowly gliding down Venice's twisting waterways in a gondola Davison has arranged for us with Vincenzo's assistance. Covered by a cashmere blanket with his arm around me, we lean back and take in the beauty of the city.

We kiss now and then, attracting the attention of passersby, mostly male, who shout various things to us that I don't care to translate for Davison despite his insistence.

"Tell me," he says, tickling my side.

I squirm, laughing aloud. "Let's just say it ranged from 'Get a room' to 'You can do better than him, beautiful.'"

His eyebrows rise in curiosity. "Oh, really? Well, in a few minutes, we won't have any spectators."

"What do you mean?"

"You'll see," he tells me, that glint reappearing in his eyes, one which I love seeing since it is now appearing much more often.

The gondola turns left, and then I see where we are headed.

The Bridge of Sighs, or Ponte dei Sospiri, appears in the distance. It is the famous limestone bridge that connects the Doge's Palace to the prison across the water. Supposedly, the legendary spot had been given that name because the bridge allowed the prisoners one last glimpse of Venice as they were being transferred.

Another legend is that if two lovers kiss under the bridge at sunset, they will be eternally united.

I turn to Davison. "You are such a sap, Davison Berkeley. But it's not quite sunset yet."

He glances up at the sky, "Close enough." Smiling at me, he leans forward. "*Aspetta, per favore*," he instructs our gondolier.

As the gondola slows, Davison reaches for something in his jacket. He takes my hand and opens it palm up, placing a red ring box in it.

I gasp. "Davison, I…I…"

"Look at me, Allegra," he commands softly.

When I stare into his eyes, I spot wetness in them. "This isn't *the* ring. We're not ready yet. We still need time to heal. But I wanted to show you how committed I am to you, how happy you make me, how much I love you."

Tears fall down my cheeks as he gives my hand a nudge. "Go ahead, baby."

I lift the top, which reveals the most beautiful round ruby, cushioned on a thin platinum band that is lined with smaller rubies, which sparkle in the light.

"Oh my God…Davison, it's beautiful," I exclaim.

He carefully removes the ring from the box, and slides it onto the ring finger of my right hand.

"Perfect," he declares.

My eyes switch back and forth between the gorgeous ring and Davison's face.

"*Andiamo,*" he tells the gondolier.

The gondola begins to move once more. As we get closer and closer to the bridge, I start crying harder as Davison holds me tight in his arms. "I love you, Davison."

"I love you, Allegra. Kiss me."

The sky overhead is eclipsed by the bridge as we sail underneath it, my lips sealed over Davison's as we kiss and kiss.

When we pull back, the gondolier declares behind us from his perch, *"Come siete belli! Vi auguro una vita di amore e passione."*

I place my head on Davison's shoulder, smiling and humming in contentment. *"Grazie. Molto gentile da parta sua,"* I thank the man kindly.

Davison puts his arm around me, turns his head, and kisses my hair. "No need to translate, my love. I caught 'a life of love and passion.'"

I nod. There is no need to say anything else as we sail until the darkness disappears, sweeping us back into the light.

* * *

Ivory candles of various sizes line the bathtub where Davison and I are soaking our tired bodies. The hot water is nearly up to our necks, the scent of the lavender bubbles intoxicating our noses.

My back leans into his strong, muscled chest. His arms encircle my waist as one of his firm pec muscles cushions my head.

I lift my right hand to take in its bejeweled state.

"You like?" he murmurs.

"I love. I can't stop staring at it."

"Good. That way I know you'll always be reminded of me."

"As if I could ever forget you, *bellissimo*."

"Damn right. Especially when I do this."

I feel a flutter beneath the water as his right hand moves down toward my cleft while his left kneads my left breast, alternating between tugging on my nipple, then massaging it.

I moan when Davison finds the opening slit of my pussy with his fingers. He caresses its plump inner flesh, his cock hardening behind me.

"Do you feel that, baby?" he asks huskily.

"Yes…"

"Should I stop?"

"Never. Oh God…never," I whimper.

I shift slightly so I can grab his shaft. With my left hand, I reach up and holding him by the nape, I bring his lips closer to me. I need to feel everything. His hands. His breath.

As he thrusts his fingers inside me, I mirror his rhythm with my own.

"Together, baby…make me come with you," he pants.

"Yes…together…always."

I feel his heart pounding behind my back. Once his hand finds my clit, it takes mere seconds until I explode. My hand tightens on his cock, and with one final pump, a fresh wave of warmth envelops me from behind.

Completely spent, I fall back onto his chest. With both hands, he spins my head around so he can kiss me full on the lips. I suck his tongue into my mouth, feeding on it like it's sweet candy.

Without warning, Davison roughly pushes me up by my hips, turning me around. "I need to fuck you, baby. Now," he growls.

I straddle his lap as quickly as I can inside the tub, my knees on the other side of his legs. He grips the sides of the tub as I reach for the lip of it behind his head, giving me more support. I slowly slide onto his lap, his hand holding his hardened cock, searching for my opening. Once he finds it, he's fully sheathed inside me.

"Ahhh," we both moan simultaneously. My head falls back as I bask in the glorious feeling of his long, hard shaft clenched by my sex.

His eyes are ablaze with need when I look into them. "Fuck me, Allegra," he commands.

The husky timbre in his voice is all I need to hear to make me want to fuck him until I pump every last drop of cum out of him.

Holding on to the marble rim, I start pounding him with my pussy. Waves of lavender-scented water lap over the tub, cascading to the floor. My body bucks as I ride him, his cock impaling me again and again.

"Yes, baby…God, you feel so fucking good," he groans. "So tight…don't stop…don't stop."

"Your cock is so hard inside me…you make me so hot," I pant. "I'm going to make you come…fuck me hard!"

As he tightens his hold on my hips, I shift to the right, angling my pussy, finding my clit. I shout in ecstasy as I slam down on him, rubbing his cock against my hard bud.

A few more pummels, and I am at the edge, cresting…cresting. "Oh God…I'm coming…Davison!"

My body shudders in release as I come, my cream oozing out of me. My sex holds on to Davison's shaft, milking every drop of cum from him.

"Ahhhh!" he yells, his body mirroring mine as it shakes from his orgasm, shouting my name as his orgasm overcomes him.

His hands encircle my waist when I drop onto his chest, our hearts pumping desperately for fresh oxygen.

I carefully untangle my legs and resume my previous position, lying against his chest with my back.

It takes a few minutes until we can speak coherently.

"You okay, baby?" he asks.

"Mmm-hmm," I reply, so blessedly content at this moment.

His chest rumbles under me with a deep laugh. "Ready to head south tomorrow?"

"I thought we already did."

He gives my butt a slight pinch. "Smart-ass. You know what I mean."

"Yes, I do," I give in. "I can't wait for Positano."

"And I can't wait to see you in a bikini."

I roll my eyes. "I can imagine. Such a guy thing to say."

Suddenly, his hands attack my ribs, tickling me and sending me into hysterics.

"Stop!" I shout as I squirm in his grip, water splashing over the edge of the tub. "Davison! Okay…okay…sorry…stop!"

He releases my sides and pulls me into him, kissing me hard on the lips. "That's enough punishment for now."

I shake my head, smiling and snuggling closer against his rock-hard chest.

I pause before I speak. "Davison?"

"Yes, baby?"

"Could we…possibly make a stop on the way down?"

"Of course. Anything you want, my love. Where would you like to go?"

"Naples."

* * *

On a hilltop with a view of Mount Vesuvius in the distance and the azure-blue water of the Tyrrhenian Sea glittering below, I stand at my mother's resting place with Davison holding my hand. A bouquet of white lilies that I brought for her sits on top of her gravestone.

A carving of Madonna and child is engraved into the stone above the inscription. I translate the words for Davison—

"*Concetta Maria Laterza Rossetti, beloved daughter, wife, and mother. An angel on Earth and in Heaven.*"

My eyes fill as I begin to speak.

"Mamma, it's me. Mia Allegra. I'm sorry it took me so long to get here. I want you to know that Carlo is dead. You don't have to worry about me. I'm a singer. I think it was all those operas you made me listen to."

I smile and let out a quiet, cathartic laugh. I tighten my hand on Davison's.

"I want you to meet someone, Mamma. This is Davison Berkeley, the man I love. I wish you could have met him. He's so wonderful. He takes good care of me."

Davison wraps his arm around my shoulders and kisses my hair.

"Papa misses you so much, Mamma. I wish you were here."

With Davison keeping me upright, I collapse into sobs. "*Ti amo*, Mamma. I love you so much. I miss you…"

I double over, but Davison pulls me up to keep me from falling. I fist his shirt, holding on to him until my knuckles hurt, soaking the cotton fabric with my tears.

"I'm here, Allegra. I'm here," he whispers.

It all comes out—my grief, my sadness, my fears. I sob until I gasp for breath.

Davison rubs my back soothingly. "Breathe, baby. Just breathe."

I shut my eyes and start to take slow, deep breaths. Once I calm down, I pull back from Davison's chest, looking up into his beautiful emerald eyes. He digs into his jacket pocket, producing a tissue for me. I smile at his kindness as I wipe my eyes and blow my nose.

"Thanks. I must look such a mess. You still love me, Harvard?"

He runs his fingertips over my warm cheeks. "Even more than I thought possible, baby."

I gently kiss his lips. I smile and take a deep breath. "I'm ready."

Pulling out of Davison's arms, I step up to my mother's grave and kiss the top of it, my lips grazing the cold stone.

"*Ti amo*, Mamma."

Davison joins me at my side, honoring my mother by placing his palm for a moment on the spot where I kissed the gravestone.

Taking his hand, I lead him out of the cemetery to our rental car, a candy-apple-red Ferrari 458 Spider convertible. I gave Davison a hard time when he first steered me to it in the parking lot in Venice. He countered by giving me the *when in Rome* line, but I argued we were in Venice, not Rome. However, once we were on the *autostrada* and he opened it up to its full potential, I quickly forgot I had ever protested his choice.

He opens the door for me. "You sure you're okay, my love?"

I nod. "Yes, *bellissimo*. I'm sure. We can go."

"*Andiamo*, baby."

I swerve my head to him as my mouth drops. "Davison! That was perfect!"

"Of course it was," he says as he puts on his aviators. "Like I said, let's go. Positano awaits."

I shake my head and roll my eyes at his flash of swagger. He gets in the car, starting the engine, revving it up before he shifts into first gear.

As we speed down the hill, I glance over at him, a wide smile curving across his lips, handling the car with total ease while wearing his driving gloves, the left one being the very one that he came looking for that night at Le Bistro, the night that we met.

I grin at him, watching him enjoying the feel of such a powerful car under his complete control.

"I meant to tell you something," I shout to him over the roar of the engine.

He pulls up to a red light. "What?"

"I spoke with Signora Pavoni before we left. I'm going to have a redo of my graduation recital."

"When?" he asks expectantly.

"In about two months. I need time to rehearse and get my voice ready."

"You know where I'll be." He beams at me, waiting patiently for me to respond.

"Front row center, Harvard," I reply knowingly.

He pulls down his sunglasses slightly so I can see his eyes. "Always, Venus," he replies, looking at me with that glint that makes me breathless and my heart beat faster every time I see it. He takes my left hand and places it on his right thigh, stroking it with his thumb, just like he did that first night.

The light turns green. He pushes up his aviators to the bridge of his nose and turns his focus back on the road ahead.

He really *is* a guy sometimes. And I love him, just like he said about me—even more than I ever thought possible.

Davison and Allegra's sinfully sexy story continues with

Devoted to Him

Available Winter 2014

Chapter One

DAVISON

Allegra Orsini is the most stubborn, aggravating, maddening, hotheaded, smart-mouthed, opinionated woman on the planet.

And I can't imagine my life without her.

She is also warm, caring, strong, brave, courageous, talented, beautiful, funny, passionate, and sexy as hell.

Which is why I'm waiting for her patiently on her father's sofa, my knees bouncing up and down in anticipation. She's getting ready for her private graduation recital, the redo, the one she missed when she was kidnapped.

That bastard Carlo Morandi died a lucky man, because if he hadn't been shot by the NYPD, I would've paid someone to leave me alone in a room with him so I could kill him myself. And I would've made sure it was slow and painful, not quick like that cop's bullet. It would've been a pleasure to torture him the way he made my beautiful Allegra, my baby, my Venus, suffer, and her mother before that. If my damn money could be useful for anything, it would've been for that.

Over two months have passed since Allegra was almost taken from me. I took her to Italy to get away from the media frenzy that was ravenous for any news of her, her recovery, and even me because I was part of her life. Most of all, I needed time to just *be* with her. We'd had a huge fight before we left when we let out all of the raw anger and emotion that had been festering inside us since she was rescued. I even destroyed a Waterford vase that my mother had given me when I finally told Allegra that I'd known all along that Morandi had planned to take her back to Italy to be his sex slave, something that I probably wasn't going to be told at all, no doubt to prevent the type of reaction I did have in the end.

That fight had actually brought us some peace. It was incredibly cathartic, and from that point on, we were determined to fight for our future together. She's already seeing her former therapist, and I'm going to start having joint sessions with her and Dr. Turner as well to continue our healing.

Our trip to Italy was amazing, especially for me, seeing the country through her eyes. Her fluency in Italian helped us when our rental, that gorgeous cherry-red Ferrari, broke down on the *autostrada* and we had to call the twenty-four-hour roadside assistance hotline.

Even more than that, I loved being able to give her the trip she deserved. Staying in posh hotels, eating at fine restaurants—it was all worth it for her because she could relax and enjoy herself. Another way I put the Berkeley money to good use. Anything for her. For Allegra.

And relax she did. I can still remember every single moan, every time she yelled in ecstasy when I'd fucked her in the bathtub of our suite in Venice. How she rode me, bucking up and down, her neck and back arching on the verge of her body exploding in orgasm, my cock sheathed in her tight cunt, milking it again and again as she shuddered…

Fuck!

I look down at my crotch. I'm hard as a rock.

I jump to my feet to bring down my hard-on. Thank God her father is still downstairs in his butcher shop. I start pacing the floor, thinking of less arousing topics like the pile of work that's waiting for me on my desk in my office or Professor Abrams's monotone timbre discussing supply and demand in my undergrad macroeconomics class at Harvard.

"Hi."

At the sound of her soft voice, I turn away from the window.

Allegra stands before me in a simple black dress that hugs all of her spectacular curves, with a thin belt that cinches her waist. With her hair pulled back in her familiar style at the nape of her neck, her legs encased in black stockings and those black stilettos I love, she is a vision.

But my favorite part of her ensemble is the ruby ring that adorns her right hand. I gave it to her in Venice when our gondola floated under the Bridge of Sighs, which, according to legend, was supposed to seal our love for eternity. She couldn't stop crying when I showed it to her and put it on her finger. My eyes welled up as well, seeing how happy she was.

Before I met Allegra, I was never such a romantic sap, not even with Ashton Canterbury, my girlfriend before Allegra. Thank

God I finally saw that shrew for what she really was—cold, unfeeling, materialistic, none of which could ever be used to describe Allegra. Meeting Allegra has opened me up in so many ways. I laugh more. She makes me want to be a better person. But most of all, I can be myself with her.

"Baby…" I murmur as I rush to her, cupping her face with my hands, my eyes roaming over her. "You take my breath away."

"Davison, you're going to make me cry, and I'm not wearing waterproof mascara," she whispers.

I'm in awe of her. "Sorry, I can't help myself. You look beautiful."

"So do you," she says, fingering my red tie, then running her hands over the lapels of my charcoal-gray suit. "This is one of my favorites."

I lean in and start nibbling on her earlobe. "Why do you think I wore it?"

"Don't start, Harvard. We'll never get out of here if you keep that up."

She wriggles out of my grip, stepping into the hallway, returning with her coat. "Now, be a gentleman and help me with this. My father's waiting downstairs."

If anything is going to crush my libido, it's the mention of her strict Italian father.

"At your service, Venus."

I assist Allegra with her coat, wrapping her cream silk scarf around her neck. I look down into her cocoa-brown eyes, which are still moist from her near tears. Even though I've only known her for a few months, I can tell what she's thinking and feeling just from the expression in them.

"Baby, you have nothing to be nervous about," I reassure her.

"You've been rehearsing almost every day. I should know because I've been missing you like crazy."

She laughs slightly at my attempt at levity, a smile appearing on her soft, lush lips.

"You've got this. You're going to be amazing."

She nods. "Thank you. I needed that. Now let's go before I lose my nerve."

She turns around, and with my hand on the small of her back, I steer my love out the door.

* * *

ALLEGRA

Front row center.

He's always there, no matter what.

I smile back in silent reply to the one spread across Davison's face. He gives me a quick wink of encouragement as I clear my throat. I signal to Derek, my accompanist, who begins playing the opening notes on the rehearsal room's piano. I open my mouth and enter my comfort zone. I forget the eyes staring at me and the ears listening for everything from pitch to pronunciation. I become Mimi introducing herself to Rodolfo as I sing one of my favorite arias, "Si, mi chiamano Mimi" from *La Bohème*, and everything is right again.

I sing the final note and shut my eyes, trying not to let the tears that are forming fall down my cheeks. I open them again to see the entire audience, all seven members of it, on their feet, applauding with Davison and my father shouting, *"Brava!"*

I bow in gratitude for the applause. Davison is the first to embrace me, of course.

"You were amazing, baby," he whispers in my ear.

My father steps up to me with tears in his eyes. "I'm so proud of you, *cara*."

"*Grazie*, Papa," I tell him. "I just wish Mamma could've seen me."

"She did see you. I know she did."

I nod as he holds me once more. A loud voice announces, "Okay, Mr. Orsini, my turn."

My best friend, Luciana Gibbons, is standing behind my father. Next to her is her boyfriend, Tomas Novotny.

"That was incredible, Alli!" she says. "Thanks to you, I'm a total mess!" I laugh as she blows her nose and wipes her eyes. I watch as Tomas places a hand on her shoulder. It makes me smile in wonder how resistant Lucy was to dating Tomas, but now she swoons over him like a schoolgirl.

"You were *vonderful*," Tomas says to me in his thick Czech accent. "Very good."

"Thank you, Tomas."

The rest of the audience, mostly faculty, comes over to congratulate me. When Signora Pavoni, my mentor, approaches me, she isn't alone.

"*Brava*, Allegra! I would like to introduce you to one of my dearest friends, Ginevra Ventura."

My mouth drops. I can't believe my eyes. Ginevra Ventura is one of the last true divas of the opera world. She's known for her passionate temperament and her famous string of lovers that ranges from film stars to royal princes. Her nickname is appropriate—"La Diva."

She is everything I imagine her to be from her album covers. Her gray eyes contrast against the jet-black of her hair with a widow's peak in the front. She is wearing a black pantsuit and a matching cashmere shawl covering her shoulders. A red ostrich Kelly bag is hanging from her elbow.

She takes both of my hands in hers before she speaks to me. "Signorina Orsini, thank you for your performance. I was very impressed by your voice. You are very talented. We will speak on Monday morning. *Lunedì, sì?*" she asks, looking back at Signora Pavoni.

My professor nods. "You made me very proud today, Allegra. Would you stop by my office then, perhaps around eleven?"

"Of course. I'll be there. *Grazie mille*," I reply, my curiosity piqued, wondering what my professor and La Diva are planning to tell me.

I keep staring at the two women as they walk away, not even noticing Davison returning to claim me.

He wraps his arms around me from the back, placing his head on my shoulder. "What was that about?"

"Do you know who that was?" I ask incredulously.

"Are you kidding? My mother would've totally fangirled over La Diva if she'd been here."

"I think my father is filling the fanboy role quite well in her place," I observe, looking over at Papa talking to her, holding his hand over his heart, probably telling her how much he and Mamma loved listening to her albums.

"What did they say to you?"

"Not much. They want me to meet them in Signora Pavoni's office on Monday."

"So basically, you won't be able to focus on anything until then," he whispers into my ear, instantly arousing me.

"Oh yeah, I'll be totally useless," I joke.

"Hmm. We'll see about that, baby. You ready to head to Le Bistro for dinner? The sooner we get there, the sooner we finish and then head back to my place for a private celebration."

I turn around in his arms, giving him a quick kiss. "I love how you think, Berkeley."

* * *

DAVISON

Allegra's head is nestled on my shoulder as Charles drives us home from dinner at Le Bistro. We're slightly buzzed from the champagne that the owner and my godfather, Elias Crawford, sent over to our table to congratulate one of his employees on her successful graduation. Seeing Allegra so happy, laughing and chatting with her father, Luciana, and Tomas, was worth every cent I spent on dinner. After her kidnapping, when I thought I'd lost my love forever, there is no price I won't pay to make sure she is always protected and taken care of, safe and happy with that beautiful smile on her face.

I watch as Charles pulls in front of my building. I look down at Allegra's peaceful expression.

"You awake, baby?" I whisper.

"Mmm-hmmm," she murmurs. "Just resting my eyes. Are we home?"

"Yes."

"Home." I love the sound of that word coming from her mouth. Hopefully, it won't be long until it actually becomes a real-ity—sharing the same home with her. I have plans for us.

She waits for me to open the car door for her, something that's become part of our routine. I clamp my arm around her shoulders and don't let go until we're inside my apartment.

I take off her coat and mine, putting them away in the hall closet. When I turn back around, she grabs my tie and pulls me to her, her lips slamming over mine. Her tongue invades my mouth, and I suck on it, feeding on its sweetness. Her hands run through my hair, bringing me in tighter.

When she pulls away, I groan in frustration.

"Fuck me, Davison," she commands.

That's all I need to hear. I sweep her up into my arms, carrying her to my bedroom. She doesn't say a word, and neither do I. We both want the same thing—me inside her.

Once we're in my bedroom, we work on each other's clothes, quickly taking turns as she undoes my tie and my shirt buttons, and I unzip her dress and pull the bobby pins out of her hair, letting it fall around her face. Both of us are now fully naked.

I roam my eyes over her luscious body.

Fuck. She is the most gorgeous creature I've ever seen. And she is mine. All mine.

I pick her up and walk with her body wrapped around mine to the bed, where I lay her down and fall on top of her.

She quickly coils her legs around my waist, her hands squeez-ing my ass.

"Hard, baby," she begs me. "Fuck me hard. I want you now."

I grunt in agreement because I'm too damn overcome with emotion. I'm dying to taste her pussy and suck on her gorgeous tits, but right now, more than anything, I need that connection with her, to feel my cock sheathed inside her.

I slide my dick into her pussy, which is already soaked.

"Oh God, baby, you're always ready for me, aren't you?" I moan. "You feel so good. So fucking wet."

I start thrusting inside her, and she quickly picks up my rhythm. She links my hands with hers, holding me in place. We are amazing together, always in sync with each other. And when we come together, it's fucking priceless.

Allegra's body is a work of art. So soft, with her sumptuous curves. I love watching her when I piston her with my cock, the way her eyes shut tightly, her lush mouth forming Os with each thrust, that angelic voice of hers that yells my name when she finally comes.

She's getting closer as her muscles tighten, going rigid, grinding the heels of her feet into my lower back. I'm impervious to the pain because it just turns me on even more, knowing I can do this to her, bring her this much pleasure with my body.

"That's it, my love. You're so fucking beautiful. Come for me now."

Her entire body shudders as her orgasm sweeps over her, yelling my name. I can feel her milking my cock harder and harder until I explode inside her, my entire body shaking from the release.

I collapse next to her, immediately reaching for her and wrapping myself around her, our bodies both slick with sweat.

Her cocoa-brown eyes open, searing into mine. I love looking into them after I make her come, completely softened. And her full lips swollen from kissing me.

"Mmmm. Thank you, Harvard," she murmurs, her head resting on my chest. "I know you probably wanted to do other stuff first."

My baby never ceases to amaze me. She knows me so damn well, and I know her.

"Hey, I was just following orders. But don't worry. It was good for me too."

"Was it? I couldn't tell," she smirks.

"Funny girlfriend."

"Davison, tonight…" She pauses.

"Yeah?"

"It meant so much to me that you were there."

"Where else would I have been?" I tell her, astonished that she'd even think I wouldn't have been there for her.

She roams her right hand over my chest. "It's just…tonight was so important, and seeing you there in the front row—"

"Center."

"Yes, center," she says with a lift in her voice. "You are everything to me, and I can't imagine not—"

"Stop, Allegra. Don't even think anything like that."

I hate it when she thinks like that. But after everything she's been through, I'm not surprised she's still afraid that something could happen to us.

"But you didn't even know what I was going to say," she counters.

"Doesn't matter. I'm here with you, in my bed, in my home, and that's all that matters. Oh, except for one thing."

"What?" she asks nervously.

"I love you."

She lifts up her gorgeous face to look into my eyes. "I love you too."

I kiss her gently on the lips as I tighten my hold on her.

Nothing will ever keep us apart, baby. I promise.

Chapter Two

ALLEGRA

At precisely eleven o'clock on Monday morning, I knock on the door of Signora Pavoni's office.

"Enter," her voice commands behind the polished wood.

When I walk into her office, Signora Ginevra Ventura, La Diva, is sitting opposite my professor. Both women are holding dainty espresso cups in their hands.

"Good morning," I greet them with a slight bow of nervousness. They're not titled royals, but for me, both women hold just as much prestige.

"*Buongiorno*, Allegra. Please have a seat," Signora Pavoni says, directing me to the other guest chair. "You remember my friend Ginevra."

I take La Diva's hand in mine to greet her. "*Certo. Buongiorno, Signora.*"

"Signorina Orsini, a pleasure to see you. Thank you for meeting us this morning," she replies in a lush, polished accent.

I settle into the chair as both women place their cups on the desk. Signora Pavoni leans forward to address me.

"Allegra, I would like to speak with you about your career goals, specifically what you envision yourself doing after graduation."

"Oh. Well, I suppose what every aspiring opera singer would do," I stammer. "Audition for roles, try to get accepted into a festival or postgrad program for young singers with a prominent opera house."

La Diva clears her throat. "Signorina Orsini, do you know that I apprentice two young opera singers every summer at my villa outside Milano?"

"Of course. Some of the greatest talents have studied under your tutorship."

"Yes, this is true," she replies in a somewhat modest tone. "I have already chosen one singer to teach in June, and now I need to fill the month of July."

Is she going to…

"When I choose a singer, I not only listen for the potential in the voice, but also in the personality, if the singer is able to convey the role with the body and the mind. What I heard at your recital moved me greatly. I saw great potential in you, Allegra, and I would be honored to have you serve as my apprentice in July."

Oh my God.

I start to shake, my eyes instantly filling with tears.

"I…I'm so honored, Signora Ventura. *Grazie mille!* But I don't have the money—"

"All of your expenses are covered," she informs me, waving her hand dismissively. "I pay for everything. *Tutto.* Your flights, transportation from the airport, and your stay in my home."

"I don't know what to say."

"The word you're looking for is '*sì*,' Allegra," my professor interjects, rather insistently.

I wipe my eyes and take a deep breath. "Before I give you my answer, Signora Ventura, I need to tell you something. A few months ago, something happened to me, and I would never want what happened to me to affect you in any way."

The two women glance at each other knowingly.

"Allegra, I told Ginevra about everything you've been through," Signora Pavoni tells me. "And I think I speak for both of us when I say that your honesty and selflessness only reassures us that we made the right choice."

A warm hand takes my right one. I turn to La Diva, who nods at me and looks at me with caring eyes.

"*Cara* Allegra, do you know how many incidents I have been involved in, both voluntarily and involuntarily?"

I shake my head.

"More than I can count with both hands. Among many things, I've supposedly ruined marriages, had an opera director fired, and seduced a young prince under the roof of his father's castle. I find you to be a strong, caring woman who has a great future ahead of her. And more important, I can teach you how to use that pain to your advantage in your performance."

I smile at her reassurance, and tighten my grip on her hand. "Then I…I…*Sì*! I don't know how to thank you. I am so honored."

"*Eccellente*, Allegra. I am thrilled that you will be joining me. I will get your information from Signora Pavoni, and I shall contact you shortly to discuss the arrangements."

The three of us stand as I shake both women's hands, telling them "Thank you" and "*Grazie*" again and again.

Before I step through the door, La Diva calls out my name.

"*Sì*, Signora?"

"You recall those three situations I mentioned to you?"

I nod.

"One of them is true," she confesses with a wicked glint in her eyes.

I smile in return before I walk out.

As I make my way to the subway, a thought stops me in my tracks.

Davison.

We're going to be apart for a month. An entire month.

Will he support my decision?

Why do I suddenly feel as if this might be a huge mistake?

* * *

DAVISON

"It's on the left, Charles," she commands.

I smile, listening to Allegra directing my chauffeur to pull over where her therapist's brownstone stands in Chelsea. She's so at ease with him, which makes me happy since he'll be in her life as long as we're together, which I plan on making permanent soon.

But my smile hides my nervousness. I hold Allegra's hand tightly in mine. This is going to be our first session together. I'd never thought much of therapy. In my family, you just keep everything inside and soothe the pain with three fingers of Glenlivet. But she's reassured me again and again that Dr. Ophelia Turner is a qualified therapist, how she helped her all those years after the trauma of seeing her mother murdered when she was five. So I need to keep an open mind. This is for Allegra, my love.

I open the door of the Maybach for Allegra. Still holding hands, we take the three steps down into the small courtyard of her basement apartment. Allegra rings the doorbell, and we're buzzed in.

Dr. Turner is standing in the foyer.

Oh, for the love of God.

She's dressed in some kind of white gauzy blouse with a black peasant skirt, her silver hair done in a braid of some kind that runs down her back, a pair of taupe Birkenstocks on her feet. I'm tempted to ask her what Woodstock was really like, Kumbaya and all that crap.

Open mind, remember? This is for Allegra, you dick.

Dr. Turner steps forward and hugs my girlfriend. "Allegra, lovely to see you, as always." She turns to me, hand outstretched. "Mr. Berkeley, I'm pleased to finally meet you. I'm Dr. Ophelia Turner."

I nod, shaking her hand in return. "Davison Berkeley. Pleasure."

"Let's get started, shall we?"

I follow the women into a small room that's covered in bookshelves and thick velvet drapes, with a Persian rug on the floor, and a Tiffany lamp on a side table. I begin to understand why Allegra feels comfortable here. I have to admit it's very cozy. Sinking into a couch upholstered in fabric that matches the drapes, I settle in and immediately take Allegra's hand, admittedly more for my reassurance than hers.

Once we're all settled in, Dr. Turner speaks.

"Where would you like to start today?"

Allegra opens her mouth, but I beat her to it. "Allegra asked me to join her for a session."

"Why did you feel that was necessary?" Dr. Turner asks, turning to her.

I quickly glance over at Allegra, watching as she clears her throat.

"A lot of feelings came out after I was rescued…well, he admitted to certain things that I wasn't expecting him to say."

"Like what?"

Allegra bends her head in embarrassment, while I shake mine in frustration.

"I told her I was angry with her because I wish she would've told me about the man who was following her before she was taken."

"It was the accomplice, yes?" Dr. Turner confirms.

Allegra and I both nod in reply.

"So you thought she was to blame for being taken?" she asks me pointedly.

"Of course not!" I roar.

This is going to go nowhere.

My face begins to warm from my frustration. "Why are we even rehashing this?"

"Good," Dr. Turner says, writing something down in her notebook.

I stare at the good doctor like she has two heads. "Excuse me?"

"Davison, you must have been incredibly frustrated and upset when Allegra was kidnapped."

"Well, that's stating the obvious."

"Davison, be nice," Allegra admonishes me.

"No, it's all right, Allegra," Dr. Turner counters before she turns back to me. "Davison, you needed an outlet, someone to place blame on for what happened."

Is she fucking kidding me?

"For crying out loud, I don't blame Allegra!"

"Of course you don't. But you felt helpless, and you wish that you could've stopped it from happening. You probably even blamed yourself."

I nod, unable to answer verbally. I don't even notice Allegra had unclasped my left hand which had formed a fist, her hand now firmly gripping in mine.

"Allegra, what happened after he told you?"

I look back at her, now tightening my grip on hers.

"The thing is…" she begins with a whisper, "he also told me that he knew about Carlo's plans to make me his sex slave when he took me back to Italy. He overheard me when he was in the bathroom in my hospital room and I was telling Detective Leary about it."

I take a few deep breaths, shuddering as I exhale.

"What happened then?"

"I threw a fucking vase at the wall, okay?" I snap at Dr. Turner.

"Davison, please."

When I look again at Allegra, her eyes are moist, begging me to stop. I release my hand, trailing my fingertips over the soft skin of her face. "I'm sorry, baby."

She leans her head into my palm, closing her eyes.

"Davison, Allegra, please listen to what I'm going to tell you."

We both shift back to Dr. Turner, my left hand now holding her right one.

"Neither one of you is to blame for what happened. The only persons to blame are the perpetrators who committed the crime. I can tell how much you care for each other—"

"I love her," I blurt out, interrupting her, not giving a shit. "Just so we're clear."

The doctor smiles patiently at me. "Yes, Davison, I can see that. Despite the time that's passed, you're still healing from the incident. And you will overcome this because of the love and trust I can sense you have established with each other. As long as you keep communicating and are honest with one another, I don't see why you won't be able to build a strong, healthy relationship."

I squeeze Allegra's hand, who's nodding her head, her eyes shut, a large smile across her lips.

Maybe this therapy thing isn't so bad after all if it makes my Venus smile like that.

* * *

"Thank you for coming with me."

We're now sitting in the Maybach in front of Allegra's building.

"Anything for you, you know that by now, don't you?" I reassure her, running my index finger along her chin.

She nods. "I do."

"Are you okay, baby? You're being very quiet."

"Therapy sessions take a lot out of me," she whispers.

"Is that all?"

"Mmm-hmm."

She's totally lying. But I don't push.

"Well, okay, if you're sure. I need to get back to the office. Dinner tomorrow at my place?"

"It's a date, Harvard."

I lean in and kiss her soft lips. She opens her mouth wider, taking my tongue into her mouth, her hands gripping my hair in a tight hold. She starts to moan, and my cock hardens instantly at that sound, growing larger under the fabric of my trousers. As much as I want to tell Charles to take us around the block a few more times, I know having sex with her in front of her father's shop is not the best place to do it, despite the car's tinted windows.

I reluctantly pull away from her mouth. "Baby, you're killing me. Not here," I plead.

She looks at me sheepishly, and nods after a few seconds. "Okay."

"Hey, listen to me," I command, lifting up her chin with my hands to make sure she's listening to me. "Believe me, I want you so fucking much right now, but I'm too afraid that your father has X-ray vision and would be able to see through the window."

She laughs.

The sweetest sound in the world.

"We'll pick this up later," I tell her.

"Promise?"

"What do you think?"

She smiles at me wickedly.

* * *

As the Maybach heads down the FDR to my office in the Financial District, what was unspoken between us bothers me. I know there was something she wasn't telling me. After what she's been through, she needs to know that I would never leave her, no matter what.

We finally reach the Berkeley Holdings building.

"The usual time this evening, sir?" Charles asks me when I step out of the car.

"Yes. But before you go, I need you to do me a favor."

About the Author

Sofia Tate grew up in Maplewood, New Jersey, the oldest of three children in a bilingual family. She was raised on '70s disaster films and '80s British New Wave music and classic TV miniseries. Her love for reading started when she received a set of Judy Blume books from her aunt when she was ten. She discovered erotic romance thanks to Charlotte Featherstone. She loves both writing and reading erotic romance. She graduated from Marymount College in Tarrytown, New York, with a degree in International Studies and a minor in Italian. She also holds an MFA in Creative Writing from Adelphi University. She has lived in London and Prague. Sofia currently resides in New York City.

Learn more at:
   SofiaTate.com
   Twitter: @sofiatateauthor
   Facebook: Sofia Tate
   Goodreads: Sofia Tate
   Pinterest: Sofia Tate